SAVANT

NIK ABNETT

First published 2016 by Solaris
an imprint of Rebellion Publishing Ltd,
Riverside House, Osney Mead,
Oxford, OX2 0ES, UK

www.solarisbooks.com

ISBN (UK): 978 1 78108 456 4
ISBN (US): 978 1 78108 457 1

10 9 8 7 6 5 4 3 2 1

A CIP catalogue record for this book is available from the British Library.

Designed & typeset by Rebellion Publishing

Printed in Denmark

SAVANT

NIK ABNETT

For Pops, who just was, and who was content for me, too, simply to be.

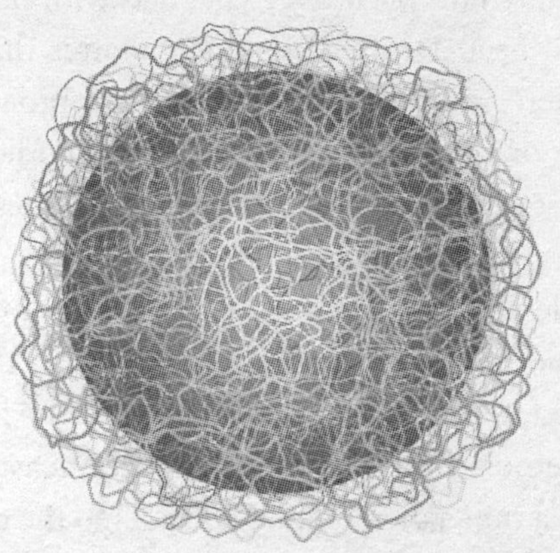

Chapter One

She wore cotpro socks in bed in High, and woolpro socks in Low. She could have had the real thing, but it seemed extravagant. She wouldn't have worn socks at all, but she disliked the sensation of linopro on the soles of her feet, with its faintly spongy finish, and Tobe couldn't bear the sound of slippers slapping against it.

It was 05:30 in the morning of an ordinary day, Metoo's perfect day.

Service and Requisites were simple, compared with the complications Civilians endured, of checks and balances, of rations and over-supply, of real and pro. She didn't know, any more, if Civilians used anything but pro. Service was daily, since she'd been with Tobe, rather than Scheduled, and Requisites fell only on mid and end days of High and Low, rather than monthly. She had not been a Civilian since she was twelve. She had not been a Civilian for more than half her life.

Metoo's family had been overwhelmed with pride and relief when she had been Drafted. It didn't matter that she'd been bred to it; there was no such thing as a forgone conclusion. Breeding was one thing, but balance was another. Never-the-less, she had stood in front of her parents, her teacher and her class, aged twelve, her future secured.

Family pride was not the best of it, the best of it was relief: the Drafted never returned to Civilian life, so there was one less mouth to feed, one less body to clothe, one less mind to... To what? Metoo's thoughts were suddenly cast back to her childhood, to a time when no one considered the mind. She had not been aware, then, of her thoughts, that they existed, never-mind mattered. Civilians were assessed for physical suitability for various kinds of work, and chipped for education and thought processing. She had been one of them, had been part of a family, but, now, she could barely remember their faces, and seldom thought about them. She was Drafted, and no one she knew had been a Civilian for four years or more. News of the Civilians was old news. She only knew that, if she fulfilled her role, they would endure.

By 05:45, Metoo was breakfasting on coffee and fruit. She chose her luxuries carefully, but this half-an-hour, alone with her thoughts, meant something to her, so she indulged herself a little. Coffee was scarce, but she grew a good deal of fruit during High, and preserved what she could to last her through Low, supplementing her supplies from Requisites. In the eight years that she had spent with Tobe, first as his Student, and then as his Assistant and Companion, Metoo had never filled her annual Requisites, giving up as much as a third to Stores, that others might enjoy the benefits.

She was privileged, but she knew it.

At 06:00, the shower was running at 40 degrees, and the

eggpro was cooking. Metoo signed in with Service, the 45 seconds it took, allowing breakfast to be perfectly cooked, ready for Tobe as he finished his ablutions. A few minutes later, she set the dish in front of him at the kitchen counter, and made her way back to Service.

"It's the same," he said.

Metoo turned, her cotpro sock squeaking slightly as the ball of her right foot rotated on the linopro. She winced, knowing that the sound would bother Tobe, that he might spend valuable time working out the physics that created that particular pitch from the cotpro formula, the wear on the linopro and the speed of her rotation.

"It's the same," Tobe said, again, without looking up.

He seemed not to be speaking to her, so, Metoo turned again, stepping this time, rather than swivelling, and went back to Service; she'd make up those 15 seconds before his tutorial at 08:30.

Back on Service, Metoo woke Tobe's Students, and set all of their Schedules and accounts for the day. It was a Companion's task, but Tobe's previous Assistant had burnt out early, and Metoo had been brought in as Assistant before she'd finished three years as his Student. She never learned what had happened to the man she'd replaced, but Kit had been brought back as Tobe's Companion, after two Lows' sabbatical, to pick up the slack. He had barely lasted the High before Metoo found herself in the dual role of Assistant and Companion. Had she found Tobe's requirements arduous, or complex, she might have failed too. In the middle of their second High together, Metoo was fully in charge of maintaining Tobe, and Service had decided that the dual role, however rarefied, should continue until a Pitu was ready to take over as Assistant, and Metoo could become, solely, his Companion.

* * *

Tobe got out of the shower, rubbed himself down, dropped the towel, and pulled a robe over his head. He never thought that someone had placed the robe ready for him, or that someone would pick up the towel. His thoughts almost never strayed to the domestic, or to Service. He had long since given up signing in, leaving it all to Metoo, except that he no longer had a conscious memory of ever having signed in, or of there being any need to. Service did not exist for him, except when it affected his practice. Metoo bypassed his need to remember it for its own sake, conscious for both of them.

He sat at the kitchen counter, as he had done every morning for as long as he could remember, except that remembering such things was arbitrary, and, therefore, redundant. He knew only this: it was the same. It was the same today as yesterday, and yesterday it was the same as the day before.

"It is the same," he said, not to himself and not to Metoo, but simply because it was.

"It is the same."

The College was home to as many as five thousand inhabitants. The Masters, with their Assistants and Companions, lived on the South side of the campus in small apartments, which usually consisted of three bedrooms and shared living accommodation. Master, Assistant and Companion were individually responsible to Service, except in rare circumstances where a Companion would be responsible for running the entire household.

The majority of the College population was made up of Students at various stages in their educations, and these included all of the Assistants and many of the Companions. The youngest were children of twelve or fourteen, who lived in family groups on the West side of the campus, and shared everything from classrooms to bathrooms in the building referred to as the School. They lived with Seniors: teachers and carers, mid-grade Drafted, who had been through the system before them. Service was taken care of by Seniors, and their routines adjusted to best suit their temperaments.

As they got older and more independent, and with first stage adjustments to their chips completed, most of the Students moved out of the School. Their education became more specific to their intellectual strengths, and some were assigned to Masters. They also moved into the dorms on the East side of campus, and were responsible directly to Service, although their choices were limited. Food and clothes rations were provided according to need, rather than taste, but Students were free to choose reading material, music and visual stimuli from Service lists. All the Students in East wore buttons, on chords, around their necks. They pressed their buttons to acknowledge Service on the Schedule, just as Civilians did.

Pitu 3 hit the Service button around his neck to acknowledge his Rouse. He had last hit the button eight hours ago for Rest, and would hit it several times throughout the day: at Roll-call, Repast, Recreation, and so on through the Schedule.

He rolled out of bed, and staggered into the small, shared kitchen, his naked feet slapping against linopro that was so old it had lost any bounce it might once have had. He put the heat on under a pan of oatpro that the Students had been topping up for most of the week. He hoped that it would be warm by the time he'd had his regulation shower in one of the stalls in the communal bathroom.

Pitu 3 wanted to get back to his room, his only private space. He'd lived in the School for the first couple of years, but was spared dorm-living; Tobe's Students were given their own rooms. There were eighteen in the block, all small and sparsely appointed, with one shared bathroom and a kitchen. Seven of the rooms were vacant, but could not be accessed by the eleven remaining Students. At least the kitchen and bathroom were less crowded than they might have been.

Pitu 3 had been Drafted for six years, and had been Tobe's Student for four. When he had begun, there were fourteen of them, now eleven; the numbers varied. New Students were moved in, and others left. Only two of Tobe's Students exceeded him in seniority, so he was Pitu 3. He had begun as 14.

Pitu had left his basic education behind, and his mind had been opened by degrees in the School. In his first year Drafted, his chip had been adjusted eight times, but the jumps in his intellectual capacity were small and unremarkable, impaired by a lack of emotional growth that he failed to recognise in himself, but which made him one of the less popular Students in the School. Later chip adjustments were subtle; the mine had been tapped, and the material found wanting.

The Drafted began by studying a broad spectrum of subjects, but Pitu's results for the first year put him squarely in the mathematics faculty, and at the end of his second year he was moved into Tobe's class.

To continue as Tobe's Student for so long was unusual; Pitu had been taking instruction from him for almost a year longer than he had anticipated. His chip had not been adjusted once during that time, and Pitu simply assumed that this was a positive. He wanted to believe that he was finally in preparation for Assistant, and wondered if 1 and 2 were also being monitored. Would they compete for the position?

Tobe's class was the smallest in College, it had the biggest turnover of Students, and any number of myths and rumours surrounded it. The younger Students fell into two camps: those who could think of nothing more exciting than working under Tobe, and those who dreaded being transferred in. Pitu just enjoyed the status it gave him. It was true that Tobe could barely tell one Student from another, that his interest in them was minimal, and that they could forget humour and affection altogether, but it was also true that Tobe was one of the top three mathematicians on Earth.

Thought might be monitored, quantified and adjusted by Service, via their chips, but ambition was not, neither was excitement, nor dread, nor pragmatism, nor interest, humour or affection.

Pitu stepped out of the shower, worked a small towel under his arms and between his legs until it was too damp to use on the rest of his body, and slung on his robe. He walked back to the kitchen, his wet feet squelching across the linopro, leaving miniature puddles where his high arches didn't connect with the surface. Ninety seconds later, he was sitting on the cot in his room, his bare feet crossed under his thighs for warmth, cradling a bowl of oatpro that proved to be hot enough, but too thick and gritty.

As Pitu ate, he cast his eyes over the facing wipe-wall, where he had written his latest calculations, referencing the list of formulae neatly arranged on the left. The work was never-ending. Tobe introduced one step at a time, methodically, but it had been four years, and Pitu had known for at least two of them that the work would not end, not with Tobe, and certainly not with him.

Tobe and Pitu arrived together for their 08:30 tutorial. Tobe opened the door to his office, and stepped in, followed by Pitu. They exchanged no pleasantries, nor would they.

The room was a regular cube, three metres, by three, by three. This was unusual among the Masters, most of whom opted for the more visually pleasing three-four-five triangle system, resulting in a room that was low-ceilinged, but with a larger floor-plan. Space was at a premium, and every room had the same volume, but Tobe did not particularly value the size of the space, only its orderly configuration.

"It was the same," Tobe said.

Pitu looked at Tobe, but his tutor did not appear to be addressing him, so he chose not to answer. Tobe usually began his sessions with, 'Tidings', which meant nothing to anybody, except that it was a sort of punctuation point that signified a beginning. Neither Student nor Master spoke, nor sat for several more seconds.

"Tidings," said Tobe.

"Sir," said Pitu.

Still, they did not sit.

"Upload Master Tobe's personal Service files for 05:58 to 06:03. The pitch of the sock, work out why it was," said Tobe.

"Sir?" asked Pitu. "I'll need specified clearance."

"Metoo," said Tobe, turning his back on his Student.

The tutorial was over. It was 08:34.

Tobe turned from Pitu, and stepped onto a low ladder that would allow him to reach the highest bookshelves on the left wall of his office. Pitu watched his Master for a moment, unsure of his next move. Tobe rose to the second step on the ladder, and shielded his eyes with one hand, against the light, as he scanned the book titles. Pitu realised that Tobe had nothing more for him, turned, and left the office, closing the door behind him.

Service sent a tone to Pitu's button, and he pressed it as he walked away.

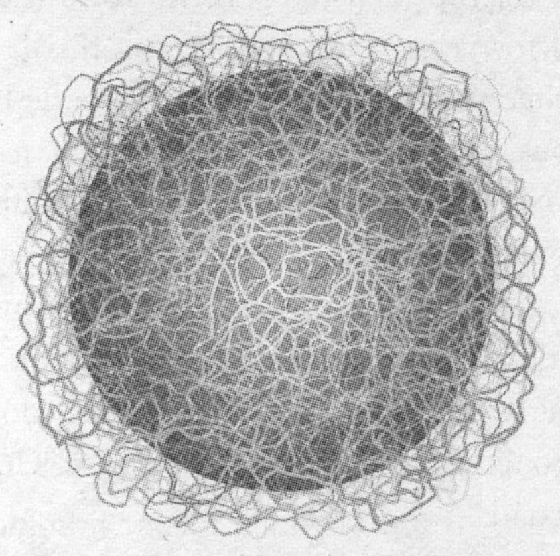

Chapter Two

SERVICE SENT A tone to Tobe's flat at 08:34. Metoo stopped stacking dishes, and went to check on it, knowing that it would concern this morning's anomaly. She was not worried.

"Metoo," she said, answering the tone.

"Pitu 3 will request specified clearance, please allow," said Service.

"Very well," she said.

Why would Pitu 3 ask for a specified clearance? And why wasn't he in his tutorial? What was happening? What was wrong with Tobe? The questions flashed through Metoo's mind, urging her to panic. She didn't. It was that damned sock. That squeak had sent Tobe off on a wild goose-chase, and Pitu 3 had, somehow, become involved. Metoo breathed more easily; it was nothing.

*   *   *

Tobe scanned the top shelf in his office for a text that he had not consulted for years. He knew it was there, he could not remember a time when it hadn't been there; he had studied it in his teens, but his work had long-since bypassed probability. The book should have been third from the right, with a blue cover. The book third from the right on the shelf had a grey cover. He checked the books to either side; both were shades of beige, not distinctly different from the grey book that sat third from the right on the top shelf. He stepped down from the ladder, and stood in the middle of the room. He didn't move for several seconds.

"Metoo," he said.

It was proving to be a strange day, not the perfect, ordinary day that it had promised to be only a few hours earlier. Service would be demanding today.

Tobe was still standing in the middle of his office when Metoo arrived a few minutes later.

"Master?" she asked, as she stepped into the room.

"Eustache, *On Probability*," he said, "it isn't there."

"Probability?" she asked.

"Eustache," he said, again. "Top shelf, third from the right."

What could he possibly want with Eustache?

Metoo squeezed past Tobe, who seemed incapable of movement, and took the first three steps up the ladder, allowing her to reach the top shelf, just. She slipped the third book from the right, off the shelf, and let it fall into her hand. The spine of the book was grey with age, and the embossed title was so old and worn as to be unreadable, but the covers of the book, front and back, were made of sky-blue book-cloth, preserved from the light, pressed against their neighbours. Metoo flipped the book open, and checked the title page, *On Probability*, Eustache et Henriot.

She handed the book to Tobe, who looked at the faded spine, and then at the blue book-cloth. He opened the book, and began to riffle through the pages. He had not moved. Metoo watched him for a moment, but decided not to ask. He needed what he needed, and, today, it was this; but what did probability have to do with the squeak her socks made?

As SHE RETURNED to the flat, Pitu 3 approached Metoo. She had forgotten to expect him.

"I'm sorry," she said.

"I've only been here a minute or two," said Pitu 3. "I hit my Service button. The Schedule's fine." He didn't know what was going on, any more than Metoo did, but, in the few dealings he'd had with her, she'd made him feel comfortable. People weren't generally nice to Pitu, so he liked being around someone whose default setting was kindness. She was one of the reasons he was hoping to become Tobe's Assistant; she would be a great Companion to work with. This might be his chance.

"Specified clearance," she said, opening the door. "Come in."

Metoo checked Pitu 3 in with Service, and, having allowed him access, turned to go.

"I have to check some personal file footage for this morning," said Pitu 3.

Metoo turned and looked at him.

"I'm sorry?" she asked.

"Footage," he answered, "05:58 to 06:03." Pitu wanted to engage Metoo, partly because he seldom had anyone to talk to, but also because she might be able to influence his promotion to Assistant; after all, it had been four years.

"I'm sorry?" she asked again.

Metoo had managed not to panic twice already this morning, and it was not yet 9 o'clock. Her regular Service had tripled almost before the day had begun in earnest, and now this. She stood for a moment, facing Pitu 3, as he turned to look at her. Her hands were clasped in front of her, but she showed no other signs of tension.

"You have specified clearance," she said, "you don't have to tell me anything."

She knew what he was doing. He was reviewing the footage of the sock incident. Pitu 3 would watch Tobe sit down to his breakfast, he would hear Tobe say, 'It's the same', he would watch Metoo turn back, and he would hear the squeak her sock made on the linopro.

The event had taken seconds, but Tobe had been careful to make sure that Pitu 3 saw everything. Why wasn't Tobe doing the maths? Tobe had instant, total recall; why waste time making Pitu 3 review the footage, work out what Tobe needed, and then do the maths? Tobe could do it in significantly less time.

What did probability have to do with any of it?

Metoo's last thought was that it should have been her. If Tobe wanted to delegate, while he did something else, why had he given the work to Pitu 3, his Student, rather than his Assistant?

Pitu left Tobe's flat with a skip in his step. He wasn't quite jubilant, but his confidence was certainly boosted. If he could get this right, and accomplish the maths in short order, he might have a chance. Metoo was not the only one who had thought about Tobe's motives.

Pitu returned to his room, hit his Service button, and took up the rag that hung from a hook on his wipe-wall. He obliterated everything but three of the formulae on the left-hand side, and set to work. This was real-world maths, and, in real-world maths, results were immediate and gratifying, unlike the theoretical stuff he wrestled with every day.

Pitu 3 was not the best theoretical mathematician in Tobe's class, but it had been his turn to have the first tutorial of the day, in rotation, and he was going to make the best of this opportunity. He had been given an Assistant's job, and he was determined to prove that he would be a fine Assistant, that he was ready for promotion.

The probability of Pitu 3 having the first tutorial of the day should have been one in eleven, but there were only four tutorial days in a week, so, in theory, there was only a one in eleven by four in seven chance that the sock incident would have fallen on a day when his tutorial was first. However, it could take up to twenty days to cover eleven 08:30 tutorials, cutting those chances from four in seven to only eleven in twenty. He had beaten odds of one in eleven by eleven in twenty. This was a good day.

When Pitu 3 had gone, Metoo returned to Service.

"Anomalies?" she asked.

"Minor and monitoring," Service answered.

"Very well," said Metoo.

Tobe stood in the middle of his room, examining the calculations on the wipe-wall, which stretched wildly from one side to the other, filling all the space that he could reasonably reach without stretching too high, or stooping too low. The answer should have been there. Probability should have been the answer. The calculations appeared to be correct. Tobe looked at his hands. He held a pen in his right hand, and a rag in his left. He looked down, and saw the book lying, open, forgotten at his feet. He bent to pick it up.

"It was the same," he said, folding the book closed, and sitting down with a sigh.

SERVICE SENT A tone to Tobe's flat ten times between Pitu 3 leaving, and their, noon, lunchtime.

Tobe had missed his ten other timetabled tutorials, and, for each one missed, Metoo had reset the Student's Schedule, and asked the question, 'Anomalies?' Each time, the answer had been, "Minor and monitoring". This was by no means the first time that Service had kept her busy because of Tobe, but Metoo could not help but be concerned. What was it he had said this morning? She could always ask Service if she could review the footage, but thought better of it; she didn't want to arouse suspicion, or give Service an excuse to bring in an Assistant. She would wait. She would wait, and talk to Tobe over lunch.

At noon, Metoo reset the Schedule; Tobe was never late, and, in five more minutes, Service would send her another tone. She wondered, for a moment, what the record was for the number of tones in one day, but only for a moment. Why torture herself?

At ten past noon, Metoo steered Tobe out of his office, by the arm. She had entered to find him sitting with a book in his lap, staring at the wipe-wall. It was the book she'd retrieved from the top shelf for him, but now the pages were stained with inky fingerprints, and were ragged at the edges and creased at the corners, as if from years of use.

"Lunch?" she asked.

"But..." he began.

"Lunch," she said again, more firmly.

"Lunch," he replied.

METOO LED TOBE to his stool at the kitchen counter, and then stood opposite him, preparing their lunch of noodles and vegetables. She vacuum sealed the noodles into the steamer, and set to work with a knife, slicing a pepper into strips so thin that they were almost transparent, and cutting slits in the spring onions before dropping them into cold water for them to flower. She watched him as she worked.

"Pitu 3 was here this morning," she said.

He looked up at her, uncomprehending.

"The maths," she said, "the physics of my socks."

"Yes," he said.

The room was silent for a long moment, apart from the scratch of her knife against the counter.

"Are you content?" she asked, at last.

He looked at her, again, without answering. At least he was looking at her.

She arranged the vegetables on small plates, and emptied the steaming noodles into two dishes. Taking cutlery from the drawer under the counter, she said, "We'll need an Assistant one day; it won't be him, of course."

Silence.

Tobe's eyes were closed, his head tilted back slightly, and his lips were moving, almost imperceptibly.

Metoo looked at him. She reached over and touched the back of one of his hands, as it lay, supine, on the counter.

"Eat," she said, and then, again, "eat."

Tobe's eyes remained closed, his head tilted, and his lips

moving. Metoo reached across the counter, and took his face firmly between her hands. His lips stopped moving, and he opened his eyes. She let his face go, but made eye contact, and kept her gaze on him.

"Lunch," she said.

PITU 3 ATE Repast with the other Students. He wanted to tell someone about what had happened between him and Tobe in their tutorial that morning, but he didn't want to jinx his luck, and, besides, he didn't really have anyone he could confide in.

The Students all had their own thoughts on why they had not had tutorials, the consensus being that Tobe was busy with something of his own. His Students expected very little of their Master, and were never surprised for long when their studies were suspended; they invariably began again, soon enough, and often with renewed vigour. The best mathematicians among them were always eager to make progress on their own, and most of the rest were content to take extra Recreation, which often included sleep. Pitu was the only member of the class who had work to do that day: a real, honest-to-goodness job, set by Tobe. He had no desire to share either the work or the credit he expected to get for it, and so he kept quiet.

WHILE TOBE NAPPED, after lunch, Metoo went back to his office. She flicked through the book that he had been referring to, checking back and forth through the pages to follow his reference points while she scrutinised the maths on the wipe-wall.

"Probability," she murmured to herself. This was kid's stuff, mandatory in the School's maths class, but soon finished with. She followed Tobe's working. One way or another, he had extrapolated every formula in the canon to try to move probability on, to get an answer, but she could not divine what he was trying to find the answer to. She scrutinised the wall again; if she could work out the mathematical problem, perhaps she could set Tobe back on his path. Much more of this and she would be creating anomalies. Much more of this, and she would have to answer to Service for her actions as well as his.

Metoo flicked through the book again. The title page and the end papers were the only pages in the book not sullied by fingerprints and ink spots. She had read the title page this morning, to ascertain that she had found the right book. She turned to the end papers and read, 'Probability extends beyond the mathematical. In the real world, probability has no memory.'

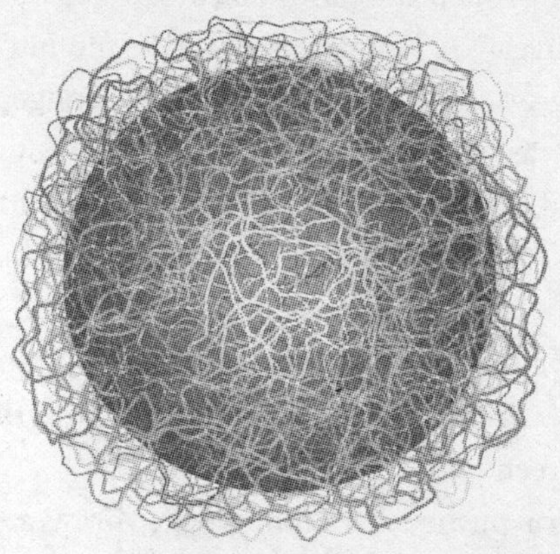

Chapter Three

A SEA OF thready lights formed a haloed globe on the screen in front of the Operator, pulsing, connecting, receding, and then repeating patterns in random order.

The screen at Workstation 2 then blinked out, fizzed and blinked out again. The Operator moved the flat bottom of his curled left fist over the counter-top, back and forth, before lifting it and thumping hard. The screen blacked out entirely, and then throbbed back to life

The Operator left his fist where it was, in readiness, and continued to watch the screen for several minutes. His other hand rested on a grubby rubberpro sphere set into the marked beige counter in front of him.

"Reset zoom to 38, 42," said the Operator, rolling the sphere left, right and then left again in ever-decreasing increments. The screen zoomed in, and the threads of light began to look like a piece of string, woven with various shades of blue, in a tangled mass.

The Operator rolled the palm-sized, rubberpro sphere again, and said, "Hover." A length of thread came into sharp focus. It was a cool grey colour, pale among the stronger blue lengths, and its pulse was barely visible.

"Anomaly at sector 38," said the Operator, hitting a button. "Tone sent." The screen in front of him blinked, and he tensed his fist slightly, as if flexing to deliver a second thump to the counter. He waited. The screen blinked again, and thrummed. When it came back up to full resolution, the threads on the screen were green.

The Operator pushed his chair back, threw a switch on the facing edge of the counter, and raised his hands.

College Service was run from a building at the North-East edge of the campus. It recruited directly from the College Students, but the Operators were a group apart, living and working away from the Student body.

When Service had been set up globally, almost two centuries before, it quickly became clear that there were no benefits to Operators fraternising with Students or Civilians; it was not only pointless, but also counter-productive. Even entry-level Operators could not talk about Service, and they certainly couldn't bend the rules for anyone, and that was what most Students and Civilians would want from them.

Selection for Service worked in much the same way as any selection process. They were Drafted as Students to the School, but their family groups tended to be made up entirely of future Operators. They were, generally, the most private people, with the lowest natural adrenalin and cortisol levels, and the highest boredom thresholds. Most were solitary in their habits, but when they did form bonds it was invariably with others like them, so there was very little hardship in being segregated.

Incoming Students never knew what they were being Drafted for, but all assumed that they were being groomed as Assistants and Companions, and that the remainder were wastage, fed back into the system, as Seniors, or moved on.

The system had endured for two centuries, and the same pattern was employed in each of the 987 Colleges throughout the World. There had been a 1,000 Colleges originally, but one had famously failed, several had amalgamated, and others had become redundant. Service Central believed that survival depended on a little over half of the Colleges having an Active in residence at any given time. There were currently 742 Actives in residence with close to three hundred more in their teens.

The lifespan of an Active could not be pre-determined, but genetic combinations were researched constantly, and potential Actives were being discovered at increasingly early ages. Breeding programs for selectable children had proven unpopular, but blood-testing all pregnant women had led to early detection of all group types. Balance did not need to be imposed. Initially, parents were told their likelihood of producing selectable offspring, and this had led to a certain pride in the status of their children, and a strong desire to provide balance. More children were being born selectable, and raised balanced than ever before, but the natural incidence of Actives seemed to be static.

Named Operator Strazinsky wove his way across the Service floor, between equipment racks, heading for the Operator's raised hands. The Service Floor was circular, the centre taken up with hardware, equipment racks for peripherals, and Techs, assessing and making repairs and replacements. The Service screens faced into the space, set eight feet apart, in an arc covering 270 degrees of the room. Operators did not often speak to each other, and could only see the screen in front of them: one Operator, one screen.

Their job was to calibrate the system, check for anomalies, and send tones. One of the nine Workstations on this Service Floor monitored the resident Active. The other eight monitored, variously, four Masters, two Companions, one Assistant, and one neutral control from the Seniors. Only data for the Active was relevant, but part of the learning curve when the system was first run involved the Operators' stress levels. Originally, Operators that had known they were working with Actives had high stress levels, despite their natural dispositions, so the system was set up to include non-Actives. As a consequence, Operators weren't kept idle for long periods of time, but could work regular hours, rather than waiting in the wings for their big moment. It also meant that Operators lived in larger communities, rather than in twos and threes, which also improved mental health.

With nips, and tucks over the two centuries since its inception, Service ran fairly smoothly across the globe. There were problems with ageing technology, and some environments proved particularly corrosive to hardware, but ongoing data showed that the entire system worked better if full Service was run at every College, regardless of whether there was an Active in residence.

It had also proved beneficial to run Colleges at the local level. No Student attended College outside his national borders, so language and customs were not an issue. Locality proved more important than colour or religion in placing Students.

Several dozen Colleges had not had an Active for more than two generations, but they were maintained, none-the-less.

* * *

STRAZINSKY HANDED THE Operator a pair of worn, stained neoprene gloves with cotton liners, and waited for him to vacate the chair. Strazinsky sat in his place, and keyed in his Morse signature, using the switch on the facing edge of the counter in front of him. Then, he pulled in his chair, which still carried his predecessor's body-heat, and rested his right hand on the rubberpro sphere.

He rotated the sphere slowly, checking the halo around the mass of green, throbbing threads. Having completed the corona, he moved the sphere methodically left and right, and up and down, covering the entire surface of the screen, checking one sector at a time. False positives were not uncommon, but Strazinsky was scrupulous in his line-check. Thirty minutes into the procedure, he had found nothing of note, but the lights remained green. The previous Operator was still standing behind his chair, awaiting instructions.

"Get me a headset," said Strazinsky.

"Verify," said the Operator.

"Verify headset," said Strazinsky, and the Operator turned and made his way quickly across the Service Floor to the equipment racks at its centre. There was no headset on the first rack, so he moved to the second. Still, there was no headset.

"Tech," said the Operator.

A Tech popped up from somewhere on the floor to the Operator's right, and asked, "Sir?"

"There are no headsets on these two racks," said the Operator. "Get me a bloody headset."

Seconds were passing, and the Operator could be penalised if he took too long; he could be demoted, or even removed from Service altogether. No Operator ever left his station without his replacement on hand, and no Operator of Strazinsky's grade would ever turn his gaze away from the screen for even a moment. When the Operator thought he could feel Strazinsky's eyes boring into the back of his head, after another 45 seconds had passed, and he still didn't have a headset in his hand, he was mistaken, possibly deluded.

After two minutes, Strazinsky was finally inserting the earpiece on the headset and adjusting the mic before saying, "Receive audio."

He listened in.

"Anomalies?" asked a woman's voice, apparently calmly.

"Minor and monitoring," said Service.

Strazinsky pulled the headset's view-screen down in front of his left eye, and said, "Receive visual."

The three-inch screen filled with drifting snow. Strazinsky waited.

"Receive visual," he said, again. The screen in front of his left eye blinked into life.

It had taken thirty-four minutes from the Operator's alert to Strazinsky getting full audio and visual: thirty-four minutes. There was nothing to see, now, or hear.

"Void visual," he said, lifting the screen away from his face. He examined the swirling, pulsing green strings of light in front of him for another sixty seconds, and then said, "Void audio."

Strazinsky took off the headset, and handed it back to the Operator, who still wore the neoprene gloves, even though his hands were becoming uncomfortably warm inside them.

"Rack 2," said Strazinsky, "and stand down."

The Operator turned his back on Strazinsky, and began to peel off the gloves. He walked over to rack 2, and placed the headset on the hook provided. He breathed once, long and slow, and left the Service Floor. The debrief on a stand-down would take a minimum of an hour, and could take much longer if he didn't remain calm.

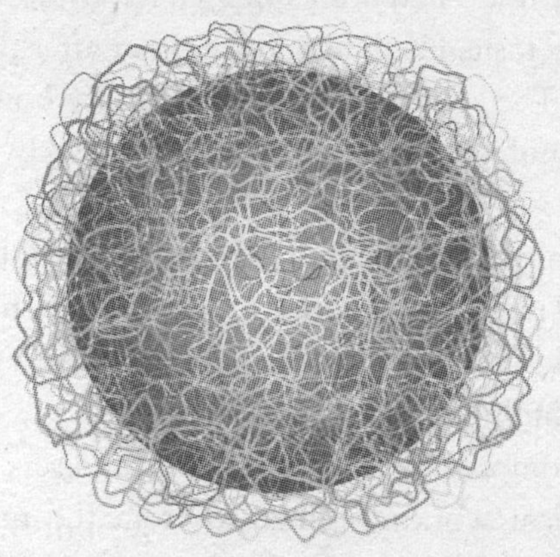

Chapter Four

TOBE DIDN'T SEE his Students for their tutorials the day after he had taken up his interest in probability. The day after that was a rest day, and no tutorials were Scheduled. It was not difficult for Metoo to switch the Schedule out so that rest days were irregular, and Tobe would not lose any work-time. The Students' hours would be made up in short order, and everything would return to normal.

PITU 3 WOKE up, hit his button, and checked his Schedule. Metoo had cancelled tutorials. Pitu had hoped to finish his sock project, and deliver the results with aplomb during his tutorial, which had been Scheduled for the afternoon session: plenty of time. He had just been given an extra day.

Pitu stood on the hard, cracked linopro of his room, his feet naked, his hands wrapped around a very mediocre bowl of oatpro; the grittiness had been swapped for a watery texture and a faintly soapy taste. He didn't notice either after the first couple of spoonfuls. The spoon sat in the half-empty bowl, untouched for several minutes as the contents cooled quickly, and began to congeal.

Pitu stared at the wipe-wall. Not only had he intended getting the maths and physics of the sock problem down, he had actually managed to do it quickly and without apparent errors. It never crossed his mind to wonder why.

He hit the compress button on the wall, and several neat pages of mathematical workings emerged from the mini-print slot. The work was both immaculate and correct. He hoped that the solution was elegant, but could not be sure.

Pitu 3 had accomplished his task, and had twenty-four hours to catch up with the other Students, and get a little further forward with the theoretical problems that tended to stretch his thinking past its natural elastic limit. He put the bowl of cold oatpro on the chair, the spoon sticking out of it at an unlikely angle created by the congealed breakfast food, and took the rag off its hook on the wipe-wall. It would take him an hour to reinstate the hard-learned formulae on the left of the wall before he could even begin to add to his learning, or at least make the attempt.

METOO PLACED THE dish of perfectly cooked eggpro in front of Tobe, and excused herself. She turned her back on him, and walked the short distance to the only closed door in the flat. Tobe liked to be able to see the space around him when he was not working. When he was in his office, he was content with his four walls and all the ideas they contained; at home, he liked to know what was beyond every threshold. He never entered Metoo's room, and her door was never much more than barely ajar, but he didn't like the door to be closed, and, beyond the door, he didn't like the room to be in darkness. It was as though it might contain something predatory.

As it was, he was a little afraid of other people. He disliked their private domains: the places that he had no reference for, and didn't understand, with their odd smells and strange, unnecessary objects, arranged without purpose, or thought to symmetry. When Metoo knew she would be spending time with Tobe, she left all the doors wide open, and Tobe's door was kept permanently open with a little wooden wedge, carved with a stylised owl. Neither Metoo nor Tobe could remember the door in any other position, nor did either of them know where the wedge had come from; it had certainly been in situ when Metoo had joined the household.

Metoo kept the door closed on the Companion's room. It was a superior space to the Assistant's room, with better climate control, a bigger floor-plan and better light. It had, originally, been intended for the Master, but he preferred the small, Spartan room at the end of the corridor, which had been designed for the lowliest member of the household: the room that Pitu 3 still believed he could earn.

She opened the door to the Companion's room, just far enough for her to squeeze through the gap, and closed it quickly behind her. Most of the flats had three bedrooms for their usual three inhabitants, and when it had been decided that Metoo should serve Tobe in her dual role, the third room had become vacant. She was at liberty to inhabit it, as she was acting Companion, but she requisitioned Service to use it for another purpose. Masters, once housed, were never moved, their households revolving squarely around them. There was no question of them taking up residence in one of the smaller units, so Service had allowed her request.

Metoo's reasoning was both sound and simple. The flat had to be heated and cooled, and she would not use any extra light, because the sun provided all that she needed through the south-facing window. The room would cost nothing to run, except for her time and hard work.

She had grown the first plants from seeds that she had saved from requisitioned fruit, putting them in saucers filled with scraps of blotting paperpro, or old cotpro socks. She was thrilled when little plants grew, and was soon producing small amounts of fruit. Gradually, over a number of weeks and months, she requisitioned more suitable receptacles and growing mediums, switching them out with her food and clothing rations, and she soon had a very viable indoor garden.

During her second High alone with Tobe, Service had offered Metoo the use of part of the garden area that backed onto the flats. It had been intended for vehicles, when they had been privately owned, but had been returned to a more natural state in the last century. The robust, year-round planting was a natural aid to global cooling, but their seemed no reason why Metoo should not grow some of her own food, especially when it benefitted the rest of the community, both in terms of rations, and the pretty garden she had built.

Metoo ambled around her room, which amounted to a combination potting shed and hothouse, spraying some of the larger plants, and releasing some of the germinating seeds from beneath their swathes of wadding. Not wanting to disturb Tobe, not wanting his company for a few more minutes, Metoo opened the tall window on the south side of the room, sat on its ledge, and swung her legs out, dropping gently down onto the grass on the other side. Her garden was only metres away, and she went to inspect the levels in her precious water-butts, and look at the seedlings she had already planted.

Tobe sat at the kitchen counter in his clean robe. His hair was still a little wet, and it dripped slightly onto his neck, leaving a spreading run of water droplets down the back of his robe. He spooned the last of the eggpro into his mouth, and looked down into the empty dish.

"It is the same," he said.

METOO LOOKED UP, suddenly. She gazed across the greensward that separated her from the flat, uncomprehending, and cast a brief glance through the garden-room window.

She caught her breath.

Tobe stood on the other side of the window.

Adrenalin threatened to pump panic through Metoo as she stood among her plants, and her visual acuity was increased to the point where she could see a tiny drop of water fall from a strand of Tobe's fringe, onto his forehead.

"It is the same," he said.

Tobe turned from the window, and was gone before Metoo could reach him. She gathered her robe in one hand, and thrust one naked leg in through the window, without ceremony. She closed the garden-room door behind her, took one deep breath, and walked into the kitchen.

Tobe stood on the other side of the counter, facing her, looking down into the empty breakfast dish that sat in the space between them. His hands were flat on the counter, and Metoo watched them for a moment. They were still. He did not seem agitated. She looked at his down-turned face, but could not catch his eye. Metoo reached across the counter and took Tobe's face gently in her hands. He looked up at her, and she smiled at him. He looked the same.

Tobe picked up the empty breakfast dish and handed it to

Metoo. Then he left the kitchen, and Metoo heard the door of the flat close behind him as he went to work in his office.

The bowl still in her hands, Metoo walked around to the other side of the counter, and sat down on Tobe's stool. She stared into the space where she had just been standing. She sat there for several seconds before she took another breath. Her shoulders slumped slightly as she stared into the space on the other side of the kitchen counter. There was nothing very much to see, certainly nothing new. Everything was the same as it had been since she'd moved into the flat.

She sat on the stool, the dish in her hand, for several minutes. Of course it was the same; that was the point. Tobe didn't like change. He liked routine. He liked to know what was coming next. He liked the familiar. He obsessed about anything new that came into his life. The garden room had been running for several years, and still he had never entered it, not until today. He had never even opened the door, before. What was going on?

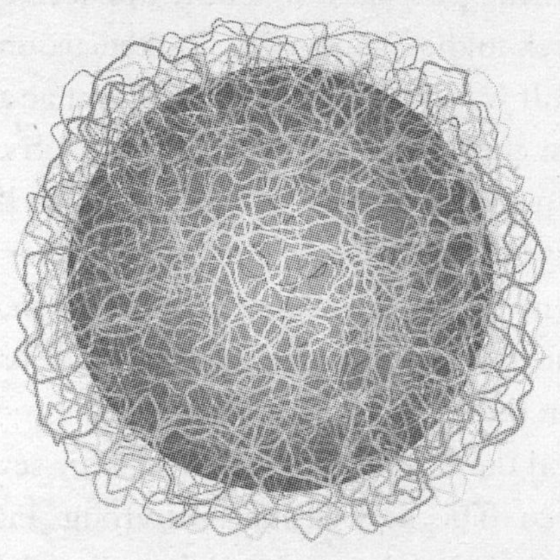

Chapter Five

SERVICE DECIDED THAT, on the third day after Tobe took up his interest in probability, the Schedule would replicate that of the first, fateful day. Anomalies had occurred during the intervening period, and there was an ebb and flow to them that might become a pattern. Strazinsky maintained the Code Green throughout that period, and all the relevant Schedules were re-set.

PITU 3 ARRIVED for his 08:30 tutorial early, and was waiting outside Tobe's office door when the Master arrived. Tobe did not acknowledge Pitu; he simply opened the door, and allowed his student to follow him into the room.

Pitu stopped on the threshold to the office, watching as Tobe tiptoed across the floor, weaving his way to the centre of the room in tiny increments, as he avoided standing on chalked workings, and ragged pages of script, apparently torn out of books and stuck to the linopro. Pitu looked around the door to the wipe-wall. It was covered in maths, formulae and equations weaving across the wall, and, often, across each other. At least two different pens had been used, one of which had obviously failed halfway through an equation, which petered out before being picked up again in another colour, so that the middle of the thought faded, and then disappeared, leaving a solitary white space on the wall.

Pitu stood on the threshold to the office for several seconds, his mouth open. This was wrong, all wrong. Pitu was thrust back into his distant past to a time when disorder meant pain, to a time when he had been too young to understand the cruelty that was meted out to him. He wanted to cry out, as he remembered, for the first time in years, the beatings, the hunger and the neglect. Then he came-to, as if out of a trance.

He took hold of the button on the cord around his neck, and pressed, holding it between his thumb and forefinger, and not letting go.

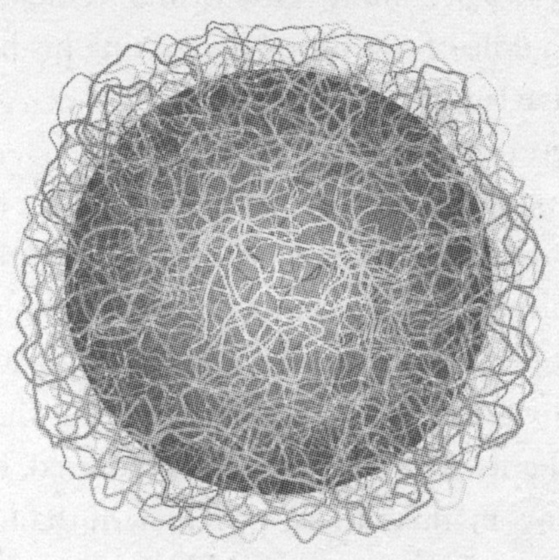

Chapter Six

TOBE LEFT THE flat and made his way to his office, a wet patch still visible on the back of his robe from his dripping hair.

He let himself into his room and set to work. His hands flew as he crossed out equations on his wipe-wall, or linked them to others. Some equations got new brackets, or were swept away altogether with the swinging of the rag he held in his left hand.

Periodically, Tobe picked up *On Probability*, thumbed through it, and lighted on a page that seemed useful. He tore out the page, leaving more ink-smudged fingerprints on it, and licked the back of it, using his spit to stick the page to the wipe-wall.

Two hours later, the office shelves were beginning to look like a crone's toothless grin, with volumes pulled out, apparently at random, and the remaining books leaning into each other, leaving black, triangular gaps.

An hour after that, the wipe-wall was full of cross-referenced workings-out, and brimming with formulae, old and new. Tobe stood in the middle of the room, examining his handiwork, as if he might have forgotten something.

He had forgotten nothing.

Tobe had a photographic memory for almost everything, but especially for mathematics, including all the work he had ever done. He could reproduce any solution to any problem that he had solved in his thirty-five years, including all the various dead-end pathways he had followed, and all the missteps he had made and erased along the way. If required, he could have reproduced any mathematical problem he had solved, with reference to the colours of pen he'd had on hand, and the ink smudges he had left behind in his haste.

The wall was full, all the reference was in place, and, still, Tobe had no solution.

"It was the same," he said, looking from the wipe-wall to the tattered book in his hands, the cover barely clinging to the remaining pages, fewer than half of them left. He tossed the book onto the chair, its cover coming free as it sailed across the room. The remaining pages scattered across the floor, and the cover landed half-on, half-off the chair, its sky-blue book-cloth hanging over the edge of the seat.

Tobe got on his hands and knees on the floor, and began to collect up the pages. He stopped, and looked at the bundle in his fist. He pulled out one of the pages and skim-read it. He licked it and stuck it to the linopro. Then he looked around for something to write with.

THE CONTENTS OF Tobe's room had not changed since he had taken it over, almost twenty years earlier. One or two things had been added, notably, more books, wedged tightly onto the shelves, which now extended to the full height of the room, beyond anyone's natural reach.

The top two shelves had been added five years earlier, and had caused a great deal of huffing and blowing on Tobe's part. He had not been able to enter his office, alone, for several weeks. The little stepladder that he needed to retrieve the books on the top shelves had lived in the corridor outside his room for two Highs, and had finally been brought in by Metoo; it had taken all day for Tobe to decide exactly where they should live in the room. Tobe's chair was the one he had inherited when he had taken over the room, and had, in its long life, had five replacement legs, two new seats, and a grand total of eight back-rests. The fact that it was, essentially, an entirely different chair to the one that Tobe had first used seemed lost on him.

Tobe seldom worked at his desk, preferring to use the expanse of the wipe-wall, and then print his work off to share it, or to illustrate his intentions to his students and other mathematicians that he corresponded with around the World. The contents of the desk drawers were constant, and the bottom drawer on the left still held the old-fashioned and obsolete mechanical drawing, measuring and calculating devices that he had collected and been obsessed by as a kid. The drawer also held a box of chalk, long sticks of dusty yellow that had probably not been used anywhere in the World for at least fifty years, and possibly more than a century, and a collection of various types of antique chemical inks.

Tobe opened the drawer, from his position kneeling on the floor, and took out the box of chalk. He turned it over several times in his hands, and then opened it. He took out the first stick of chalk, and then replaced it. He looked at the dusty residue on his forefinger and thumb, smelled it, and licked it. He took the same piece of chalk out of the box, again, and, tentatively, made a mark with it on the linopro. He looked down at the mark, and started to get off his knees to go to the wipe-wall. As he stood, he realised that he had smudged the chalk mark, not quite obliterating it, but fading it dramatically. He looked down at his robe, and saw a yellow smudge on it. He took the rag from its hook on the wipe-wall, and went back to wipe away the chalk mark. When he had finished, it was even less distinct than it had been when he'd knelt in it, but it could still be seen, as if the colour had faded from a tiny patch of the linopro.

For the next two hours, Tobe stood, bent double at the waist, working out his mathematical problem using chalk on linopro. He worked around his feet, and then moved them carefully to bare patches of floor so that he could continue his calculations.

As Metoo walked along the corridor, towards Tobe's office, he emerged, closed the door behind him, and turned. She raised her hand in greeting, and they walked towards each other. Then she turned, took his arm, and walked with him back to the flat.

Her relief was palpable. Metoo rarely went to his office, unless Service needed her to, or Tobe asked for her, but he seemed not to think it strange to see her there. She had not known what she would find, or what to expect. Yesterday had been disturbing in so many ways, and Tobe's actions this morning, entering the garden-room, had done nothing to alleviate Metoo's concerns.

He had been gone since six o'clock this morning, starting work at least a couple of hours before his usual time, so she was relieved to see him leaving his office at his regular lunch hour.

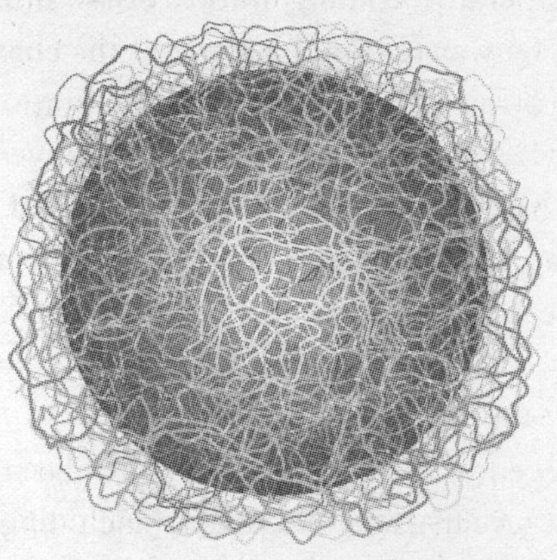

Chapter Seven

The Operator had been out for the rest of the previous day, being de-briefed. He could tell Service nothing that they didn't already know. He had followed Protocol, and could answer for every decision. In fact, he had not made any decisions; he had simply done what was required of him. There would be no reprimand, or demotion, but neither had he done anything of note; he would not be hailed a hero. He would return to his Workstation at Service as soon as Code Blue was re-established, and maintained for a specified period, which had not yet been decided, but which would, undoubtedly, mirror the length of time that the station was in Code Green. His stand-down could be of any duration, but he did not expect it to be longer than a few days, at most, and he looked forward to the respite. No Operator was ever assigned to an alternate Workstation: one Operator, one screen, one Station.

Strazinsky, on the other hand, had a very full timetable. As the Named Operator coming into a crisis situation, with a Code change, he was required to see out the change. However long it took, Strazinsky must remain on-Station throughout the crisis, until all settings were restored and verified, or until the situation hit critical mass for a change of Code-status to Yellow. He had expected a long night. What he did not expect was ever to be relieved of his post because of a Code ramp-up.

In the two centuries that Service had been global, two extraordinary events had occurred, including the famous failure of one of the Colleges.

On that occasion, Code Red had been reached in less than thirty minutes, and had seen four changes of Operator, from Blue to Green and then on, in turn, to Yellow, Orange, and finally Red. The staff change-overs had not happened fast enough, and there had been a massive loss of life at the American College in the Old Mid-West. The College had not survived. More than decimated, it had lost almost three in four of its inhabitants. Death fell democratically across all ages and grades: a thousand Students, Seniors and Assistants died, along with more than a hundred Masters and Companions. Two Actives had also perished.

The event, known as 'the Meltdown' had happened because of a naive and fundamental mistake. The premier Active's Companion, Abel, had been a charismatic, who had developed a religious cult, and placed his Master at the centre of it. His Master also happened to be, although it was not known within College, Active. Religious tolerance had been a basic tenet of global government since the historic struggles of the twentieth and twenty-first centuries, and no thought was given to the elevated, God-like persona that was imposed on the Active. It did not appear to impair his work in any way, and it resulted in a docile College workforce, and a sense of purpose among the Companions and Assistants. Within two Highs, cult members were being recruited from the Drafted, and, within five, all Assistants and Companions were promoted according to their status within the cult, rather than their suitability for the job.

The religious fervour of the majority of the inhabitants of the College seemed to aid its smooth running rather than impair it, and Service, both Daily and Scheduled, worked virtually without a hitch.

Without the stimulus of personalities clashing and shifting, and, without the usual office politics, Service at the College became lazy and bloated. Shift patterns were regular, and Named Operators barely worked at all.

The Active, who was entirely benign in the venture, was considered elderly in terms of effective Masters, and was increasingly infirm, but his ailments had been kept from his followers. Service Central decided to maintain the Active as the figurehead of the cult, in his dotage, and introduce a new Active. That was when the problems began, and, although it was some time before the scenario played out, it was already beyond College Service to recognise or forestall, let alone prevent, the inevitable.

No one quite knew how, but Abel, the instigator and effective head of the cult, had somehow detected that his Master was Active, and he was also able to sniff out the new Active when he arrived, as a boy of fourteen, to replace a Master who was hospitalised for dementia at the end of High that year.

Selection procedures had changed and developed over the hundred and fifty years since, evolving into a system that was virtually flawless, and which, certainly, would never allow another Abel to be Drafted.

In the College's final hours, Abel set about testing his influence over the Active's disciples. It proved so widespread, so pervasive, and so utterly outside the control of Service, that he was able to mastermind an announcement, setting out the Messiah's deathbed wishes, and instigating a mass suicide.

Service had no warning of the announcement, hearing it simultaneously with the rest of the College.

After that, everything happened very fast. In half-an-hour the event was over.

In the aftermath, when the situation was analysed from all angles, by experts in the field, new rules and regulations were set out. It took some time to formulate guidelines that would not restrict freedom of religious expression, but it was finally accomplished. A system was also initiated whereby rules and regulations were constantly tested and verified.

SERVICE WAS TWO hundred years old. It did not run like clockwork, but no one had seen a Code Orange or higher for fifty years, and Service Central was proud to claim that it would never see another Meltdown.

THE OTHER MAJOR incident had happened within thirty years of the first. It had been much less dramatic, and, as it turned out, less damaging, but no one had known that at the time.

A very well-established College in the Urals came under some criticism from Service Central for corruption, and the decision was made to bring in an entire new Service team. The team of brightest and best had been assembled from all points of the globe, when personal travel was still widespread. Specialists were brought in from South America and Western Europe, and the bespoke team was trained together and all started work on the same day.

On paper, the new system had looked perfect, impenetrable, with more built-in fail-safes than would ever be required. It had taken two years for the College to fall apart. The collapse was slow, but the problems were deep-seated, political and incredibly divisive. The imposition of an entire new Service team proved too much for the Masters' entourages, and the Seniors and Students to bear. The problems went deeper than anyone had realised, including Service Central, and proved impossible to solve. The situation at the College became progressively worse, and culminated in a stand-off between East and West. Sensibilities and prejudices through centuries of back-biting and in-fighting had caused a rift that could not be solved by shared education alone.

Ironically, the College did not have an Active in residence at the time of the collapse, and, for the most part, the Masters, who had very little interest in political and cultural differences, were oblivious to what was going on.

There would never be another Meltdown, but, to prevent it, the College was dismantled, wholesale. The oldest of the Masters were retired, with their Companions and Assistants, and, those that could be, were re-assigned. Some took years to settle in their new positions, and others never managed it, and were, eventually, put out to pasture. The Service team was broken up, and all members re-assigned to Colleges close to their birthplaces, some returning to the Colleges where they had been to School.

At that point, it was decided that, as far as possible, all College inhabitants should be local, and any new Colleges should be populated slowly, over a number of years. It also became clear that trying to move Masters from one College to another was all but impossible, and the rules were changed so that Masters could not be moved without their express permission; it was understood that the very nature of Masters meant that this was extremely unlikely ever to happen.

There was always a free-flow of ideas across the World, especially where education was concerned. Masters, and particularly Actives, did not understand prejudice, and connected only at a cerebral level. They might not be able to make eye-contact, or answer a combination question, but they could share ideas and information at an incredibly esoteric level with complete strangers, without any thought of prejudice.

Their social currency was ideas, not religion, routine, habit, custom, dress, or basic education, and, as such, their prejudices were limited. They felt nothing for those who did not communicate ideas back and forth with them, neither good nor bad.

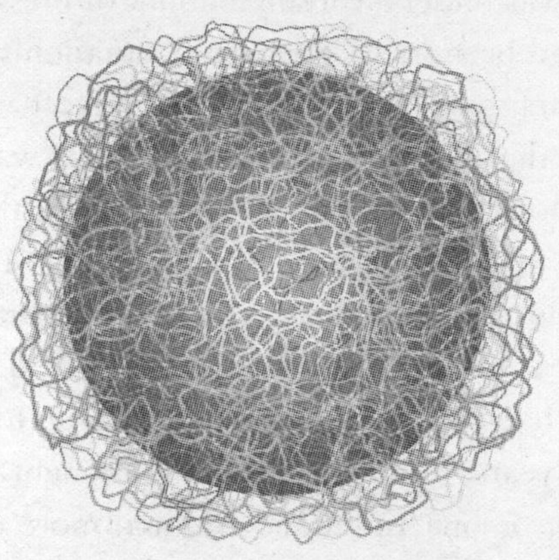

Chapter Eight

PITU 3 WAS still pressing his Service button between his thumb and forefinger when Metoo arrived six minutes after he had first taken hold of it. She would have been quicker, but Named Operator Strazinsky had no precedent for making his next decision; his adrenalin was flowing, and he had almost no concrete information. It took him four minutes to make his move.

His station was reading Code Green, unverified by any tangible threat, and Strazinsky had used his seventeen years of experience in Service, including five as a Named Operator, to conclude that, not only was he working a Master's station, but that his subject was 'away with the fairies': a not terribly kind, but essentially benign phrase that Service used, informally, to describe the many and varied occasions when a Master, or an Active, veered harmlessly from the norms ascertained for his particular character.

Strazinsky was under a certain amount of pressure, not least because he had been in a Code Green situation for more than thirty-six hours, and he knew that his subject was a Master, which meant that he could also be Active. It was the general consensus among Named Service, worldwide, that there was very little to choose between a high-grade Master and an Active, beyond the very specific brainwave pattern that was critical to the safety of the planet. Nothing had been proved, and scientists had been working on the syndrome for more than two hundred years, but it was generally thought that one gene here or there, or one childhood trauma, more or less, could mean the difference between an inert, but useful, beard, and a fully fledged, dyed in the wool, unalterable, unfathomable Active.

Diagnoses were being made increasingly early in the lives of potential Actives, but tests were, even now, by no means conclusive.

Strazinsky's experience in Service played a significant part in his decision-making abilities in this particular instance, and, after the metallic taste in his mouth subsided, and his hands stopped shaking, some four minutes after Pitu 3 compressed his button between his index finger and his thumb, Strazinsky took the conservative route.

If it had been Code Blue, the Operator would have taken Pitu 3 out of the equation; he was probably just a frightened kid, witnessing some of his Master's stranger behaviour for the first time. In the five years that he had been a Named Operator, Strazinsky had worked on Code Green situations a number of times. The Code often got ramped to Green by novice Assistants panicking, or by Students, like Pitu 3, being inexperienced. Things usually cooled off pretty quickly, the problem was resolved, without incident, and the Code Green disabled.

This Code Green had been active for longer than any he had worked before, and Service had not found the problem or neutralised it.

As an Operator, Strazinsky had hit tone buttons that had activated Code Green; as a Named Operator he had never precipitated the ramp-up to Code Yellow.

Strazinsky hit the button on the counter in front of him, despite being fully aware that doing so could change his career, and even his life, forever.

SERVICE SOUNDED IN Tobe's flat.

It took less time for Metoo, hopped up on adrenalin, to make it across campus to Tobe's office than it had for Strazinsky to take the decision to press the Service button on the faded, grubby countertop in front of him.

Metoo arrived, breathless, outside Tobe's office. She looked into the room at him before she did anything else. She looked startled as she peered into the office, her skin pale and her eyes wide as she feared the worst, without knowing just how the worst might manifest.

Tobe did not seem to register her anxiety at all. He stood in the middle of the room, surrounded by torn pages from academic texts, and swathes of handwritten calculations. As things stood, they did not look unduly troubling to Metoo. Tobe was in his office, in the room where he was most comfortable. He had been working, albeit frantically, and obsessively, but she had witnessed similar scenes before, during her time with him. Service had not been quite so trigger-happy on those other occasions.

Metoo did not know that Tobe's station was at Code Green, or that Service had been monitoring the situation for so long.

She did not know that Strazinsky, tired, frazzled and not a little afraid, had been obliged to make a potentially career-altering decision on the Schedule Service button of a second-rate Student, whose standing in the College hierarchy was certainly significantly lower than the man in question preferred to believe.

Tobe was safe, and oblivious, so Metoo, tense, and sweating slightly, dropped her chin onto her chest and drew in a deep breath, before turning to face Pitu 3.

His face was pale and drawn, elongated by the drop of his jaw that had set fair since it had taken up the position more than six minutes earlier. Pitu 3 had clearly never seen anything like this before.

Metoo had seen Tobe like this two or three times a year for as many years as she cared to remember. As a Student, she had admired his ability to cut out the World completely, in order to concentrate on his mathematics. As his Assistant, she had watched Kit dealing with Tobe, inadequately, she had thought at the time, dosing him with anti-depressants and sleeping draughts, and putting him out of action for days or weeks at a time.

Her breathing back to a more normal rhythm, Metoo took hold of Pitu's hand: the one that was gripping the button around his neck so tightly that his knuckles were white.

"You need to let go now," she said. "Pitu, you did the right thing. You did well, Pitu. You can let go of the button now. Let go, Pitu, I'm here. Pitu, it's safe. The Master is safe. Let go of the button, Pitu. Service has sent me. You can stand down."

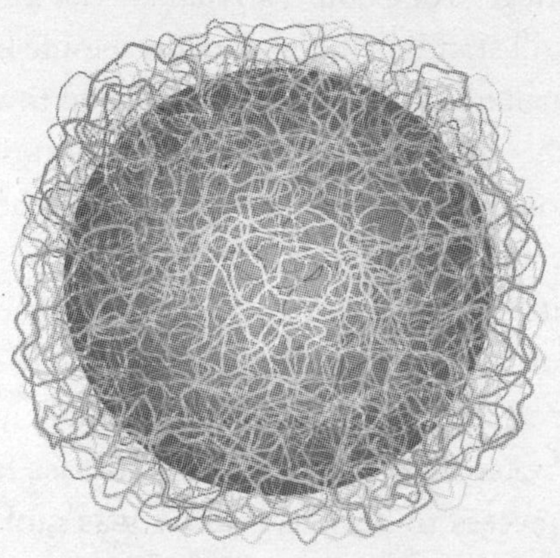

Chapter Nine

"TOBE," SAID METOO, "it's time to go home."

"I've got a tutorial," said Tobe, standing, his feet apart, where he had positioned them in gaps between the chalk calculations and the pages of text books that he had torn out and stuck to the linopro. He seemed completely oblivious to the predicament that he had thrust his Assistant-Companion and Student into.

"Service cancelled the tutorial," said Metoo. "Your Student..." she began before trailing off, and looking at Pitu 3 for inspiration. "Your Student has been taken ill."

Tobe looked at Metoo, who stood in the corridor next to his Student. She could not tell what he was thinking from the expression on his face, but he did not appear to be unduly distressed. The odd situation, and, particularly, the break in his routine was bound to unsettle him, but Metoo's panic was subsiding, and her only immediate concern was to deal with

Pitu 3, and then get Tobe home, so that Service could do its job.

Pitu 3 was still standing in the corridor beside her, his button still hanging around his neck. Metoo reached towards it.

"May I?" she asked, gently taking the button in her hand. Pitu looked down at the button, and then caught her gaze. He looked like he might cry, and she realised that he was in shock.

"It's all right," she said. "I'm going to get some help."

Metoo typed C-Q-D into Service, using Pitu's button and an old Morse signal that she had been taught when she had become Tobe's Assistant-Companion. If all else failed, and she had no other access to Service, Metoo was authorised to use any Student's button, which would relay her individual three letter code, overriding the Student button ident.

Service arrived on the scene in less than two minutes. One of them wore the Medic Operator's armband that reassured Metoo that Pitu 3 would be taken good care of, and one was a Police Operator.

"Ma'am," he said, "did you identify yourself on a button override?"

"Yes," said Metoo.

"Which button, ma'am?" the Police Operator asked.

Metoo pointed at Pitu 3, who was having his pulse and temperature taken by the Operator with the Medic's insignia.

"Mudd," said the Police Operator, speaking to the Medic, and gesturing towards Pitu 3's button, hanging on the grubby chord around his neck. The button was illuminated. Neither Pitu 3 nor Metoo, nor Tobe for that matter, nor half of the Service Operators standing in the hall, had ever seen a lit button. "Remove that, immediately, for verification and processing."

Pitu suddenly broke out in a sweat, and his knees buckled beneath him.

"I..." he began, and then he went down.

The Medic knelt down beside his patient, put him in the recovery position, and slipped the button from around his neck.

"Piggy-back to your Schedule," said the Police Operator, and Mudd removed a length of flat nylon ribbon, from his belt, with a loop and buckle at each end. He buckled one end firmly around Pitu 3's right wrist and the other around his own left. Until Pitu 3 was safely back at Service, he was physically and electronically linked to his Medic Operator. It was for his own safety, as well as for the good of Service, the College, and, potentially, the planet.

Within another two minutes, Pitu 3 had been stretchered out of the corridor. Metoo and the Police Operator remained outside Tobe's door, and Tobe remained, where he had been standing, in the middle of his office.

Two more Service Operators had set themselves up outside Tobe's office, in the corridor on either side of his door.

Metoo realised that the Police Operator was about to cross the threshold, without any thought to the data that covered the floor.

She anticipated the move, and put her hand on his upper arm, firmly.

"Don't," she said.

"He needs to be extracted," said the Operator.

"Not like that, he doesn't," answered Metoo.

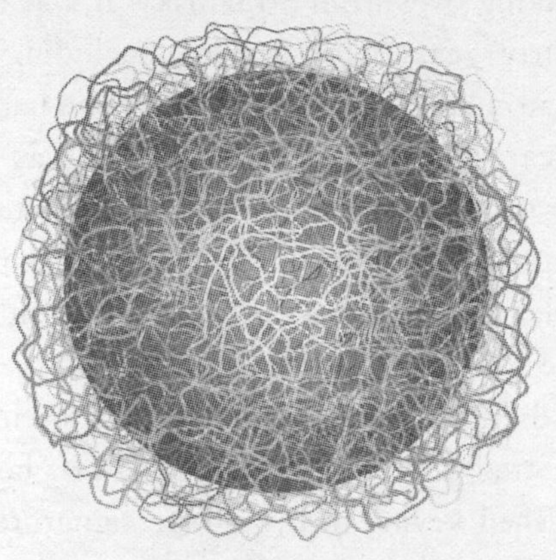

Chapter Ten

NAMED OPERATOR STRAZINSKY had pushed his chair away from the screen in front of him, and thrown the switch on the facing edge of the counter. He was running his hands up and down his thighs, partly to relieve his anxiety, and partly to wipe away the sweat that had collected in his palms. His hands should have been raised. He remembered Protocol, and lifted his hands into the air, as if in a gesture of surrender.

A TONE SOUNDED on the Service Floor. The remaining eight Operators stopped what they were doing, pushed their chairs back from their screens, and threw the switches on the facing edges of their counters. Eight pairs of hands were raised into the air.

The first man into the room was Ranked Operator Dudley. He was on duty on the Service Floor, and had the dubious privilege of taking over from Strazinsky. It was his first Code Yellow in thirty years with Service, including twelve as a Ranked Operator. He had found his niche and had no ambition to climb the career ladder any further. He was a short, neat man with the sort of dry sense of humour that was virtually unheard of among Operators. He was also, completely and utterly, reliable, and there was a little more confidence in the room when he was there.

"Verify headset," he said, before he had even sat down in the seat that Strazinsky vacated for him. The headset arrived just as he finished keying in his Morse signature. He did not hesitate for a moment, and was already reviewing visual and aural material before his second had arrived, and even before Strazinsky had left the Service Floor with his escort.

No one on the Service Floor that day had ever witnessed the phenomenon before. No one working at College Service had ever witnessed such an event, and only a handful of the most senior staff at Service Central had ever been part of so potentially serious an incident. They had all trained for such an eventuality, but it was still virtually impossible to know what any man would do in a crisis, even an Operator.

A genuine Code Yellow required a total change of Service Floor staff. All Operators were suspended from their duties and replaced with two of their colleagues. This meant taking Operators out of Recreation and Repast, in the first instance. If the problem persisted, Resting Operators would be Roused, and, finally, supplemented from senior staff at Service Central. Tech and support were not switched out, but were supplemented with an additional pair of hands for each rack.

Each of the eight original Operators donned his cotton-lined neoprene gloves, and stood behind his chair as the new Operator took his seat, and his colleague pulled out the dicky seat from under the counter, and took up position a little higher and to the left of the primary Operator.

Strazinsky was escorted to an interview room directly off the Service Floor, so that he was close to his station, if he was needed. The room was a two metre cube with a table, two chairs, and, on the wall to the left of the door, a vid-con screen.

THE COLLEGE ONLY had five Ranked Operators, so that only one of them was on duty at any one time, but there was always a second available for emergencies. Strazinsky was relieved that McColl was on-call. They had known each other for some time, and McColl was the only Ranked Operator that Strazinsky still found approachable. The tendency for Service Operators to be insular ran deep, and, for the most part, there was a direct link between how naturally private an Operator was and how far he advanced in his career. McColl was a rare being, in that he was both psychologically self-sufficient and affable.

The meeting required the presence of at least three people: the interviewee, the interviewer and the observer.

"Who will observe?" asked Strazinsky as he and McColl sat on the chairs in the interview room, facing the screen.

"I will," said McColl. Strazinsky looked at him, slightly baffled, and then realised what was happening.

This was big.

"Who will interview me?" asked Strazinsky.

The vid-con screen lit up with drifting snow, and then settled, showing a chair and a computer array, somewhere that Strazinsky didn't recognise.

"Let's see, shall we?" asked McColl.

A man walked into shot on the screen, his back to the camera. He turned to sit in the chair, but Strazinsky didn't recognise him. The man wore a dark suit with a light shirt and a dark tie. The picture seemed indistinct, and, while he didn't recognise him, Strazinsky thought that the man on the screen could be mistaken for half-a-dozen different people that he did know. He had an anonymous, regular face. He was medium height, medium weight and average colouring, apparently without any identifying marks or features.

The man cleared his throat and looked out of the screen at Strazinsky and McColl.

"Agent Operator Henderson, interviewing," he said. "Interviewee?" he asked, and there was a pause before Strazinsky answered, leaning forward slightly, and speaking more slowly and clearly than usual. He was nervous.

"Named Operator Strazinsky, Agent Operator," he said.

"No time for titles," said Henderson. "Observing?"

"Ranked Operator McColl, sir," McColl said, briskly.

"Initial Protocol," said Henderson. "Yes/No questions and answers only, if you please."

If you please, thought Strazinsky. *If you please?*

Henderson cleared his throat again, bringing Strazinsky to his senses.

"Yes," said Strazinsky.

Over the next couple of hours, Strazinsky said yes and no thousands of times. The interview technique was not new, but it proved highly efficient in times of heavy stress. It did not allow for the interviewee to analyse his thoughts too much or try to describe a situation that he didn't have the imagination or the vocabulary to do justice too. The Yes/No system allowed the interviewer to follow any path he chose, picking out what was important, and homing in on it with the interviewee.

Civilians were seldom required to undergo such intense interviews, and the method was seldom used on them. Creatives often found it difficult to stick to the Yes/No formula, with their tendency to use more qualifications, both verbal and gestural, and often did better telling a story, wholesale, or making pictures or acting out scenes. The best interviewees were the empirical personality types, which included most grades of Drafted, particularly Service Operators. The Yes/No interview was fast and efficient, and a low-stress way of getting the best information in the shortest time. Interviewees were not asked to think or speculate, so, during the course of the interview their answers became automatic responses, which were considered more reliable as evidence, if and when the time came.

"Is your name Strazinsky?"

"Yes."

"Is your designation Ranked Operator?"

"No."

"Do you work station 3?"

"No."

"Were you called in on a Code Green?"

"Yes."

The first dozen questions established the basic facts that were already a matter of record, and by the end of them Strazinsky was feeling a little more relaxed. He would have to explain nothing. If he was asked to explain what had happened, he might not have been able to.

His instincts had told him that there was no case for upgrading to Code Yellow, and yet, he had done it. He would not be asked about his instincts or about his decisions. He would not be asked to explain himself. There was no wrong answer. He would not be asked, "What were your criteria for instigating Code Yellow?"

Interviews were used to glean the facts of an event on the

Service Floor, quickly, without recourse to surveillance, which was always reviewed, but not always prioritised. When it was prioritised, as on this occasion, it could take twice as long to review footage as it would simply to view it in real-time, and as much as ten times as long to review footage as it would take for an experienced interviewer to extract the same information.

Strazinsky had spent more than 36 hours at Station 2, Code Green, before the ramp-up to Code Yellow. Service Central needed all the relevant information now, not in three days time. Agent Operator Henderson had allowed a four hour window for the extraction of the key facts.

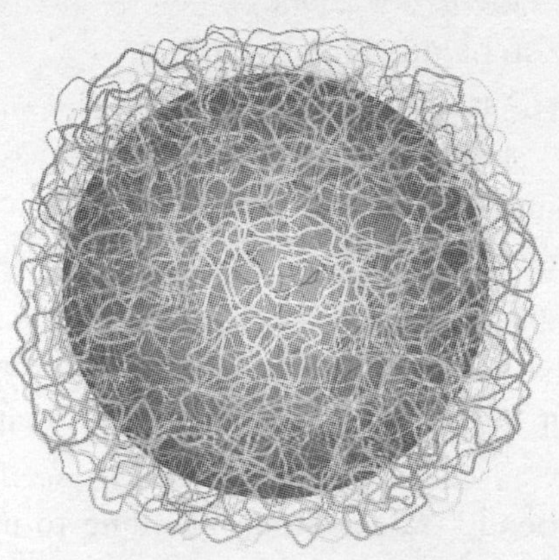

Chapter Eleven

"TOBE," SAID METOO, "it's time to go home."

"I've got a tutorial," said Tobe.

"It's been cancelled. The Student isn't well."

"I'll work."

"It's time to go home."

"Who's that?" asked Tobe. Metoo didn't know who he was referring to; he seemed to be looking right at her. She hesitated.

"Who's that?" asked Tobe. Metoo turned, and realised that the Police Operator was still standing at her shoulder. She'd been so busy trying to work out how to keep Tobe calm and get him home that she had quite forgotten he was there. She fished around in her mind for a benign, plausible answer.

"Who's that?" asked Tobe.

"Nobody," said Metoo, answering reflexively. She knew as soon as she said it that it wouldn't work.

"Somebody's there, not nobody."

He could be so bloody literal at times.

"Who's that?" asked Tobe.

"This is..." she began, hesitating as she turned to the Operator, gesturing up at him with a shrug.

"... Saintout," said the Police Operator.

"French," said Tobe.

"Yes... French... a long time ago," said Saintout, pushing his bottom lip out in an oddly Gallic expression that was not lost on Metoo.

"He's my friend," said Metoo, intending to make Saintout seem as unthreatening as possible.

"Tobe's your friend," said Tobe. "French is not your friend."

"You are my friend," said Metoo, glad to have something useful to latch on to. "Do you remember what friends do?"

"Tobe's your friend, so Tobe helps you," said Tobe.

"Exactly. Will you help me now, Tobe?"

"Tobe's your friend."

Metoo took that to mean yes.

"Just hop across the floor, and come home with me."

"The floor," said Tobe, looking down.

Metoo was afraid that she'd drawn attention to the wrong thing, and was annoyed at herself for asking the sort of combination question that Tobe found impossible to answer. She tried to bring his attention back.

"Let's go home," she said, quickly. Tobe continued to look at the floor, turning his body slightly away from her.

Metoo waited for a moment, gesturing frantically with her hand to Saintout to get out of sight. Saintout moved to his left until he could no longer see into the office, or be seen from it, but stayed close enough to be useful if Tobe became a threat.

"Tobe," said Metoo, and then again, "Tobe."

Tobe swivelled back to face her again. His head was still bent, but he was looking up through his fringe at her.

"Take me home, please?" she asked.

Tobe tiptoed out of his office, gently stepping into the small gaps left between his calculations. He crossed the floor without apparently disturbing anything.

Metoo put her hands out, her arms horizontal to either side of her body, keeping the Operators at bay. The two men on either side of the door nodded at her to acknowledge that they understood her instruction. Saintout brought his right hand up to his waist, in case he needed to deploy his weapon.

As Tobe crossed the office threshold, Metoo reached out and placed a hand on either side of his face. His eyes were cast down.

"Thank you, Tobe," she said. "Now, let's go home." She turned him as she spoke, still holding his face, so that his vision was, effectively blinkered. They were soon walking down the corridor away from the office, with Saintout at a discreet distance behind them. Tobe had not seen any of the Service Operators.

The Operators on either side of the office door turned to face each other, and then turned to face into the room.

"Bloody hell," said the man on the left.

SAINTOUT ESCORTED TOBE and Metoo back to the flat, and waited outside. Metoo set the bath to run, and told Tobe to undress. He went to his room, and she ducked back into the corridor to speak to Saintout.

"Thank you," she said. "I think he'll be fine now."

"I'm sorry, Assistant-Companion," said Saintout, "but I've been assigned, and I'm not going anywhere. By rights, I should be in that flat with you. In fact, Assistant-Companion, I must insist that I accompany you back into the flat."

Metoo looked at him.

"Now," said Saintout.

Metoo would not jeopardise Tobe's work or life by having someone, anyone, come into the flat while he was there. From time to time, a Student would come in, usually for something to do with Service, but she always ensured that their visits happened when Tobe was in his office. Since he kept to a fairly rigid timetable, and, since he tended to work longer hours than Students, their visits had never been a problem. It helped enormously that Tobe was a creature of habit. He had established routines, and he hated to deviate from them. Leaving his office so early in the day, today, would cause enough trouble. There was no way that Metoo was going to allow Saintout to walk into the flat.

Saintout, however, was insistent.

TOBE WALKED, NAKED, to the bathroom, leaving the door open as he stepped into the bath and sat down in the water that was still running.

Metoo went to the closed door of the Companion's room, opened it, barely far enough to let her pass through, and closed it quietly behind her. She crossed the room to the window, without looking at any of her plants. She opened the window as wide as she could, and stuck her head out.

"You really ought to be careful of that, Assistant-Companion," said Saintout, who was standing with his back to the wall adjacent to the window.

"I didn't think you were there," said Metoo, clutching her chest with the shock of suddenly hearing Saintout outside the window, before she saw him.

"I was told, most emphatically, that I must not be seen by the subject, Assistant-Companion," said Saintout.

Metoo didn't answer him. She knew he was being amusing for her benefit, but none of this was funny; she needed to be particularly vigilant with Tobe. Things had not been going well for days, since the stupid sock thing, and she had no idea what the fallout would be.

Colleges were set up with the sole purpose of catering to the upper echelons of the Drafted, which, basically, meant the Masters, since no one ever knew who was Active. Things did not go wrong. Companions kept their Masters' home-lives simple and regulated, with specific reference to their individual personality maps. Assistants did a similar job in the Masters' offices. Beyond that, Students were Scheduled according to their Masters' needs, and Service was on hand at all times to monitor everything.

She had asked more than a dozen times in the past two days, "Anomalies?" They had answered, "Minor and monitoring". What the hell was going on?

Tobe was in the bath, and Saintout was in the Companion's room. Metoo signed into Service.

"Anomalies?" she asked.

There was no answer.

"Anomaly status on Master Tobe?"

"Thank you for signing in," said Service. "Service will resume shortly."

Metoo sat, rigid, for several seconds. She could hear Tobe in the bath. She had never known him to take a long bath, so she didn't have much time. She wondered, for a moment, whether she had remembered to put out a towel and a robe for him. Why did she wonder? Of course she had.

Metoo willed herself to stay where she was. Tobe was fine; that was all that mattered. So long as Saintout was in the garden room, and did not do anything stupid, Tobe would be quite happy pottering about. He would not wonder, for a moment, what she was doing signed in to Service. He didn't care about Service. It struck Metoo how odd it was that Service watched Tobe's every move, while he totally ignored its very existence. He had everything he needed, and he did not need Service. Service needed him.

"Anomaly status on Master Tobe?" she asked.

Service buzzed faintly for a moment or two, as if with very distant static.

Metoo's hands were sweating slightly, and her eyes were big in her face, again.

"Anomalies?" she asked, so short of breath that she could not repeat the entire formal request.

Service buzzed again. Then she realised that it wasn't buzzing at all, but that her aural acuity was heightened, just as her visual acuity had been heightened when Tobe had been in the garden room, yesterday morning, and she had watched the droplet of water fall on his forehead.

Tobe had been in the garden room.

Metoo's temperature rose, instantaneously, and her skin began to prickle with a sheen of cold sweat.

Metoo heard Tobe step out of the bath.

Tobe had been in the garden room. He had been there once, and so he might go there again. Something must have mattered to him very much for him to enter the room for the first time. If the thought occurred to him again, it would be much easier for him to enter the garden room a second time.

Metoo found herself in the corridor outside the bathroom. She watched as Tobe, his back to her, dropped the towel and threw the robe over his head. He turned to face her.

"Come into the kitchen and have a cup of tea," said Metoo. She tried to hold down her panic so that he wouldn't see it, while knowing, all the time, that he had never been able to read her face; she was in no danger of being caught with her feelings.

They walked to the kitchen together, and Tobe sat on his stool, while Metoo began to make the tea. The initial rush of adrenalin had subsided. Tobe was safe, and, apparently, oblivious.

"MODERATE AND MONITORING," said Service, to empty air.

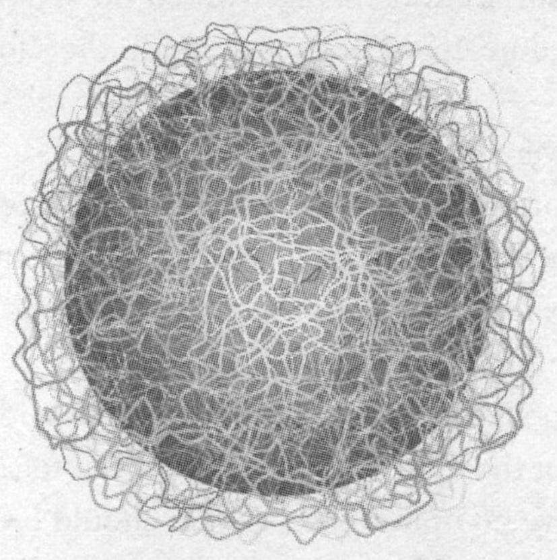

Chapter Twelve

SERVICE SENT TWO Techs to Tobe's room. There had been a long discussion, first between the Operators who had guarded the door, during Tobe's extraction, and then between the three Ranked Operators, who had been brought in from Repast, Recreation and Rest, mobilising the entire Service team, for the College, at Ranked level. McColl was still observing for Strazinsky, and Ranked Operator Dudley was manning Station 2, alongside the Named Operator that had replaced Strazinsky.

The three Ranked Operators could not come to a unanimous decision about what to do with Tobe's office, so they called in Service Central.

The two Techs stood outside Tobe's room for over an hour, alongside the Operators, who were guarding the entrance. No one went in or out. The door remained open, and the four men standing in the corridor outside barely dared to breathe.

A decision was made. Service Central was already reviewing

footage, various sections being worked on simultaneously, so that the procedure could be completed in the shortest possible time.

The Techs were sent in.

After two or three minutes watching the Techs wrangling with each other, trying to decide who should enter the room, one of the Operators stepped towards them.

"The little bloke goes in," he said.

The Techs looked at the Operator, who had said less than any of them during the tense hour they had been together, and had claimed to have no opinion as to what should be done.

"Stands to reason," he said. "Small feet, less likely to make a mess of what's there."

The smaller of the Techs, who had 'Estefan' stencilled on the back of his regulation overalls, unlaced his work boots, and, using the toe of the other foot, against the back of the boot, removed them, without having cause to use his hands. It was mandatory for Techs to have clean dry hands when they were working, and they all developed habits relating to their hands, either rituals or shortcuts, depending on their personalities. Estefan preferred shortcuts; another Tech might take his boots off with his hands because the last thing he would do before starting a job would be to wash his hands, regardless of whether they were clean.

Despite not touching his boots, Estefan took a vacuum sealed pack from his pocket, opened it, and wiped his hands with the alcohol swab inside, dropping the pack and the swab, where he stood, when he had finished using them.

Estefan's socks were too white to be cotton. Techs were allowed to Requisition clothes made from natural fibres, even though they were rare and came at a price, because of the ingrained habits passed down through generations. Old, manmade fibres had been prone to static electricity, and could cause excess sweating, neither of which was compatible with old electronics. Many Techs were still superstitious about natural fibres, and would rather wear them beyond the point of decency than switch to pro. Modern Tech, even the knackered obsolete stuff that most Techs had to work with was not sensitive to foreign bodies, including dust and liquids, and all electrical components were self-insulating at the molecular level. Estefan had no qualms about wearing pro, and preferred to spend his Requisites on other things.

Estefan turned to the Operator.

"I'll leave my socks on, if it's okay with you," he said. He wasn't asking.

"Fine," said the Operator.

The other Tech erected a mini-crane in the corridor outside Tobe's office, to transfer hardware into the room without having to walk back and forth, and Estefan found his way across the linopro, following in the Master's footprints.

Estefan reached the compress button on the wipe-wall, hit it, and waited to see what would come out of the mini-print slot. In theory, the print-out should include everything on the wipe-wall, but neither of the Techs had ever seen a wall that was such a collage of various bits of paper stuck down with spit, and acres of scrawled, and cross-written calculations.

The compress button was designed to rationalise the work, and print it out in a format that could be followed by others in the same field. It didn't matter what was on the wipe-wall, in so far as it could be handwritten musical score, a story in any language, mathematical calculations, or a combination of many things. It didn't matter how many times things were crossed out, or how many arrows, circles or lines were used to link thoughts together. It didn't matter how many symbols were used or whether punctuation was correct. The job of the compressor was to track the process, and then present it in a way that was succinct and accurate, without bypassing any of the creativity or thought processes of the author.

Pages started to emerge from the mini-print slot. Estefan cast an eye over them, but they meant nothing to him, and he couldn't easily ascertain whether the text book pages were being included. After 20 pages, or so, the mini-print began to make an odd sucking noise.

"Toner," said Estefan.

"You're kidding," said the other Tech.

"No," said Estefan. "This thing needs toner."

ESTEFAN HIT THE switch on the mini-print to turn it off, and set to work fitting a compress button and mini-print slot to the floor.

In theory, the system could be fitted to any surface, and the best of the newer models could be retro-fitted, so that the memories in the surface of the vibrations, which had resulted from the pressure of pen on wipe-wall, or, in this case, chalk on linopro, could be picked up and analysed after the event. Neither of the Techs had fitted one in practice, and neither knew anyone that had retro-fitted a mini-print system, let alone in linopro with a none standard, frankly unknown, unstable writing medium, which was also littered with pages of text from various books, including diagrams and non-standard mathematical symbols.

Fitting the system was not difficult or complicated. The unit came in two, self-contained sections with one broad-spectrum flat sensor to pick up vibrations on the surface that was being used as a wipe-wall. It should only have taken about 20 minutes to fit the system, but Estefan was hampered by having to stand on the surface he was working on, not to mention the fact that he was being constantly admonished by the Operators not to step on anything that might be classed as evidence. He must not obliterate the material, either by wiping out the chalk marks, or by interfering with the floor's memory of the vibrations it had collected while Tobe was making his calculations. He didn't have much of a margin for error.

Metoo left Tobe in the kitchen with his cup of tea, and went to the garden room to try to get rid of the Police Operator. She hoped that she might be able to persuade him to leave the way he had come, and only return if she needed him, which she considered extremely unlikely.

She closed the door of the garden room behind her. Saintout was standing with his back against the wall adjacent to the window. He looked very relaxed, leaning against the wall, with his feet crossed, casually, in front of him.

"Toner," he said.

"I'm sorry?" asked Metoo.

"I was just coming to find you," said the Operator, "something about the mini-print in his office needing toner. What the hell is toner?"

"Tobe has never allowed anything to be changed in his office, and, when he moved in, the equipment was already pretty-well obsolete. I've been trying to persuade him to have everything upgraded for about a year, but I hate to push; we went through massive traumas over the bookshelves and library steps."

"Sorry I asked," said Saintout.

"Tobe's mini-print still uses toner, a chemical that needs to be topped up at regular intervals," said Metoo, by way of speeding things up. "And do not leave this room through that door," she added, pointing at it.

"Service doesn't have any toner, and I'm guessing they need to extract information," said Saintout, ignoring Metoo's last comment.

"What are they doing to his room?" asked Metoo. She was anxious, even though she had known that this would happen, that they would dismantle his office. She also knew that, no matter how careful they were, Tobe would know that someone had been there without his permission. It could take weeks or even months to get him happy and settled again.

She looked at the Police Operator.

"His desk," she said. "Bottom drawer on the left."

Saintout began to relay the information back to Service.

"Get Service to send me a tone if you need anything else," said Metoo, giving up on the idea of getting rid of the Operator, at least for now.

ESTEFAN WAS JUST finishing the retro-fit when the call came in. He opened the bottom drawer of the desk, carefully, so as not to drag the underside of the drawer over the stuff on the linopro, and looked inside.

"You should see what's in here," he called to the Tech still standing in the corridor, shouting instructions.

"Put everything in the bucket, and I'll crane it out," said the other Tech. "Any toner in there?"

Estefan started going through the drawer, dropping things into the bucket that was suspended next to him.

"Hey," he said, "this could be the stuff he wrote on the linopro with." He held up the box of chalk for the other Tech to see.

"Great, stick it in the bucket," said the Tech. "Toner?"

"Looks like it," said Estefan, lifting out an ancient cardboard box with an old-fashioned screw-top bottle inside, half-full of liquid. "This lot belongs in a museum."

In less than half an hour, all the data possible had been collected from both mini-print slots. Neither of the Techs had a clue whether any of it would be readable, but that was why this Operation was being carried out in four phases: the principals were being interviewed, the footage was being reviewed, the Techs had printed out the data for dissemination, and now, the specialists would come in.

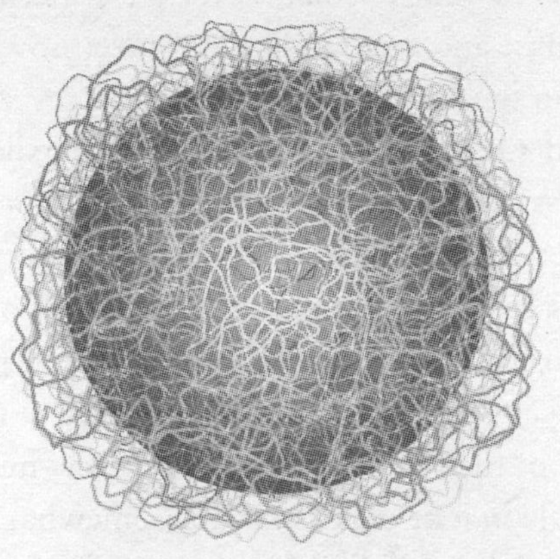

Chapter Thirteen

Pitu 3 was stretchered back to Service. The Medic didn't think there was any urgent need for him to go to the infirmary, and planned to stay with him. Interrogation was far more critical at this point than Pitu 3's health status. He could be hospitalised after he was interviewed.

Pitu 3 was transferred to a chair-stretcher and carried in an elevator up to the Service Floor. He did not enter the main Service Floor where eighteen Operators were still busy monitoring the screens, and a dozen Techs were milling around, but came in through the exterior gallery, a walkway on the outside of the circular room, half a storey lower, so that no one passing along it could be seen at screen-height inside the room, proper.

Pitu 3 was put in the interview room next to the one occupied by Strazinsky and McColl. Pitu 3 was there because of Strazinsky, and Strazinsky was there because of Pitu 3. If either one could get hold of the other, who knew what might ensue?

As it was, the two men would never have met in the normal course of things, and were unlikely to meet now, despite their involvement in the same, potentially critical, event.

No Ranked Operator was available, immediately, as they were in discussions about how to treat Tobe's room, but Pitu 3 was considered to be a minor player in the incident, so a Named Operator was sent to de-brief him, along with one of the few female Operators, who was really only there to put him at his ease. Mudd was also with them. The interview room was the mirror image of the one next door, and it was unusual to have so many people in it at once, so it was somewhat cramped, not least because of the chair-stretcher.

"Let's get you out of that, shall we?" asked the female Operator. "My name's Bim. How are you feeling, Pitu?"

"I'm fine, really. It was just a bit of a shock, that's all," he said, trying to get out of the chair-stretcher.

"Just sit back, Pitu, we need to unstrap you first. We'll have you out of there in no time.

"This is Operator Bello. He'd like to ask you a few questions, if you're feeling up to it," said Bim, gesturing to the man who had just entered the room. "I'm going to step out for a moment if that's all right."

Pitu nodded, although he still looked pale and pitiful.

There was no rush. Pitu would be allowed to tell his story in his own words. With all the other information that was available, his testimony was insignificant, and he was not considered a reliable witness. He had been Tobe's Student almost as long as anyone had, but he was kept there so that Tobe had familiar faces in his class, rather than because he was any real long-term asset. Pitu 3 would, no doubt, be moved back to the School as a Senior, eventually. When, would depend on how restless he became. Most Students didn't last more than four or five years with a Master, and a six-year stint, while not unheard of, was very rare.

Pitu 3's involvement in this incident almost certainly assured his departure from Tobe's class, and it would not be because of a promotion to Assistant.

Bim returned to the interview room with two fold-up chairs, after Pitu had already been removed from the chair-stretcher and seated in one of the chairs that belonged in the room. She wheeled the chair-stretcher out into the corridor, while Bello unfolded one of the chairs and placed it next to Pitu for the Medic Operator to sit on. All three men were sitting when Bim returned, unfolded the last of the chairs, and sat down opposite Pitu, next to Bello.

"Are you all right to start?" Bim asked Pitu 3.

Pitu nodded.

Bello removed a small electrical device from a case that he had brought into the room. He placed it on the table, and took out a cord of plaited wires, which he handed to Medic Operator Mudd.

"Perhaps you could prepare the subject," said Bello.

Mudd took the cables and began to run through Protocols with Pitu 3, who had a strange look of excitement on his face.

Tobe stood in his room, the door propped open, as usual. The room was a two metre cube with a low cot on the left and a narrow bookcase opposite. There was a small window close to the ceiling, on the wall opposite the door, which he never looked out of, and the wall opposite the bed was a wipe-wall, partially obscured by the bookcase. There was no storage space, other than the bookshelves, but there was a small table under the window, which served as a desk of sorts. The room was more like a monastic cell than a bedroom, but it suited Tobe. He didn't care about clothes, which Metoo always organised for him, since he always dressed and undressed in his bedroom or on his way to the bathroom, and he didn't really have any belongings. The few things he had become obsessed with over the years lived in the desk in his office.

Tobe sat on the cot for a few minutes. He didn't need to take so much as a pace to stand in front of the bookcase, so he stood, and pulled a copy of *On Probability* off the top shelf, all in one, measured movement. He sat down on the cot, again, and began to thumb through the book.

Metoo was in the garden room. She had told Tobe that she wanted to check on her plants, and perhaps he'd like to work in his room. Tobe had said that he didn't work in his room, because he worked in his office. Never-the-less, he had turned his back on her, and walked away down the corridor.

"Service needs to interview him," Saintout told her.

"That's impossible," Metoo answered. "He wouldn't understand it, and it'd frighten him. He's not good with questions."

"You don't seem to understand," said the Police Operator, "Service needs to interview him."

"I understand, perfectly. I just don't see how it's going to be possible."

"They could do it here."

"He can't have strangers in the flat. He can't bear anyone in the flat, not even his Students. He won't talk to anyone from Service. He doesn't even sign in for himself. I don't know if he even remembers that Service exists."

"We'll get a doctor in. We'll medicate him," said Saintout. "He'll be fine."

"Over my dead body."

"You know," said the Police Operator, "that isn't out of the question."

Metoo thought for a moment that he was joking. She almost laughed. Then she looked at him, and realised that he was, literally, deadly serious.

"It's that important?" asked Metoo.

"I don't know," said Saintout, "I don't have clearance to that level, but the fact that I don't have clearance to that level tells me all that I need to know. I'm sure you understand what I'm saying."

Metoo's head dropped, and her thumb came up to her mouth, as if she was going to chew the nail on it. She stood that way for several seconds.

"They have to interview him," said Saintout. "Do you want me to call a doctor, or what?"

Metoo was pacing the room. She stopped in front of a shallow shelf where she was growing some ornamental plants, including an old English plant called 'Honesty'. She was growing it because it had become very rare in the past two hundred years, in Britain, and a plant enthusiast that she corresponded with in Siberia had offered her some seeds. She also liked that it was called 'Honesty', and was even more pleased with the name that her friend had given to the flat, oval seed-pods that he had sent to her. They were delicate, papery, silver objects that she almost didn't want to submerge in soil, because they were so beautiful. The English translation for their Russian name was 'Moon Pennies'.

Metoo relaxed, visibly, as she ordered her thoughts: Tobe was as honest as the day was long. He did not know how to dissemble, let alone lie. There had been occasions, when she first became Tobe's Student, when Metoo had cringed at his lack of tact, but anyone who worked in College eventually got used to that; it was a common character trait among the Masters, especially the scientists and mathematicians.

Service knew Tobe's profile, so they knew that he was incapable of lying. That being the case, surely it didn't matter who interviewed Tobe, or how. If he was asked a direct question, providing that it wasn't a combination question, he would offer a direct answer.

Metoo stopped pacing, and turned to face Saintout.

"Or what," she said.

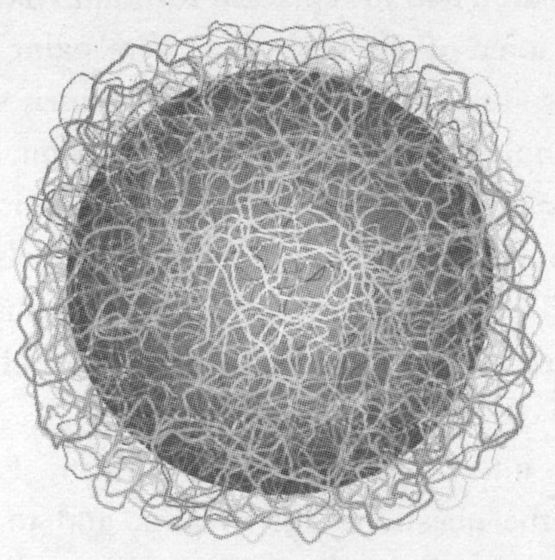

Chapter Fourteen

"I HAD THE first tutorial of the day, 08:30 with Master Tobe," said Pitu 3.

"Before that?" asked Bello.

"When before?" asked Pitu 3, bewildered. "There wasn't a before."

"Okay. That's good," said Bello.

"It's fine," Bim said, reassuring Pitu 3.

"So, I went to my tutorial for 08:30, and we arrived together. He might have said something, I don't remember," Pitu 3 continued, lifting his eyes to look at Bim, searching for approval before he went on.

He was sitting forward on his chair, with his forearms resting on the table between him and Bim. The other three were all sitting back in their chairs. He kept his head low, sometimes holding it in his hands, sometimes dropping it down between his shoulders, and once, knocking one of the sensors off his skin, so that Mudd had to replace it for him. His hands moved a good deal; some of the time they were palm down on the table, stroking the surface, where the finger sensors made odd clicking noises, at others they were in his hair. He also touched the back of his head a good deal, certainly more than was usual. Every time his hands moved, the ribbon between him and Mudd tightened, or went slack, or rustled with an odd, harsh sound, and the sensors and wires clicked against the table-top.

Part of the interview involved monitoring Pitu's physical responses to the questions put to him, and to his answers. The Medic had taped sensors to Pitu's chest and finger tips to monitor his heart-rate and breathing, and how much he was sweating, the plaited cord of wires running from the sensors to the small device that sat on the table next to Bello. Pitu 3 seemed very pleased with the equipment; at last he was being valued. At last, someone was taking notice of him... Everyone was taking notice of him.

Service Central was also uploading footage of the interview in real time, so that the process could be completed as quickly as possible, and the College could be brought back down to Code Green, at least.

"I'm pretty sure he did say something," Pitu 3 said, "but you can check that on the footage, right?"

"Depends if you were in the corridor or already in the office," Bello answered. "It'd be a big help if you could remember, son."

Pitu 3 smiled slightly, and sat a little straighter in his chair, the sensor wires straining slightly.

"Oh, right, okay," he said. "Let me see... He did say something, I'm sure. Maybe it was something to do with maths, maybe it was to do with a text book. That was it. I think he mentioned a book."

Bello's machine sensed that this information wasn't accurate, but he continued with his questions; all the data would be decoded later.

"Did he always greet you the same way when you met?"

"Tobe? No, he didn't talk much. He didn't really speak to me. Oh, yeah, sometimes he said 'tidings' instead of 'come in'. Yeah, he did that a lot," said Pitu 3.

"So, you're in the office?" prompted Bello.

"Yeah. He said to check out his footage, and gave me a time code for the morning. He said I should ask Metoo, so that's what I did.

"I went over to Tobe's flat, and Metoo signed me in to Service. We had a bit of a chat, and then I got to work with the material. I was thinking, *What are the odds of this happening?* I mean, he gave me my own calculation to do, real world. I guess he needed me to do it, so that he could figure out something else, or maybe my thing was a small part of his thing. Anyway, it was pretty cool.

"I went back to my room and got started on it. I was pretty pleased that he'd picked me for the assignment. It's about time. I've been with him four years, you know?"

They did know.

Bello had uploaded Pitu 3's profile before he'd entered the interview room. Every Drafted individual, however minor, however close to the margins of usefulness, underwent a series of psychometric tests before being placed at the College. Bello already knew that the interviewee liked to feel important, but didn't like taking responsibility for anything. He knew that his observation skills were poor, but that he would happily switch facts around to fit the circumstances if there were gaps in his knowledge.

Bello also knew that Pitu 3 was more ambitious than he

was talented, and more selfish than compassionate. None of this boded well for Pitu 3 becoming Tobe's next Assistant. Pitu 3 appeared to be the only one not to have realised that, self-awareness being one of his lowest scored, measurable characteristics. He also scored a virtual zero for empathy. The one useful trait he had, in abundance, was his tendency to the literal. It was what had got him into Tobe's class in the first instance. He was stolid in his thinking, lacked imagination, and didn't work at an aggressive pace, so he was the perfect choice as one of the anchors in the class, giving Tobe the continuity he needed.

By extension, he did everything by the book, and never took a risk. Compared to the Student body, as a whole, he was 50 percent more likely to precipitate a Service Action. The benefit to Service, under Code Yellow, was that he was 70 percent more likely to be erroneous in his judgements and emotional responses. Service still hoped that the Code Yellow was an aberration.

"That was the day before yesterday. So, then some stuff was cancelled," said Pitu, "and I didn't get another tutorial until today. I was first, again, so I guess Service, or someone, messed about with the Schedule. I just thought Tobe was working on something. Everyone thought that."

"Did you talk to any of Tobe's other Students?" asked Bello.

"I had the job, I had the maths to do, and I did it, too, so I didn't want any of them taking the credit," said Pitu 3, becoming flustered, the machine responding more and more to the tensions in his body. "I didn't want to let on that I knew anything. They were all talking, you know, but I just kept quiet. I've been Tobe's Student for a long time, longer than anyone... almost. I didn't think he was going nuts or anything."

"By which you mean?" asked Bello.

"Yeah, sorry. I mean, I didn't know there was anything wrong until that second tutorial. I just... he looked so...

"We're trained, you know," he said. "They train us to keep an eye on things. The Masters are important people, us Students look out for stuff. We spend time with them, more than anyone else, so we see things."

"But you didn't see anything at the first tutorial, two days ago?" asked Bello.

"No. Like I said, I just got on with what he told me to do. Then, when I went to the second 08:30 tutorial... well... You saw it," he said, looking at Mudd. "There must be footage," Pitu 3 insisted.

"What exactly do you remember about what you saw?" asked Bello.

Pitu 3 was leaning over the table, his arms outstretched across its surface, his chin almost touching the tabletop. He looked up at Bim, and said, "He opened the door. He didn't look at me, or speak, or anything. He just opened the door and started to walk in. Only, he couldn't walk because of all the stuff on the floor.

"It was weird. He was tiptoeing through all this stuff: pages from books, and equations all over the place. I couldn't even tell what it was. It didn't look right.

"We were trained," he said. "We were taught to recognise when there was a problem, and he obviously had a problem."

"So the Master was upset?" prompted Bello.

"Yeah, that's right," said Pitu 3, and then hesitated for a moment, before contradicting himself.

"Well, not exactly upset. More... I don't know... It was weird. He was holding his robe and tiptoeing across the floor, only stepping on the bare linopro, and there was all this stuff. It wasn't normal."

"So was it the Master that was upsetting, or was it the state of his room?"

"You can never tell with him, anyway," said Pitu 3. "None of them give much away. It's not as if we really know what they're like. It's like they've got something missing, or something. You can tell what they're thinking by what they're doing, and he was doing weird stuff on the linopro. He wasn't even using a pen. I don't know what that yellow stuff was on the linopro, but it wasn't right."

"Did the room upset you, Pitu?" asked Bim.

"Yeah, I guess," said Pitu 3, slightly sullen. "But if something's wrong, we're supposed to hit our buttons. That's all I did. I just did what I was told."

"We know, Pitu," said Bim. "There's nothing to worry about. Now, why don't we get you over to the infirmary, and have you checked out properly? Then you can get some rest."

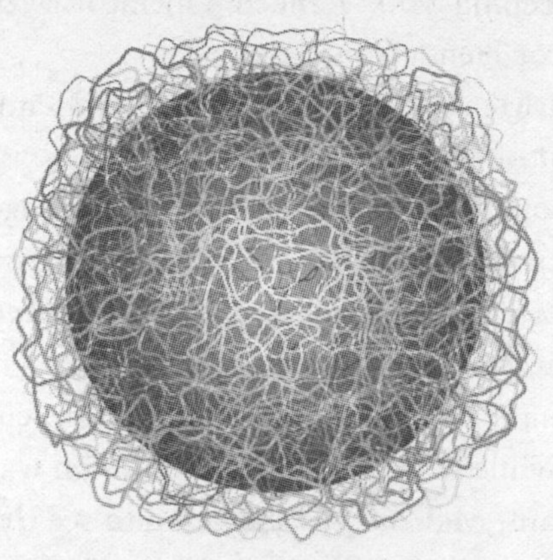

Chapter Fifteen

RANKED OPERATOR MCCOLL was tired. Strazinsky had to be tired. McColl looked up at the screen, at Agent Operator Henderson; he looked as fresh as the proverbial daisy, although McColl still wasn't sure whether he reminded him of someone, and if so, whom.

McColl tried to glance at his watch, without drawing attention to himself. Agent Operator Henderson was halfway through asking a question, and couldn't possibly notice what McColl was doing. It felt, to McColl, as if the interview had gone on for a long time; so many questions had been asked and answered. Several times, he had thought that Henderson had come to the end of his questions, but still they came, homing in on very small, very specific target areas.

"Yes," said Named Operator Strazinsky in answer to the question.

"Are we keeping you, Ranked Operator McColl?" asked Agent Operator Henderson.

"Yes," said McColl, looking directly at Henderson on the screen in front of him.

"No, sir. Sorry, sir," said McColl, stumbling through the embarrassment brought on by his less than professional response. "Seriously, begging your pardon, Agent Operator Henderson, sir, I –"

"At ease," said Agent Operator Henderson, cutting McColl off, casually, while he looked down at his own watch. When he looked up again, McColl was staggered to see that Henderson appeared to be smiling, even though the screen never showed a very distinct image, and expressions were almost impossible to read.

"It might interest you to know, McColl," he said, "that your position as observer was required simply to make sure that we were getting as close to the truth as, if you'll excuse the um... Well, as close to the truth as humanly possible. None of my questions to Strazinsky, and none of his answers could be validated without your presence."

"Yes, sir," said McColl. "Still, sir..."

"Don't worry about it, McColl," said Henderson. "If it's any consolation, I was had in that style not once, but twice when I was Ranked, and one of those times was on Manoeuvres. I'm not sure I've lived it down, to this day. That's why I worked my arse off to make Agent; I couldn't take the mockery any longer."

Henderson appeared to be smiling again, but it was still impossible to tell, for sure.

"That will be all," he said.

As Agent Operator Henderson got out of his chair, the screen switched to drifting snow.

McColl and Strazinsky looked at each other, and sagged, visibly, with the relief of having got through the interview.

"Well, that could've been worse," said McColl.

"Only for you," said Strazinsky.

"Take your point," said McColl. "I'd be surprised if you didn't get a pat on the back at the end of all this, though. It sounds like you played it down the line."

"Let's get through whatever this is, first," said Strazinsky, "before we start some kind of mutual appreciation society."

"Yeah," said McColl, wearily.

"Code Yellow," said Strazinsky.

"Code Yellow," said McColl. "It doesn't look like they're going to lift it, does it?"

"It doesn't look like it, no," said Strazinsky, "not if that interview was anything to go by."

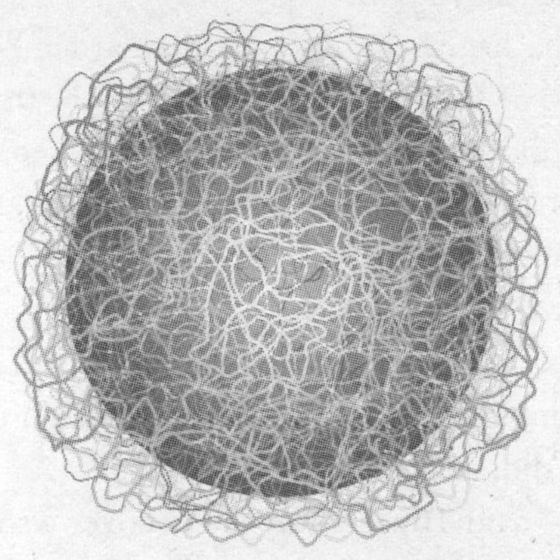

Chapter Sixteen

Tobe took up the pen for his wipe-wall, and stood at the far right hand corner of the room, closest to the window.

"It was the same," he said.

"Tobe works in his office, not in his room.

"Tobe always works in his office.

"What is the probability of Tobe working in his office?"

He held *On Probability*, in his left hand, scrutinising the cover. It was a soft edition with graphics on the cover, of probability trees with fractions and percentages shown, in various type-sizes and fonts. He read the information on the front and back, and then looked at the book, quizzically. The information was wrong; it was jumbled and unclear, and misleading. Perhaps all the information in the book was wrong.

"Metoo," he said.

A minute later, when there was no reply, Tobe stepped out through his bedroom door.

"Metoo," he said, again.

This time, he heard the door of the garden room opening and closing, so he stayed where he was, on the threshold to his room. Metoo did not go into Tobe's room when he was there. The door was always open, but Tobe still thought of it as his private domain when he was in the flat.

"Yes?" asked Metoo.

Tobe handed her the book, which she opened, and began to look at, thinking that he wanted to share an idea with her, which he still did, occasionally.

"The cover," said Tobe. "Why is the cover wrong?"

Metoo flipped the book closed, her thumb acting like a bookmark somewhere in the text, and glanced at the cover. She looked from the cover of the book to Tobe, baffled.

"How is it wrong, Tobe?" she asked.

"The maths," said Tobe.

Metoo looked back down at the cover of the book. She had not thought of it in terms of the mathematics; it was simply a graphic illustration that this was a maths book, and, in particular, a book about probability. She felt herself tense slightly as she realised that this was another edition of the book that Tobe had been looking for in his office.

"OK," said Metoo, "the maths is wrong. The cover of this book isn't meant to have real maths on it. It wasn't designed by a mathematician it was designed by... well... a designer."

"But the maths is wrong."

"Yes. The maths on the outside of the book is wrong, but the maths on the inside of the book is correct."

"Why?" asked Tobe.

Metoo thought for a moment. She didn't want to cause Tobe any anxiety, but she knew that Service needed something from her. She must make things as easy and normal as possible to get them all through whatever it was that was happening to them.

"A mathematician made the inside of the book, because he understands maths. A designer made the outside of the book, because he understands books," she said.

Tobe thought for a moment.

"Inside, the book is the truth? Outside, the book is lies?"

"I suppose so," said Metoo, touching his arm, and smiling at him as she handed the book back. "Is that all right?"

Tobe took the book from Metoo. He folded the back cover and the front cover away from the inside, grasped their outside edges together in his left hand, holding the body of the book in his right, and tore the covers off, so that only the spine and the pages of the book glued to it still remained. He handed the front and back covers of the book to Metoo. She took them.

"All books?" he asked.

"Some," said Metoo, "not all."

His action was perfectly logical, to anyone who knew Tobe at all, and Metoo wasn't worried about him. She was worried about Service. She was worried about the situation, which she still knew almost nothing about, but she wasn't worried about Tobe. He didn't seem agitated or unhappy, and he seemed to be dealing extremely well with everything that was happening around him.

Tobe turned from Metoo, and stepped over the threshold back into his room. Metoo took this as a sign for her to leave, and walked back down the corridor to the garden room, and to Police Operator Saintout.

Tobe opened *On Probability*, and began reading on the title page, still standing in front of the wipe-wall, the pen held between his right palm and the last page of the book. He remained patient and methodical, reading the title page, acknowledgements, international codes and translations, edition numbers, publisher's information, years of publication, author credentials and so on.

He began again at the beginning. After reading the first chapter, and following Eustache's examples, Tobe put the book down on the desk to his left, open at the appropriate page, and began to make a simple probability tree based on the toss of a coin: obverse/reverse, obverse/reverse, obverse/reverse. His working was very neat and precise, forming a beautiful tree pattern across the wipe-wall. Tobe looked at the wall. The probability of the same thing happening over and over again just got smaller all the time: a half times a half, times a half, times a half... It could never actually reach zero, but it got closer and closer to it. Besides, everyone knew that a fair coin would land on its obverse on half of the occasions when it was tossed, and on its reverse the rest of the time. The first step was, at least, logical.

Tobe wiped the wall clean with the rag that was hanging on the hook next to the bookcase, and, standing in front of the wall, set to reading the second chapter of his maths text book.

After a few more minutes, Tobe turned back to the beginning of the book, and read the first chapter again. He closed the book and put it on the table.

He stepped over the threshold to his room and said, "Metoo."

This time, Metoo heard Tobe the first time, her ears pricked, because she didn't want to risk missing his call, and, as a consequence, have him walk into the garden room as he had done the previous morning.

As Metoo came into sight, around the corner of the corridor to his room, Tobe asked, "Have you got a coin?"

* * *

IN COLLEGES IN Canada, India, North Africa and South America, the other four of the five best mathematicians in the World set to work on the printouts from the mini-print slot in Tobe's office. Service Central had glanced at them, but quickly realised that they might as well be written in Welsh or Walloon, or some other dead language, for all they could understand the densely packed pages of symbols and devices.

It was common practice for experts to share ideas across the College system, worldwide, so Masters Gilles, Sanjeev, Mohammad, and Rosa were not surprised to receive the pages, apparently from Tobe. They were, however, required to work harder than usual to understand the half-finished thoughts and ideas, and examples of wild stabs in the dark that could not be considered as thorough extrapolations at all. Tobe was meticulous, and these pages of maths were not. Never-the-less, Tobe had, apparently, sent them, and there were some interesting ideas buried in the morass of numbers and symbols. If they were surprised that Tobe had sent them incomplete ideas, they didn't show it, and they quickly became so embroiled in the maths that nothing else mattered.

They were soon talking to each other, comparing notes, trying to discover what Tobe was thinking. It was all logical, but none of it seemed to lead anywhere.

Probability was an old discipline; it had to be taught, of course, but none of the specialists could understand why Tobe had gone back to a subject that had nothing left to offer. It was not the sort of theoretical, unsolved mathematical puzzle that any of them specialised in, but, if Tobe was looking into it, there must be something there.

They worked on everything from quantum mechanics, Schrödinger's Cat and Einstein's EPR article, to the law of large numbers and the central limit theorem, all of which were hundreds of years old, and all of which were so familiar that no one expected anything new to come out of them.

Tobe had tried to get beyond the hay-day of mathematical thought, and had applied more modern ideas to his problem, including Qiu's Statement and Calvert's Synchronym.

After hours of working separately and together, of sharing results and extrapolations, all four Masters of mathematics came back with the same question, *What was Tobe trying to find the answer to?* None of them could work out what the initial premise had been, other than that it was broadly related to probability. There was no sense of the precise nature of the question.

Service Central, masquerading as Tobe, had no way to answer the question, and so stalled, while they collected information, and waited for the opportunity to interview Tobe.

Metoo, when she was asked, could not answer the question, even after she had spent some time reviewing the data in the garden room, watched over by Operator Saintout. She was a good theoretical mathematician, but no one considered that there were any remaining problems where probability was concerned, so she had not studied it since School.

She was certain of one thing: Tobe was looking for the answer to a question. She knew, only too well, that Tobe might not know the nature of that question, might not be able to express it in any language, mathematical or otherwise. Why something happened the way it happened could not always be explained; some things simply were. Tobe did not understand that. The chances of Tobe ever understanding that were, in Metoo's vernacular, "Slim to none".

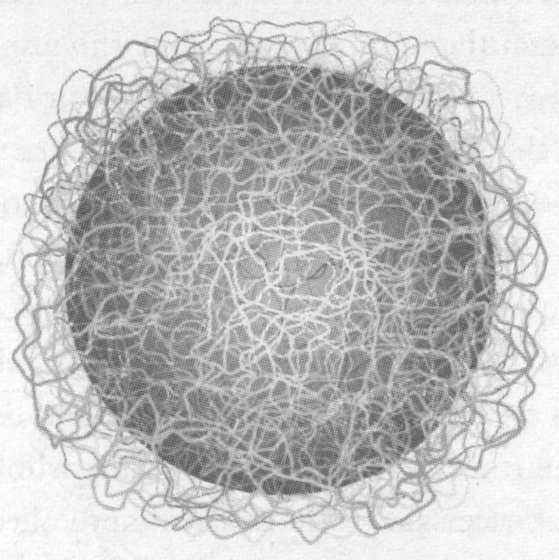

Chapter Seventeen

RANKED OPERATORS MCCOLL and Dudley continued with their duties. Of the three remaining Ranked Operators, Patel was the best rested, and she had eaten, so she was sent out to Tobe's office to supervise the extraction at 18:00.

She had to take the room apart, starting with the floor, for logistical reasons, and then moving on to the wipe-wall, the bookshelves, the desk, and finally the fabric of the room. There would be nothing left when she was finished. Of course, she would not be doing the job alone, in fact, it was not intended that she would be doing the job at all.

Estefan and his colleague were stood-down for debriefing, and two more Techs and two Operators were brought in at the end of their Rest periods. Service Central wanted fresh men working the room; what came out of there could prove critical.

One Operator and one Tech began the process of working their way across the linopro, under Operator Patel's instruction.

Patel was aware that the information on the linopro had not been drawn from the door, inwards, but she also knew that it was the only way to collect and record all of the data. She began by instructing the Tech to make a 30 centimetre square on the threshold of the room, using pins and string to mark out the area. When everything was collected and bagged from that square, including copies of all the handwritten data, they could move on to a second square. All the squares would be numbered to form a grid, with the corresponding number on the bag containing the information from each square, so that the whole lot could be reconstructed if necessary from the data they collected.

It was difficult, painstaking work: collecting the tatty pages from books without leaving bits stuck to the linopro, copying out complex equations, including crossings out, errors and smudges that nobody present understood, while trying not to impose their own values on the artefacts.

The first square took almost half an hour to dismantle and bag up. When they were finished there would be a hundred bags just for the floor, and it could take fifty working hours to complete. By the end of the second hour, Operator Patel was viewing the process almost as if she was performing a kind of forensic archaeology. With one person copying and another documenting and bagging, per square, it was important to have both teams working the room at the same time. She worked out the optimum order for the squares to be completed in. Both teams working together would cut the time in half, to twenty-five hours. The team in the left half of the room worked in rows back and forth, across the room, while the team on the right of the room worked in columns along the length of the room.

Increased familiarity with the process, and the fact that the mathematical data seemed simpler and clearer, the closer to the middle of the room the men worked, made everything go faster than expected, and collection of data on the linopro was completed in a little under eighteen hours. Operator Patel did as much work as any of them; four people were working at any given time, and one was resting, or bringing refreshments. They also only worked fifty minutes to the hour to allow for comfort breaks and to keep the workforce relaxed. It was an efficient system, and Operator Patel got more out of her team than anyone at Service Central had dared to hope.

Operator Patel preferred to keep the teams that she had trained for the job, rather than bring in new staff, and, having made her case to Service Central, she was allowed to continue with one of the teams after a four hour rest period. The second team would come in after an eight hour rest period, and the first team would get their second four hours of rest. Then, both teams would go back to working the original system until the next task was accomplished and the wipe-wall was dismantled.

Tobe had worked on the first day, when he should have been taking tutorials. He had started work early on the second day, which should have been a rest day, and a rest day was imposed on him on the third day, after Pitu 3 had hit his Service button at 08:30 in the morning.

It would not be impossible to impose a second rest day on Tobe on day four of the event, if things were not sorted out before then, but Metoo did not relish the thought. She could still hardly believe that things seemed to have gone so far. Tobe was in his room, apparently tossing a coin and collecting the data, quite happily, while Saintout was wondering about in the garden room, doing goodness only knew what, and waiting for her to make one of the most important decisions of her life.

She signed in to Service, and asked, "Anomalies?"

The answer came back, "Moderate and monitoring."

Metoo took a deep breath.

"Please advise," she said.

"Maintain the subject," Service replied.

Metoo wanted to scream. It was her job, to maintain the subject. She had been maintaining the subject for her entire adult life. She was on-call twenty-four hours a day, seven days a week. She fed him and clothed him. She had set his routine when she had first become his Assistant-Companion, moulding her predecessor's regimen, as she went along, to better suit Tobe's needs, without changing things so dramatically that she upset him. She had even weaned him off all the drug therapies that her predecessors had used for their own convenience. For the past eight years, she had maintained the subject.

She had watched him while she was his Student. She had liked and admired him then, but her relationship with him now was much deeper and more profound than it had been when she had merely sat in his classroom.

How dare they tell her to, "Maintain the subject"? How dare they? It was all she had ever wanted to do for him, not because she had to, but because of the relationship they had. In fact, it was less than she wanted to do for him, less than she wanted to do for them both. She didn't want to 'maintain' she wanted to nurture.

Metoo understood Tobe; she knew him. Service had profiles on him, they had his dossier, they knew his mental status, they had completed every kind of test on him, possible, including several that she considered cruel and unusual, but none of that mattered; Metoo lived with Tobe, and her life belonged with his.

It didn't seem to matter to them. No matter what she did for, or said to, Service, if they couldn't test it, count it, or quantify it, they could not understand it.

She signed out of Service, and tiptoed towards Tobe's room. He was sitting on the cot, his feet apart, on the floor, looking down at where he had dropped the coin she had given him. She had been listening to the coin bouncing off the linopro for most of the day. He was content, untroubled, breathing easily and physically relaxed. Service was the one panicking, not her, and not Tobe. If there was something wrong, she would know it. She didn't know it, couldn't feel it.

Confident that Tobe would continue his activity until suppertime, which was still a couple of hours away, Metoo ducked back into the garden room.

"Okay," she said to Saintout, "this is what we're going to do."

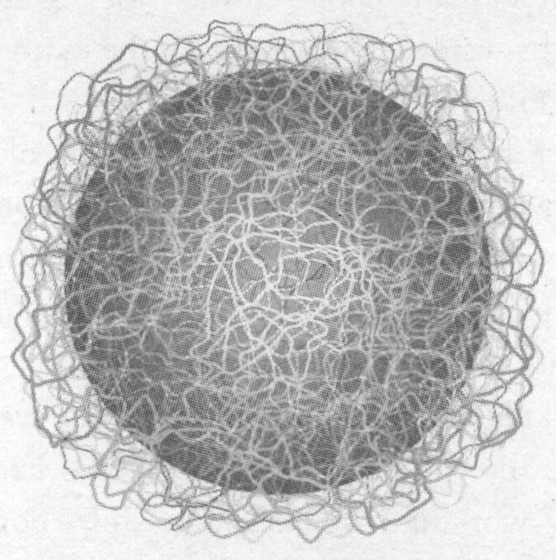

Chapter Eighteen

It took two hours for the Service Floor change-over to be completed. Each of the eight screens, not immediately involved in the Code Yellow, switched out to Service Central, and an Agent Operator relayed instructions for the following shift.

For the next eight hours, the outgoing Operators would have an enforced Rest/Repast period, regardless of their shift-status, so that they could be back on-call as soon as possible. The eight men, who, half an hour before, had thrown the switches on the facing edges of the counters, and put on cotton-lined neoprene gloves, were dismissed. They took off their gloves, and one or two of them wished their colleagues luck, or exchanged words with their Techs. As they left, there was a small sigh of relief from the remaining Operators on the Service Floor, who finally had room to breathe; so many bodies made the place claustrophobic.

All Techs more than four hours into a shift were also put on compulsory Rest/Repast, for the same reason, which alleviated the pressure of so many bodies in the room, a little more. The remaining Techs were supplemented by the extra pair of hands that was brought in for each rack.

By the end of the first two hours, the number of bodies on the Service floor had dropped from fifty to a much more comfortable thirty. It was still almost double what it would normally have been, and the pairs of Operators at their screens had to get used to the proximity of another person very quickly.

It was one of the few situations where no one really knew who was better off: the participants, or those who had been spared the anxiety of working that particular shift. For some of the more ambitious outgoing Operators it was a missed opportunity, for others it was a relief; some of the incoming Operators were thrilled at the chance to prove themselves, while others began to doubt their abilities. It was the same for the Techs.

All of the Techs and Operators had faced precisely these circumstances in Training Simulations and Manoeuvres, but the real thing was very different. Some would sink and others would swim, but Service Central was adamant that they would prevail.

Conditions on the Service Floor were difficult. The tension in the air was palpable, and some of the Operators' and Techs' bodies were reacting to the stress in ways that didn't endear them to the people they were working with.

So far as anybody knew, and nobody knew very much at all, only one Workstation was registering a Code Yellow, so monitoring ought to continue as usual for the remaining eight stations. The only difference in this shift was that every Workstation had two Operators, and Service Central was monitoring all the stations in rotation.

The Service Floor worked two eight-hour shifts, during which time nothing changed. Two hours into the first shift, when everyone had settled down, and the Techs had got the racks up to prime-spec with everything to hand, where it should be, and duplicates waiting, everyone began to relax.

The change-over to the second shift was a little tense, those incoming not knowing what to expect, and anxious to find out what had happened in the intervening time, particularly those who had switched out and been put on compulsory Rest/Repast. They had eaten and slept, and were either keen to get back into the fray, or were returning to the Service Floor anxious and reluctant.

The hand-off went slowly, but smoothly, with each Workstation being monitored, again, in turn, by Service Central. The Service Floor was too full of people again for almost an hour, which caused the room temperature to rise, and stress levels to increase.

Two hours into the second shift things had returned, once more, to something resembling normality, regardless of the fact that there were twice as many Operators as usual, and half as many Techs again as on a regular shift.

"It's about bloody time," said one Tech to another. The second man looked at the first as if he was insane.

"You're enjoying this?" he asked.

"I like the fact that the racks are fully stocked, and we've been allowed to do our jobs, properly, for once," said the Tech. "How long have we been under-supplied for? No hardware, no tools, no extra labour. Now, suddenly, we have all the equipment we can handle, and enough Techs to install it and run it properly."

"You're insane," said his colleague.

"So sue me," answered the Tech, running his finger along a row of lights on a brand new piece of hardware, sitting on rack 3, next to him.

Two shifts had passed, nothing had happened, and, still, no one had made a decision about the Code Yellow. The Operators began to talk to each other, in their pairs, and the Techs speculated that human error was more likely to be to blame than their beloved machinery, but that the obsolete, over-repaired machinery was more likely to be the culprit than any dangerous malfunction in the Service system.

THERE WAS NEVER any natural light on the Service Floor. Studies on variations in light levels, colours and luminosity had proven that people worked most efficiently, and calmly, at a particular bandwidth for electro-magnetic radiation, so that all Service facilities were lit to that particular bandwidth. In theory, it made it impossible to tell what time of the day or night it might be, and, at the beginning of training, some Service Operators suffered minor collapses in their circadian rhythms. These seldom lasted long, and were thought of as a necessary evil within an adjustment period. One in a thousand Operators, most of whom lived close to the tropics, never finished basic training, because they could not tolerate the light-levels they were expected to work at. Service Central considered this a statistically insignificant figure.

It was well into the night, when the Service Floor generally worked at its lowest staffing levels, yet none of the Techs had been relieved.

What the Operators and Techs on the Service Floor had not been told by Service Central was that two other College Service Floors were experiencing ramp-ups. By the last hour of the second shift, one had been in Code Green for four hours, and one had been ramped up to Code Yellow.

It was 02:30 on day four of the incident and Service Central was working with Operators in Colleges in Lima, Peru, and in Winnipeg, Canada.

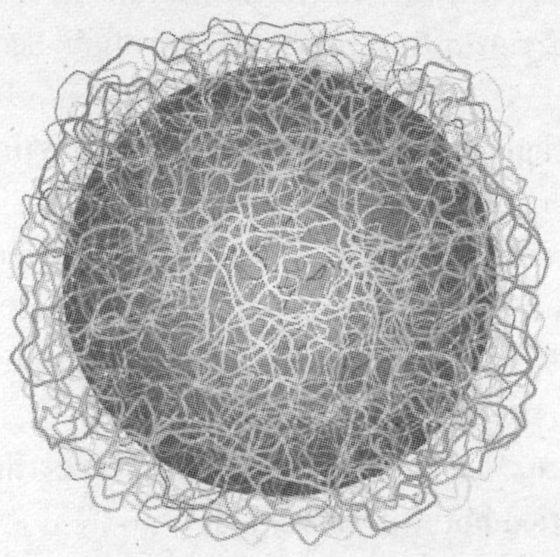

Chapter Nineteen

Tobe and Metoo saw out day three. He worked on simple probability problems, almost making a game of them, while continuing to collect and collate the data, and Saintout stayed in the garden room. Once or twice, a tone sounded in the flat, but it was always Saintout relaying information, or requesting Metoo's presence.

On one occasion, she went into the garden room to find him eating from a tray, with domed covers over the plates.

"What the...?" she began, almost laughing.

"Combat Repast," said Saintout, "double helpings.

"How are things?" he asked her.

"That's just it," said Metoo, "he seems rather happier than usual. I'm telling you, there's nothing wrong with Tobe."

"Well, we'll know, one way or the other, tomorrow. Are you still prepared to go through with this?"

"Absolutely."

"In that case, someone from Medtech needs to come in."

"Why? You can adjust my chip through Service Central, can't you?"

"There's a slight problem with that," said Saintout, "which I'm not at liberty to divulge."

"If you're going to send in someone from Medtech to mess with my brain, you'd better find some damned liberty," said Metoo, approaching the door. "Send me a tone when you've got something useful for me."

"Yes, ma'am," said Saintout. His respectful use of an honorific startled both of them.

"What did you call me?" asked Metoo, turning back to face him.

"Sorry, but you seemed terribly serious. It just came out."

"I'm not your superior, but thank you." Metoo left the room, closing the door quietly behind her.

"Oh, I think you are," said Saintout.

Within five minutes, the tone sounded, again, and Metoo signed in with Service.

"Yes," said Metoo.

"Service Central has requested Medtech to perform a procedure, regarding brainwave analysis. Subject: Assistant-Companion Metoo."

"Why can't you make the adjustment to my chip, remotely?" asked Metoo.

"That is not possible, and all information relating to the matter is classified."

"So, give me specified clearance, because, without it, this isn't going to happen. Send me a tone when you have an answer for me." She signed out of Service.

Metoo sat, slightly anxious, but no less determined, as she waited for the tone. She would do anything for Tobe, if she had to. He was the only person on the planet that she would kill or die for, but she would not be manipulated, and she was not afraid of Service Central. As far as Metoo was concerned, they could not tell her anything about Tobe that she didn't already know. She would not be made to betray him.

No one had ever told Metoo that Tobe was Active, and Tobe certainly wasn't aware of it. Metoo had known that he was special the moment she first met him, and he had not even known her name for the first year she had spent as his Student. He had never previously remembered the names of any of his Students, which was why, almost immediately after Metoo moved into his flat, everyone in Tobe's class was given the same name with the addition of a number. When none of the 'Neda' group proved suitable as an Assistant, the name and some of the Students were fazed out, and replaced with the designation 'Pitu'.

Metoo lived and worked with Tobe for two years before she began to suspect that he was Active. It was nothing in particular that he said or did; it was just something about him that was different from the other Masters. Tobe was the Master that she was close to, so she told herself that she had elevated him to the status of Active, in her mind, simply because of their relationship.

The thought had drifted into her head at regular intervals ever since, but Metoo had always disregarded it. It made no difference to her. She knew that no one in College was supposed to know the identity of the resident Active, or, indeed, whether the College had one.

The events of the last three days were the straw that broke the camel's back: a pretty damned big straw. Metoo was confident that Tobe was Active, certain of it, even. She didn't want to have a chip adjustment unless it was vital to Tobe's well-being, because she thought that if Service Central knew that she was aware of Tobe's true status, they would relieve her of her position in his household, and she could not bear for that to happen.

She reminded herself, after a few minutes' thinking about it, that she could, and would bear separation from Tobe, if it was in his best interests. She took a deep breath, and waited for the tone. It felt like a long wait.

"Yes," said Metoo, answering the tone almost before it had sounded.

"Operator Saintout will speak with you," said Service Central.

"That isn't specified clearance. Does he have someone from Medtech with him?"

"Not at this time."

"You are not giving me specified clearance?" asked Metoo.

"Not at this time. Police Operator Saintout will advise."

Metoo was puzzled, but signed out, none-the-less.

She cast a glance in Tobe's direction, but he seemed happy enough with his probability puzzles, so she went back to the garden room and Saintout.

As she closed the door, quietly, using both hands behind her back, so that she was facing Saintout, she opened her mouth to ask him a question, but he cut her off.

"I've found some liberty," he said, gesturing to Metoo to take a seat.

METOO LOOKED AT Saintout for a moment, her back still against the door. He stood up from his position leaning against the wall.

"I'll stand, thank you," said Metoo. She wanted to stay close to the door so that she could hear Tobe if he called her.

"I think you should sit," said Saintout, picking up one of the chairs, and putting it as close to the door as he could, without blocking Metoo's exit.

Metoo sat on the chair, the colour draining from her face.

"It's Tobe, isn't it?" she said. "Something's wrong."

"No," said Saintout, quickly, "Tobe is fine, so far as we know. He certainly isn't physically ill or in any immediate danger. There is no need to worry about him."

"I do worry about him," Metoo said, dropping her voice, and her head.

"Yes," said Saintout, "you do.

"I've been instructed to answer some of your questions with reference to your chip," he said.

"Okay," said Metoo, preparing herself for the worst.

"You are reluctant to have a chip adjustment, and you are particularly reluctant for Medtech to do work on your chip, is that right?"

"Yes."

"You would rather have a chip adjustment through Service Central."

Metoo nodded.

"I told you that it was impossible for you to have your chip adjusted by Service Central, and there is a reason for that."

"You want to extract more information from me, regarding my position, than I prefer to give, and you don't trust me to tell the truth."

Saintout sighed, and Metoo looked up at him, instead of down at her hands, resting in her lap.

"I certainly understand why you are so valued by Service Central," he said, under his breath.

"The truth is, Metoo, your chip was permanently disabled six years ago."

Metoo looked at Saintout for several seconds, her hands clenching and unclenching, slightly, in her lap.

"I don't understand," she said. "Everyone is chipped. Chips are permanent, but adjustable. No one could live without a chip."

Metoo put her hands up to her head, and held them there, as if she was protecting her mind with them. The chip should have been her protection, and they had taken it away from her. Why?

"A handful of people, worldwide, function with a disabled chip," said Saintout. "I can't tell you who they are, but one or two are in Service, a few are Masters, and one is a Civilian, the only one of his kind. There is also an Assistant in, I think, in the Middle East, somewhere, who has been functioning with a disabled chip for three months. His Master is doing very important work in Ethics and Philosophy."

"Why me? Why did nobody tell me?"

"Would it have made a difference?" asked Saintout.

"To what?"

"Would it have made a difference to your work with Tobe? Would knowing your chip had been de-activated make you any happier?"

"Leave Tobe out of it," said Metoo, warily.

"But isn't he the point of all this?"

Metoo stood up quickly, and was out of the door before Saintout could say anything more to her.

She stood on the other side of the door from him, breathing hard, as if she had run across the campus. Her back was to the door, and she held onto the door knob, as if trying to prevent Saintout from opening it. It was foolish; if he wanted to open the door, Metoo would not have the strength to stop him.

Metoo took a couple of deep breaths, and walked towards

the kitchen. It must be supper time by now, and it had been a long day. She needed to do something. She couldn't bear the thoughts that were tumbling through her head.

Metoo measured out rice for the two of them, and found a packet of fishpro to go with it. She vacuum sealed them into steamers, and began to prepare a salad of tiny yellow tomatoes and frilly lettuce, from her garden, the type that Tobe seemed to like so much.

A tone sounded in the flat.

Metoo tried to ignore it, but, within a few seconds, she was worried that Tobe might be disturbed if Service sent two tones too close together. She wiped her hands on a cloth and went to sign in.

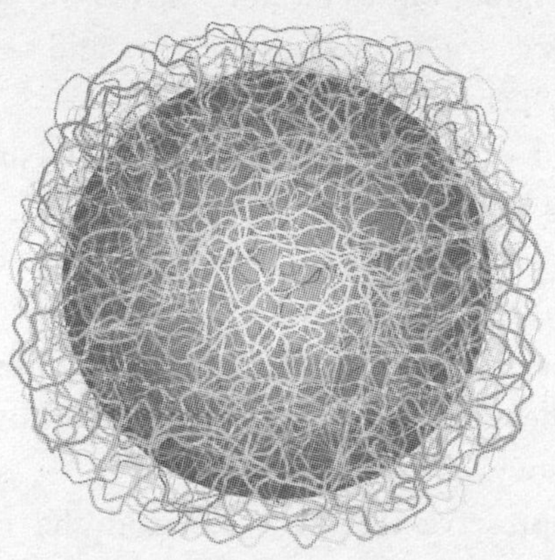

Chapter Twenty

Sixty hours into the event, Service Central had no protocol for dealing with the escalating problem.

They needed to know what Tobe was working on to try to keep him Active, but, by sending his work to other maths Masters, between hours fifty-two and fifty-three, they had, apparently, accelerated the problem. Was there a mind-virus in the works? How did the information, transmitted via the mini-print slots, effect the minds of the mathematicians without them knowing what was going on?

Control Operator Branting had hastily put together a team from his political, psychological, medical, educational and esoteric advisors. Twelve people sat in the room, each with his specialism, from ethics to sub-molecular biology, from neuroscience to nano-virus recognition. No one had an immediate answer.

No one had an answer, because no one was allowed to review the data that had been collected.

"For the first hour of this meeting, there is no such thing as a bad idea. Let's get rid of the junk, people, and see what's left," said Control Operator Branting.

They got rid of the impossibilities, but, having done that, there was very little left.

"We need to be empirical," said Mr Johnson, one of the medical specialists. "Let's not theorise, let's experiment."

"How?" asked Branting. "We gave the data to the four greatest mathematical minds in the World, wasn't that experiment enough?"

"We must preserve the Actives," said the neuroscientist, sitting to the Control Operator's left.

"So, don't involve the Actives," said a woman's voice from the far end of the conference table.

"Miss Goldstein?" asked Branting. "What are you suggesting?"

"I'm not sure, yet," said Goldstein, "but could we consider exposing the data to other groups, perhaps outside the College system, or maybe among volunteers from lower ranks."

"We don't know how the problem is being transmitted," said the doctor.

"Do we have data from the original outbreak on this?" asked Branting.

"Master Tobe's room extraction is barely begun and will take some considerable time to complete, sir," said Qa, his private secretary.

"No, I mean, what about other people exposed to the data... to the room?" asked Branting.

Several of the specialists at the table began to look at each other, while others started making furious notes.

* * *

The room emptied quickly at the end of Pitu 3's interview. It had not been a particularly pleasant experience for anyone present, although Pitu seemed to mind it less than the others. Mudd was thoroughly sick of his charge, and his work was not yet done.

Bello packed his electrical device and attendant cables away, and left the room first. Bim followed him out, but she returned within moments, and began to fold up the temporary chairs. She took them out of the room, one at a time, and, when she entered again, with Pitu's chair-stretcher, Mudd was already on his feet.

"Let's be having you then," he said to Pitu 3, trying for all he was worth to remain cheerful, and get through this assignment. "The infirmary will take good care of you, and I'll be out of your hair."

"Won't you stay with me?" asked Pitu 3.

"I'm due a Rest," said the Medic, "but, if I'm required –"

"Good," said Pitu 3, cutting him off, and sitting down in the chair-stretcher, which Mudd was convinced he didn't need.

Medic Operator Mudd would have liked to hand Pitu over to someone else. He had worked beyond the end of his shift, and was tired, hungry and irritable. There was no way that he could leave Pitu 3, though, without serious repercussions. He was manacled to his subject, because of the Schedule piggy-back, and Students were not allowed to go off-Schedule under any circumstances, particularly, Mudd thought, not in these circumstances.

Mudd almost wished he'd insisted that Pitu 3 be taken straight to the infirmary, and saved himself the misery of spending so much time with him. That manoeuvre would also have landed him in trouble, of course, when Service Central found out that he had delayed an essential interview.

"Why is it always the morons who get away with this shit?"

Mudd mumbled under his breath. Bim was standing close to him, securing the straps in the back of the chair-stretcher.

"I heard that, Medic," she said.

Mudd looked at Bim. He was partly crestfallen to have been caught out at all, and partly annoyed because he had unwittingly left himself wide open for censure.

"Bugger," he whispered.

"Yep," said Bim, grinning, "heard that too."

Mudd smiled, awkwardly, back at Bim, and she held the interview room door for him as he wheeled the chair-stretcher back out onto the gallery.

FIVE MINUTES LATER, Mudd wheeled Pitu 3 into the reception area of the infirmary. A doctor and several Medics were, apparently, waiting for them.

"First things first, doctor," said Mudd. "We need to get this man back onto his own Schedule."

The receptionist leaned over his desk with a large, heavy grade, tear-proof, paperpro envelope in his hand.

"You'll need this then," he said.

Mudd took the envelope, but did not have clearance to break the seal.

"Anyone?" he asked.

The doctor took the envelope from Mudd, and smiled at him.

"I'm guessing your replacement is overdue?" asked the doctor with a smile.

"What replacement?" asked Mudd, reduced, by his fatigue, to sarcasm.

"We'll have you out of here in no time," said the doctor.

A tone sounded in the reception area, and the receptionist

signed in to Service. He was only on the line for a matter of seconds before signing off.

"Doctor Narinda," he said, "there's a large group coming in from Service for Medtech. I've been instructed to alert you."

"Thank you," said the doctor.

"Excuse me," said the receptionist to Mudd, "you wouldn't be Medic Operator Mudd, by any chance?"

"I'm going to regret answering that question in the affirmative, aren't I?" asked Mudd.

"Only if you'd rather not spend an indeterminate amount of time in Medtech," said the receptionist, "starting immediately."

"Bugger," said Mudd.

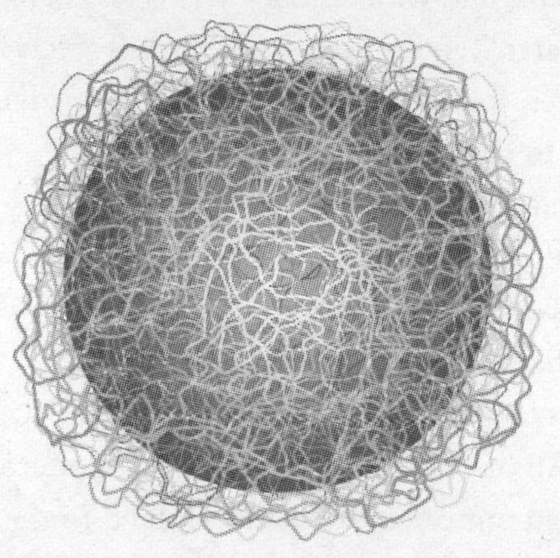

Chapter Twenty-One

"IT'S BEDTIME, TOBE," Metoo said, walking towards the open door of his room.

He was sitting on the cot, looking from the coin on the floor between his feet, to the wipe-wall where he was collating his data. He stood up, made a mark on the wall, sat down and picked up the coin.

"Bedtime," said Metoo from the threshold.

"It's working," said Tobe, smiling.

"It's supposed to," said Metoo, making the effort to smile back. "You have to go to bed, Tobe. You can do some more tomorrow..." Her voice trailed off. Tomorrow, Tobe wouldn't be tossing coins. In the moment, she had forgotten what tomorrow would bring, and she hated herself for lying to him, even accidentally.

Tobe stood up, lifting his robe off over his head as he made his way to the bathroom. He dropped the robe on the floor, carried out his ablutions, and walked back to his room, naked, less than five minutes later. Ten minutes after that, Tobe was asleep.

Metoo waited for a further ten minutes, steadying her nerves for what was to come.

A tone sounded in the flat.

Metoo signed in to Service.

"Yes," she said.

"Operator Saintout will speak to you, now."

"Does he have a Medtech with him?"

"He does. All of your questions will be answered."

Metoo signed out of Service, and walked to the garden room door. She took two deep breaths, and smoothed down the front of her robe. Her hands were still and dry, and her skin felt cool. She dropped her shoulders, took hold of the door knob and entered the room.

She stood with her back to the door, as she had several times during the day, so that she could hear Tobe, and respond if necessary, and so that she could escape if she wanted to. Saintout took a couple of paces towards Metoo, and smiled at her.

"What do you need to know?" he asked.

"What will they be able to read in my mind?" Metoo asked.

"That isn't the point of the exercise."

"Never-the-less."

"Theoretically?"

"Theoretically."

"More or less, whatever they want to read," said Saintout, "but, I repeat, that is not the purpose of the exercise."

"What is the purpose of the exercise?"

"It was your idea. In fact, I seem to remember that you insisted on this as the best, if not only, course of action. We don't need you to sanction anything, you realise that?"

"Of course I do," said Metoo, resigned.

"We are trying this as a first step," said Saintout. "Service Central is unconvinced."

"But they sanctioned this," said Metoo, frowning.

"I've said too much."

"Service Central told me that you would answer all of my questions."

"I believe that Service Central told you that all your questions would be answered, I don't recall any mention of who would furnish those answers," said a voice to Metoo's left.

She had seen the woman, bending over a collapsible, stainless steel table, setting out instruments, had recognised her as Medtech from her overalls, but had, otherwise, disregarded her presence. She had dealt with Saintout throughout her ordeal, and it was him she turned to, now.

The woman from Medtech gestured to Saintout. He stood in front of Metoo for a moment longer, and then reached out, and touched the top of her arm with his open palm, very lightly.

"I don't have clearance," he said, "and I'm all out of liberty. I have to go, now."

"I'll order specified clearance, through Service Central," said Metoo, but she knew she was grasping at straws. She clasped her hands lightly together in front of her, and said, "Don't go far, okay?"

"I won't," said Saintout. He turned his back on her, opened the large, south-facing window, onto darkness, stepped onto the ledge with his right foot, and out into the garden with his left. The window closed behind him.

"Questions?" asked the woman from Medtech.

"What's your name?" asked Metoo.

"Wooh. Doctor Wooh. The procedure is very simple. I need to locate the atlanto-occipital joint, and insert the chip. I will immobilise your neck for a few moments, while I'm doing the procedure, but it shouldn't be painful, and we should have immediate results."

Wooh gestured at the instruments on the tray table beside her, and picked up a device that looked like a pen.

"This is the only instrument I should require. I keep the others on hand, merely as a precaution. If I can't gain access to the joint in the cervical vertebra, we might need to use a light anaesthetic, and make a small incision, but there won't be any scarring."

"Apart from the emotional kind," said Metoo, tersely. She didn't like this woman, and she didn't like what was being done to her.

"I assure you, I won't allow you to be in any pain."

"I don't care about pain. This isn't about pain. Pain, Doctor Wooh, is the least of my worries.

"The procedure will no doubt be exactly as you describe, but I have questions before you start immobilising me and sticking things in the back of my neck; I take it that's what you mean by atlanto-occipital joint?"

Wooh looked at Metoo, caught entirely off-guard. Most of her patients, in the past, had been eager Students having adjustments to their chips; Service advised that Medtech should continue to use doctors and medical professionals to perform the task, because it seemed to reassure the kids, even though there was generally no reason why the adjustment couldn't be made remotely. Wooh wasn't used to patients that talked back, and she had never inserted a chip into a patient more than a year old. In fact, Doctor Wooh hadn't inserted a chip in anyone for ten years, or made an adjustment for that matter, outside of her lab, but she was the superior on duty in Medtech, and she outranked the superior on duty at the infirmary, so it had fallen to her to do the procedure. Her clearance was among the highest, in College, and she outranked Saintout by several levels.

Saintout had been given specified clearance for some of the information that Metoo would need to know, because Service Central realised that she had begun to trust him during their day together. It was up to Wooh to deliver the rest of the information, and she didn't relish the prospect.

"Let's sit, shall we?" she asked, gesturing towards a chair.

"I need to be close to Tobe," said Metoo, "in case he needs me."

"That, I can help you with." Wooh produced a headset, identical, in appearance, to the ones worn by Operators on the Service floor, and handed it to Metoo.

"You can wear this," she said. "Put it on. It's tuned to Master Tobe's wavelength, so that you can monitor his activity, remotely. If he should wake up, you'll know about it before he does."

Metoo looked at the contraption in her hands.

"I can see and hear Tobe through this?"

"No. We avoid invading anyone's privacy; in fact, there are laws against it. We can only monitor basic brain activity with this type of headset. You don't have –"

"The necessary clearance," Metoo said, cutting Wooh off.

"Visual and Audio are available to higher ranking Service Floor Operators," Wooh continued, "but if you put the headset on, and tell me what you see, I can guide you through it."

"And I just have to take your word for it?" asked Metoo.

"I'm afraid that's all you have," said Wooh. "I should also warn you that a lot of people find this a deeply unsettling experience, the first time around, so if it becomes too much for you, let me know, and we'll take it off."

Metoo slipped on the monitor, which sat high on her head. A bead extended down from it, which she inserted into her ear, and then she pulled down the screen in front of her eyes. All she could see was a swirling mass of yellow threads, which appeared to be throbbing slightly, and all she could hear was a soft, low tone, which had a lilt to it.

"What can you see?" asked Wooh.

"A ball of yellow, stringy lights," said Metoo.

"And hear?"

"It's like someone humming. It's almost like a lullaby."

"Good. The lights will probably stay yellow, but that's not what you're interested in. You need to look out for changes in individual strands, which might show up brighter or duller than the rest, or the pulsing that you can see... Can you see pulsing?"

"Yes, a little."

"Okay, good. You want to watch out for the pulsing getting faster, or for different areas pulsing at different rates."

"And the sound?"

"Listen for changes. Lower in pitch and slower ululations means he's more relaxed, and faster and higher means he's more active. From what you describe, he's obviously sleeping soundly at the moment. Let me know if things change, or if you're worried."

"Okay," said Metoo.

"Just one other thing," she said, after watching and listening for a minute. "The outcome of all this could change my status with Tobe, couldn't it?"

"It could," said Wooh, "and it probably will."

"I thought so."

"Are you ready?"

Metoo kept watching and listening, engrossed in the experience. She began to say something, but thought better of it. After tomorrow, she might never be so close to Tobe again, and she was determined to enjoy these last peaceful moments.

She breathed deeply, inhaling and exhaling to the pulse of the light-threads and the lilt of the hum.

"As I'll ever be," she said.

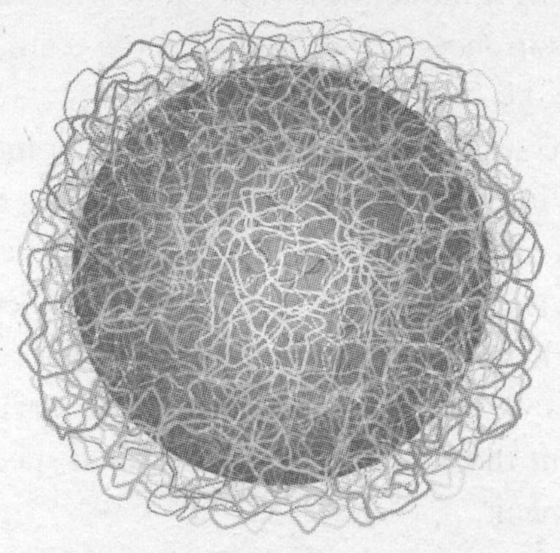

Chapter Twenty-Two

"IF WE ASSUME that everyone who had direct contact with the room, and/or the data, is contaminated, what are the parameters for containment?" asked Control Operator Branting.

"We need to work out a safe zone," said Mr Johnson, "to include Companions and Assistants of the five Masters."

"What about Students?" asked Miss Goldstein. "Some of them would certainly be susceptible, if we include persons with similar mental acuity or personality types."

"What about maintenance personnel?" someone else asked.

"By which you mean what?" asked Mr Johnson. "Cleaners? Technicians? Ground crew?"

"We should put a ring between those directly in contact with the data, and the people who have come into contact with them since. We should be able to trace their activities, but let's hope they didn't do too much socialising in the last couple of days."

"Medtech should be isolated too," said Miss Goldstein.

"We'll put a ring around them. They can work with the subjects in isolation, but once we've established the team, no one goes in or out."

"One of the subjects, the Student, was also interviewed, so anyone in the interview room should be taken to Medtech, and their contacts monitored," said the neuroscientist.

"This thing is growing fast," said Branting. "Let's begin with a curfew, and keep everyone where they are. We can call people to Medtech as we need them, and give them Service escorts."

"What about the Schools?" asked the viral specialist, whose name was Nowak.

"We should isolate them, immediately," said Branting, gesturing to Qa. "See to it.

"It is unlikely that there has been any contact between the Schools and any of the subjects, but we'll cross-check, and isolate any Students and Seniors who have come into contact with any of the subjects. The numbers will be small to none."

Qa returned before Branting had a chance to pursue his thought any further. He put a finger up in front of his chest in the smallest of gestures.

"If you would excuse us, ladies and gentlemen," said Branting.

Chairs scraped back, and the dozen men and women that had been sitting around the table, filed out of the room.

Branting turned to the console in an alcove close to the door. He sat down, keyed in his Morse signature, and followed it with the letters C-Q-D. He pulled in his chair, and put on a headset as the screen came to life.

Five minutes later, Branting signed out of Service Global, and gestured to Qa to bring his advisors back into the room.

Once they were all seated, Branting got to his feet.

"We have a problem," said Branting. Some of the advisors present looked at each other. How could their problem possibly be any worse than it was five minutes ago? "The mini-print slot system is not secure."

"No, sir, it isn't," said Mr Ahmed, "not locally, and not globally. It is intended as a medium for the free exchange of ideas, and so, anyone can access anything."

"Precisely," said Branting.

"The mini-print was used to distribute Master Tobe's data?" asked Mr Ahmed, his skin turning a pale, ashen colour. He clenched his teeth together, so that the muscles under the sharp cheeks on his gaunt face tensed, visibly. Mr Ahmed thought he was going to vomit, and he fumbled in his pocket for a handkerchief to catch it in. He gagged slightly and swallowed hard, the bulge in his neck bobbing alarmingly.

"So, isolation plans are pointless?" asked the neuroscientist.

"Probably," said Branting. "Anyone tuned in to a mathematics-based channel, or even the news, could fall prey to whatever is causing these problems. We will continue with quarantine procedures at the Colleges, but we must remember that we're casting a net, rather than locking anything down.

"What's our legal position, Schmidt?" Branting asked, turning to the man at the far end of the table, who had not yet spoken.

"It's a civil liberties issue," said Schmidt. "I know that you know this, but, for the record, 'Neither Service Central, nor Service Global is empowered to censor, interpret, interrupt or remove any intellectual property made freely available by any Drafted member or by any Civilian'."

"Where do we stand on interpretation of the law?" asked Branting.

"We can't do it. I just quoted the first sentence of a three hundred page document. This thing has been around for as long as Service has, and no one gets to mess with it."

"Are there no extenuating circumstances?"

"Extenuating circumstances would have to be fought in the courts at the global level," said Schmidt. "It's do-able, but, I fear that it's grossly too late for this event."

"Let's set the wheels in motion anyway," said Branting. "If we get through this thing, it might be a useful statute to have on the books for next time."

"I think we'll hit a major sticking point there, too."

"How so?"

"I think you'd have trouble defining terms, and there's no way to cover all eventualities."

"So, we could cover this situation, retrospectively, and guard against the same thing happening again..." began Nowak.

"But the chance of the same set of circumstances recurring is –"

"Let's quote Assistant-Companion Metoo, shall we?" asked Branting, "And just call it 'slim to none'."

"That's about the size of it," said Schmidt.

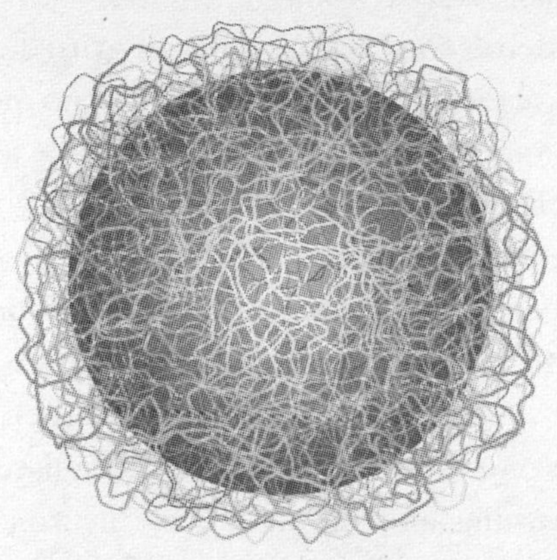

Chapter Twenty-Three

WOOH SHOWED METOO a deep neck brace. It had solid, tilted rings, top and bottom, with curved, vertical bars holding the two together. The rings seemed hopelessly far apart, but the vertical supports had threaded sections on them, so that the collar could be made deeper or less deep, depending on the length of the subject's neck.

The rings were covered in grubby, orange neoprene that Metoo thought looked particularly unattractive. She didn't comment.

"My neck's nowhere near that long," she said.

"You'd be surprised," said Wooh, but she shortened the supports, never-the-less, before wrapping the collar around Metoo's neck. When it was securely in position to the correct circumference, Wooh began to elongate the vertical supports. Metoo felt as if her neck was being stretched beyond its natural limits.

"Comfortable?" asked Wooh.

"Hardly," Metoo tried to say, through gritted teeth, but her neck was so extended that her lower jaw had no movement in it, what-so-ever, and she found herself talking like a ventriloquist with her jaw clamped shut.

"It won't be long," said Wooh, by way of reassuring Metoo.

Metoo did not care. Her discomfort was minor, particularly compared to the fascination that the video and audio feeds held for her. There was a subtle ebb and flow to the rhythm of the lights and the pitch of the sound. She recognised the cadence of Tobe's breathing and the timbre of his voice in the low hum, and saw the sparkle in his eyes, when he was following a thought to its logical conclusion, in the pulse of the lights in front of her. She only thought that his mind was not yellow, that it could never be yellow.

Metoo was vaguely aware of a flash of pressure on the back of her neck, not like a prick, more like an insistent thumb-print, or an emphatic poke. The next thing she knew, the collar was released from her neck, as if being torn away in one swift move, and she felt something icy cool and moist: a swab, she supposed.

"All done," said Wooh.

"That's it?"

"That's it."

"Now what?"

"Now you rest, and I climb back out through that damned window. I'll need that, first, though," she said, gesturing at the headset.

"How do I shut it off?"

"Just flip up the screen and take the ear-bead out, and the rest is automatic."

"Let me wear it again, sometime?"

Wooh was surprised; it wasn't the usual response. Most people found the experience difficult. Either it gave them a headache, or vertigo, or made them nauseous or agitated. Metoo was oddly calm.

"Of course," said Wooh, "if I can."

Wooh put her instruments away in a neat doctor's bag, and then collapsed the table and attached it, by a strap, to the side of the bag. She opened the window, lifted her equipment out over the ledge, and dropped it onto the grass on the other side.

Metoo held out her hand, and, after a moment, Wooh took it, and shook it firmly. Metoo was grateful to Wooh for giving her Tobe back for a few minutes, and Wooh was oddly impressed by the calm, strong little woman in front of her.

"Send Saintout back in, would you?" asked Metoo. Wooh nodded and smiled. She sat on the window-ledge, and swung her legs out. She stepped out onto the grass, picked up her bag, and looked around.

Saintout wasn't there.

"He's gone," said Wooh, just as a tone sounded in the flat.

Metoo held up one hand to Wooh as she turned to the garden room door, "Don't move," she said, as she left the room

"Yes," said Metoo, signing in to Service.

"All current occupants must remain in the building," said Service.

"Anomalies?"

"Moderate and monitoring."

"What's going on?"

"All current occupants must remain in the building."

"Where's Saintout? Does that mean Doctor Wooh has to stay?"

"All current occupants must remain in the building."

Metoo signed out of Service, listened in the hallway for a moment to make sure that Tobe was still asleep, and, reassured by his slow, steady breathing, she let herself back into the garden room.

Wooh looked up at her from where she was leaning against the wall, adjacent to the window, her feet crossed, casually, in front of her, and her arms by her sides.

"I guess we're going to get to know each other a little better than either one of us expected," said Wooh.

"Have they told you what's going on?"

"Not yet, but I'm guessing that if they haven't told you now, they're not likely to tell you at all. Do you know if there's a status change on Master Tobe?"

"They're not telling me anything. I ask for anomalies, and they tell me 'moderate and monitoring'. I don't even know what that means. I've never been past 'minor and monitoring' before, and it's generally 'minor and momentary'. What are they keeping from me?"

"Anything and nothing."

Metoo visibly jumped, and put her palm high on her chest, shocked, and Wooh turned to see where she was looking. Saintout was standing on the other side of the window.

Wooh opened the window, while Metoo got her breath back.

"Did I startle you?" asked Saintout, stepping onto the ledge and then into the room in two easy strides. "Didn't mean to, sorry.

"I got the order to remain in the building, and I was still in transit. It's a lovely evening, so I was taking the long route around the building. I decided I'd better come back to the last building I was in. I hope three isn't a crowd," he said, looking from one anxious face to another.

"Four," said Metoo.

"I don't –" Saintout began, before he was cut off by Metoo.

"There are four of us in the flat."

"Service should have known that you were outside," said Wooh.

"It would appear that they've got better things to keep an eye on than me," said Saintout. "Without wishing to alarm anyone, things don't appear to be getting any closer to being resolved."

Metoo looked from Saintout to Wooh. Her face was pale and her eyes were large, but her skin was cool and her hands were still. She was calm.

"Will someone please tell me what's going on?" she asked.

"Doctor Wooh?" asked Saintout, stepping and turning, so that he stood next to Metoo, as though physically taking her side.

"I don't know any more than you do," she said.

"But you do have the means to find out," said Saintout.

"If they haven't even bothered to put your tracer on," Wooh said, "I'd be prepared to bet that they're too busy to bother talking to me."

"You have the trump card, though, don't you, Doctor Wooh?" Metoo asked.

"How so?"

"Think about it. Tobe is the primary subject in all this, whatever it is. Presuming everyone in College, and not just us, has been locked down, that puts you in charge of Tobe. He's stuck in here, and so are you. You out-rank Saintout, and nobody's telling me anything. Doesn't that put you in the perfect bargaining position?"

"I'm not sure bargaining with Service is at all wise," said Saintout.

"Well I've got nothing to lose," said Metoo. "They've put this damned thing in my head so they know what I'm thinking; I might as well say it, it won't be news to them."

"It really doesn't work like that," said Wooh, "although, I do take your point.

"It's late, Master Tobe's asleep, and no one is going anywhere, so why don't we try to relax and get some rest; we might have a long day ahead of us tomorrow."

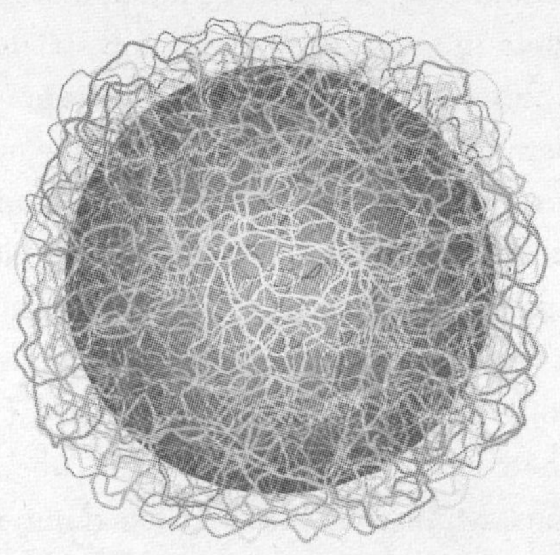

Chapter Twenty-Four

Pitu 3 was enjoying the attention. He was in a medical gown, in bed, in a private room, in no time at all. His Schedule was even hooked up to the infirmary, so that he wasn't required to press his button if he didn't feel like it, providing he wore a tag on his finger.

For the first hour, he was visited at least half-a-dozen times by one Medic or another, and twice by doctors. It seemed to him as if they were just chatting with him. It was the most attention he'd ever had in his life, and he was revelling in it. He had alerted Service to Tobe's problems, and he'd suffered a minor physical and emotional breakdown as a result. It didn't matter how the affair played out; he would be a legend in College for a long time to come.

During the second hour, visits to Pitu 3's room were fewer and further between. During the third hour, nobody came to see him at all. Early in the fourth hour, he was woken up, so that a Medic could remove his tag, leaving him responsible for his own Schedule again.

Worse than all of that, he could hear things going on beyond the door to his single room that he was not a part of.

Of the thirteen obvious candidates for contamination in the College, Tobe and Metoo were in their flat. Pitu 3 was the first taken to the infirmary, but it was not yet known if he had suffered from contamination, and a more immediate concern was his emotional well-being; he was destined for the infirmary before there had been any evidence that Tobe's work could prove dangerous. Mudd was the first signed into the infirmary, purely as a potential contamination patient, but he was also Service and a Medic, so he helped to open the quarantine ward that would house the rest. The Service Operators that had stood outside of Tobe's room, while he was extracted, were the next to be escorted to infirmary ward Isis, followed by Estefan and his colleague.

"Just fill these in for me," said the receptionist, handing the Techs clipboards with multi-page questionnaires on them.

"Why?" asked Estefan. "What did we do?"

"It was probably the toner," said his colleague, "or maybe the stuff he drew on the floor with. Stands to reason it was something in that room. It can't be too terrible though, I haven't got any symptoms."

"And nobody's wearing masks, or sticking us in suits or anything. What is it then?" asked Estefan.

"You'll be quarantined in ward Isis, where you'll be given more information," said Mudd, "but first we need you to fill in the forms. Pay particular attention to question 12b if you wouldn't mind: human contacts. Then we'll get you processed."

"Bren's going to go mad," said Estefan, "and what about the kids?"

"Lockdown on Estefan's residence," Mudd called over his shoulder at the receptionist, who was thrusting a clipboard at the Operator that had delivered Saintout's tray to Tobe's flat.

"What do you mean, 'Lockdown on Estefan's residence'? I live alone," said Estefan. "I went over to see a Senior at the School, a friend of mine for a... I guess you probably don't need to know what for."

"Get Doctor Narinda in here," said Mudd. "We need to interface with Service at a superior level, right now."

The faculty building where Tobe's office was situated was the first to be locked down. Patel and her crew would have to manage as best they could. It didn't matter how long it took, because no one else was going to enter that room. None of the other rooms in the building were open, so, except for some basic sanitation, and access to lockdown rations, which were both ancient and meagre, they could do nothing but work. The best rest that any of them got while they were in the building was the sleep that they snatched, propped up against the wall in the corridor outside the office, which was filling up with cartons of bagged up material that could not be extracted under the terms of the lockdown.

Workstation 4, on the Service Floor, rotated between control subjects, but was currently taken up with a Senior at the School. The cool, blue threads were virtually stationary, with low luminescence. Watching the feed felt like watching paint dry, so station 4 tended to be the busiest Workstation on the Service Floor, because its Operator was switched out every two hours; no one could be expected to concentrate for longer than that. Most two hour slots also involved a line-check, which the regular Operators chose to do, simply to have something to occupy them during their shifts.

Station 4 collected and collated the most data, and yielded the fewest results of any Workstation on the Service Floor.

AT 05:30, ON day four, someone from Medtech came into Pitu 3's room and woke him up. He placed a breakfast tray over Pitu's knees as he sat up, and turned to go.

"Press your button for Rouse," said the Medic, without looking back.

At 05:32, Pitu pressed his button, and moved the tray so that he could get out of bed. He was back within a minute, and lifted the cover from the dish on the tray. Oatpro, great, but he was hungry, so he picked up the spoon and began to eat.

The Oatpro was only barely warm enough, and wasn't giving off any steam, at all, but it didn't matter, because it was sweet and creamy, and hadn't been topped up by Students for a week in a crusting pan; it had been made fresh that morning.

Pitu 3 was still sitting on the edge of the bed, eating his breakfast, when the Medic returned with a clipboard, and a thick file.

"We need you to review some material for us," said the Medic, handing Pitu 3 the file without any further ceremony. Pitu made to open it, but the Medic reached down and placed his hand on the plain, drab cover. "After I've gone."

He stood next to the bed, and began reading from the questionnaire on the clipboard. Pitu felt sure they were the same questions he'd answered when he was admitted the night before. The Medic ran through them quickly; too quickly for Pitu's liking. He barely had a chance to answer the questions, and had no time at all to speculate or draw the Medic into conversation. The man was terse and far too businesslike, not at all like the staff from the evening before, who'd been so attentive.

NAMED OPERATOR BABBAGE was brought on for the 04:00 shift change on Workstation 4, and would remain at the station until further notice. He was paired with Named Operator Siemens, who would take the dicky seat. As they entered the floor, the room grew more than usually quiet.

Babbage took his seat, keyed in his Morse signature, pulled his chair up to the scratched counter, and placed his hand over the rubberpro ball mounted in the tabletop. Siemens pulled out the dicky seat, and sat next to him.

"Verify headset," he said to the Operator he was taking over from.

"Verify," said the Operator, and, before he had a chance to move, a Tech had placed a headset in his hand.

"Thank you," said the Operator, taken aback. The Operators, who worked the Service Floor, never observed the niceties, but neither were the Techs ever this diligent.

Babbage dismissed his predecessor at the station, and began to conduct a line-check, including audio and visual. The line-check was completed in just less than five minutes, and no anomalies were recorded. No anomalies had been recorded at station 4 for over twenty years. Never-the-less, Babbage felt the tension growing in the room.

"Subject switch-out at 05:30," he said to Siemens. Three... two... one... monitoring switch-out."

The perimeter of the ball of threads on the screen in front of Siemens and Babbage altered slightly, and the threads appeared to be a little more densely packed, but a rookie Operator would have been unlikely to notice either change, and the colour-discrepancy was negligible and invisible to the naked eye. Babbage and Siemens saw enough to know that the switch-out had been completed without a hitch. They had not been told who they were monitoring, but they were both seasoned Operators, and had been briefed with all the latest updates on what to expect.

Nothing happened.

"05:32," said Babbage. "Subject has acknowledged Rouse. Line-check."

"Verify," said Siemens.

"Verify line-check," said Babbage.

Station 7 monitored one of the Companions. It was part of the upper echelon of the control group, and the same Companion had been monitored on it for two Highs. The normal minimum was a year, and the normal maximum was three Highs, so, she was the optimum candidate for a switch-out, particularly given that she would be switched with another female of a similar rank. The data for the switch-out itself could make for very interesting reading at this stage in the event.

Ranked Operator Chen came onto the Service Floor at 04:30, so that the shift change-overs were staggered. She was followed by Operator Goodman, who had never been promoted during his thirty-plus years with Service, but who was, when push came to shove, everyone's favourite go-to guy. He had more eye-years in front of a screen than anyone, and he could summarise any and all activities with his own particular brand of line-check, which he could perform completely and efficiently in less than three minutes. He had done it in ninety seconds, once or twice, just for the guys on a quiet shift.

Goodman held the lowest rank on the Floor, but he was the specialist. He was also the only man to whom the adage 'one Operator, one screen, one station' did not apply.

"Ma'am," he said, approaching Workstation 7, and pulling out the chair for Ranked Operator Chen to sit.

"You've got to be kidding," said Chen. "I'm not sitting there with you watching over my shoulder. I'll take the dicky."

"Oh, right you are," said Goodman, stepping to one side, and pulling the dicky seat out from under the counter. "If you're sure?"

"I'm very sure," said Chen. "I have no desire to make a total idiot of myself in front of you, Goodman. I'm only here to observe."

"Expecting something funky?"

"Expecting something. You weren't briefed?"

"I'm six hours into a Rest," said Goodman, "so I'm guessing there wasn't the time, or they'd have brought in someone else."

"There is no one else. You're it."

The other Operators in the room all outranked Goodman. They were all stressed, working in close proximity with one another, and no one seemed to know what was going on. They all began to breathe a little easier, and relax a little more when they heard Goodman's voice. No one turned to look: one Operator, one screen. They didn't need to look; his presence was enough to soothe them.

Goodman sat in the seat in front of the screen, and began to enter his Morse signature, using the switch on the facing edge of the counter in front of him.

"No," said Chen, "allow me."

Goodman reset the switch before getting up from his chair. Chen perched on the seat for just long enough to enter her own Morse signature, and then vacated the chair for Goodman.

"Whatever I do here will have your name on it, ma'am," said Goodman, "are you sure you want that?"

"I need you to have my clearance level if you're going to be any use to me at all," said Chen, "and this is the fastest and most efficient way to get you specified clearance, without going through channels."

"We are eager beavers, aren't we? This is almost as serious as waking me up before I've had my eight hours." He chuckled low in his chest, and Chen looked up, mildly astonished, before smiling warmly at him.

"Let's get a headset, shall we?" asked Goodman, pulling his chair closer to the counter, and resting his huge right hand gently on the rubberpro sphere set into its surface

"Verify," said Chen.

"Verify headset, Ranked Operator Chen."

A Tech dropped a headset into Ranked Operator Chen's hand. She leaned forward and handed it to him.

"Things could start to happen fast in here," she said, "so why don't we drop the formalities; you can call me Chen."

"Bob," said Goodman, offering Chen his hand to shake, and twinkling all over her. "Can't have us on an equal footing, now, can we? And, since you're the boss, let's piggy-back a couple of headsets."

A Tech appeared at Ranked Operator Chen's elbow with a brand new, out of the box, state of the art headset that was half the size and weight of the great lump that Goodman was wearing, but the contrast was somehow appropriate to their comparative ages, sexes and sizes.

"If you're ready, Bob," said Chen, "that completes the change-over." She looked over her shoulder at the outgoing team, and said, "You may stand down, gentlemen, but please sign in, for changes to your Schedules."

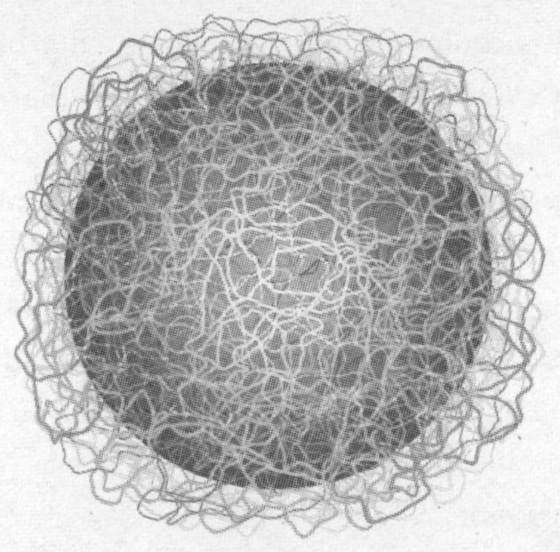

Chapter Twenty-Five

METOO SLEPT FITFULLY, but got out of bed, as usual, at 05:30. Her cotpro socks hit the cool linopro, and she sat on the edge of her bed for a moment, looking down at her feet, and remembering what had happened the night before.

She took a deep breath, stood up, and walked across her room and out to the kitchen. She put her coffee on, and then went to the bathroom, washed and dressed, quickly, and tidied the room ready for Tobe, leaving out a clean robe and towel for him.

Time would be tight this morning, and she really wanted a little of it to herself, before she had to confront Saintout and Wooh, and face the day. She stood in the kitchen, drinking her coffee, feeling quite unable to eat anything, even the fruit that she usually enjoyed so much.

She poured herself a second cup of coffee, and braced herself.

At 06:00, the shower was running at 40 degrees, and the eggpro was cooking. Metoo signed in with Service.

"Yes," she said.

"All current occupants must remain in the building," said Service. "Rest cycle complete, please ensure that all occupants are provided with the sustenance they require."

"What happened to...?" Metoo began, but then she remembered that expecting a tray for Saintout would give away the fact that he was still with them, and his tracer didn't appear to be working. He might be an ally if things went badly, so she didn't want to risk giving away his location to Service.

"You have a question?" asked Service.

"No, no question."

Metoo couldn't risk Tobe bumping into Saintout and Wooh, so, while she could still hear his shower running, she dashed back to the kitchen, scooped the eggpro into a dish, added some crackers and the fruit that she had planned to eat that morning, and slipped it to them through the garden room door, on a little tray with a couple of spoons. It would have to do.

At 06:03 Tobe and Metoo bumped into each other in the corridor, as Metoo made her way back to the kitchen.

"I'm so sorry, Tobe," she said, as they stepped into the kitchen together. "I was in the garden room, and I forgot the time. I'll make you some breakfast now. Sit."

Tobe looked at Metoo, baffled.

"There's no breakfast," he said.

"I'm going to make your breakfast for you now," said Metoo, mixing more eggpro: two scoops of powder to one of powdered milk, a pump each of salt and pepper, out of the dispenser, and let the steam do the rest.

"Is it the same?" asked Tobe.

"You always have eggpro," said Metoo, automatically; she had other things on her mind.

After 45 seconds, breakfast was perfectly cooked, and she set the dish in front of him at the kitchen counter, and picked up her cup of coffee, which would be cold if she didn't get to it soon.

Tobe spooned some eggpro up to his mouth.

"No!" shouted Metoo.

Tobe sat with the spoon an inch from his lips, looking at Metoo.

"Breakfast," said Tobe.

"It's too hot," said Metoo. "It usually cools on the counter for a few minutes while you're in the shower. I'm sorry."

"It's not the same?"

"You just have to wait a minute. I'll tell you when it's ready.

Tobe sat on his stool with the spoon up close to his face, and waited. He made Metoo want to smile. She drained the last of the coffee from her cup, and put the cup in the auto-clean, walking around the counter and behind Tobe to do it. When she turned, he still had the spoon up to his mouth, but the eggpro in the dish had stopped steaming.

As she left the kitchen, Metoo called over her shoulder, "You can eat now, Tobe. I'll be back in a minute."

Metoo went to the garden room, ducking in, quickly, so that there was no risk of Tobe hearing movement in the room.

Tobe ate some of the eggpro. He looked down at it after three or four mouthfuls.

"It's the same," he said, and carried on with his breakfast.

SAINTOUT AND WOOH were in the garden room, finishing the breakfast that Metoo had taken to them on the tray.

"Good fruit," said Wooh as she entered. "How did you manage to get it?"

"I grow it," said Metoo, spreading her hands wide to encompass the room they were in.

"Stupid. Of course," said Wooh, embarrassed.

"You whip up a decent egg, too," said Saintout, by way of letting Wooh off the hook.

"Eggpro," said Metoo.

"Eggpro?" asked Saintout.

"Eggpro," said Metoo. "It's a matter of proportions."

"Bloody good," said Saintout. "What's the secret recipe, then?"

"Thank you. It's two scoops of eggpro powder to one of powdered milk, a pump each of salt and pepper, out of the dispenser, and let the steam do the rest: 45 seconds."

"That's how you keep him in your thrall, then?" asked Saintout.

"Sorry?" asked Metoo.

"You and the prof," said Saintout.

"Sorry?" asked Metoo.

"You and Master Tobe. You're unusual, the two of you."

"How so?"

"Nobody expects it."

"Expects what?"

"Nobody expects a Companion to last for so long. And an Assistant-Companion should be wiped out in months. Most of us gave you a year at most, and it's been what? Three highs? Four?"

"Eight years," said Metoo. "Two years as his Student. I had some help from Kit at the beginning, but –"

"You've been enabling this guy for six years?" asked Saintout, incredulous.

"How is that even possible?" asked Wooh.

"Oh, not you too," said Metoo. "How do I keep him out of his office?"

"He can't go there, today," said Wooh. "They haven't finished collecting the information."

"And, when he goes back, it won't be the way he left it," said Metoo. "He'll know the difference."

"Of course he'll know the difference," said Saintout. "They're going to strip that room! There'll be nothing left: no sign that anything ever happened in that room. They've taken everything! Okay, maybe they're in the throes of taking everything, but the next time he goes in his office, it will be like the first time."

"He can't cope with that," said Metoo. "You can't take his work away from him. It'd be like taking his life."

"What else do you expect?" asked Wooh.

"Why can't they leave him in peace?"

"Fear," said Saintout. "Service lives in fear. They have nothing and no one, and they haven't got a clue how the Actives make this whole thing work. Wouldn't you be scared?"

"The only thing that scares me, is the effect of all this on Tobe. He's only human, you know!"

"Human?" asked Wooh.

"You're the doctor," said Metoo. "He's more human than you or I.

"What is wrong with you people?"

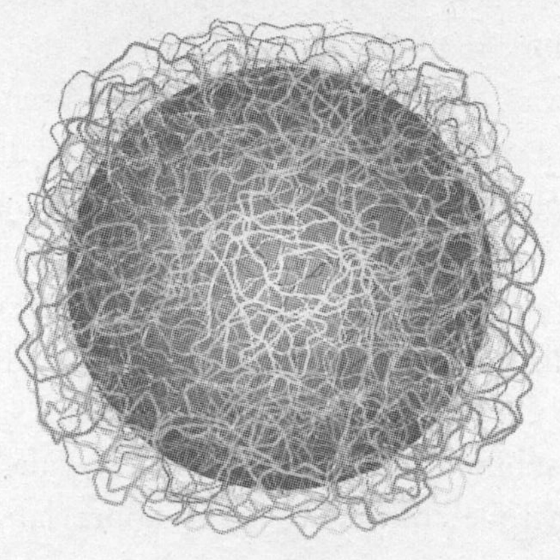

Chapter Twenty-Six

THERE WAS, EFFECTIVELY, no change at Workstation 4. Babbage and Siemens were specialists, brought in, specifically, to monitor the anomalies at station 4, and collate information on the subject. There was nothing to collect or collate. Workstation 4 was inactive. It was as if the station was wired to an inert test subject.

"This can't be right," said Siemens, who had expected fireworks from the start, and had seen nothing. It wasn't that she hadn't seen anything of any significance; she had, literally, seen nothing: nothing at all.

"It so can be right," said Babbage. "We're brought in to monitor these great mystery cases, and, nine times out of ten, they prove to be inert, benign, inconsequential. Getting the call is one thing, getting a reading is quite another."

* * *

Pitu 3 sat in his hospital bed. It was 07:02, and he had eaten the oatpro more than an hour before, but the tray had not been taken away, and, however good it had been at breakfast, the oatpro had congealed around the lip of the dish and in the bowl of the spoon, and was stiff and grey and unpleasant.

Pitu 3 had been doing as he was bidden. He had spent the last hour and a half looking through the file that was delivered to him with his breakfast. He had waded through the material that had been extracted from Tobe's mini-print slot, but it still did not interest him. He recognised that it was the material that he had seen in Tobe's office, even in its abbreviated state, but it meant nothing to him.

If the folder had included material on the cotpro and linopro, and the physics of the stuff that Pitu 3 had been working on, he might have found something to take an interest in, but he didn't understand the other stuff, and he hadn't been included in it, so, his interest was negligible. He simply didn't care. Besides, the maths didn't add up; it was too esoteric, too theoretical, too deranged for his liking.

Pitu 3 had reached the last few pages of the file. Ranked Operator Patel had taken pictures of Tobe's room, and got them back to Service Global before embarking on the task of dismantling the office. The first was a close-up of a section of the wipe-wall, slightly degraded by an inadequate zoom lens, and didn't offend Pitu too much. The second was of the floor. Pitu began to feel uncomfortable. He didn't want to look at the pictures, but had been told that he should scrutinise the entire file, and he was used to doing as he was told.

It was the last picture that really made him shudder. It was a composite, panoramic view of the entire room, showing, not only the maths, but also the dislodged and torn books, and the untidy bookshelves. At the centre of the picture was a chair, which had a book hanging off it, showing a bright blue square of book-cloth. The sight of the splash of colour right in the middle of the picture somehow made Pitu want to wretch. He closed the file, and placed it face down on the breakfast tray.

"I CAN'T GET a reading," said Siemens, at Workstation 4.

"Who can't get a reading?" asked Babbage.

"Okay," said Siemens, "you can't get a reading. What the hell is going on?"

"This guy is inactive or, passive. We're not getting a reading, because we don't have a significant intellect."

"So, what are we doing here?"

"You tell me," said Babbage.

Station 4 was almost entirely static for more than an hour. There appeared to be no change in the structure, intensity or variability of the cloud of threads on the screen in front of them

"We'll do another line-check at 07:00," said Siemens, "but this looks like a negative to me, and we only get two hours with this guy."

At 07:02, when Babbage was only a couple of minutes into the line-check, he and Siemens both spotted something.

"Where was that?" asked Siemens, "68, 71?"

Babbage checked the grid reference.

"Reset zoom to 68, 71," he said. The screen refocused, and Babbage and Siemens looked at the result.

Babbage rolled the palm-sized, rubberpro sphere again, and said, "Hover." A length of thread came into sharp focus. It was a cool grey colour, pale among the stronger blue lengths, and its pulse was barely visible.

"Anomaly at sector 68," said the Operator, hitting a button. "Tone sent."

"And there it is," said Siemens.

"Except that it's out of the intellectual range in that sector," said Babbage.

"We'll need authorisation," said Siemens.

"Okay, said Babbage," but it'd better be quick."

A single grey thread at 68, 71 began to fade, and then another, and another. Within ninety seconds, the threads had become cold, frayed-looking and fragile. This was not an intellectual response. This was an emotional response. Feelings came and went in very different patterns from thoughts, and time was of the essence. They needed to capture this moment, and exploit it quickly. The problem was, circumventing the law on emotional privacy.

"We need to know the stimulus for the subject," said Siemens, "and we need his psych file."

GOODMAN AND CHEN prepared for the switch-out. It was 05:58 and they had two minutes to go. The tension in the air was palpable.

"Subject switch-out at 06:00," said Bob Goodman.

"06:00," said Chen.

Bob Goodman looked at Chen, sitting in the dicky seat.

"Are you really going to do that every time I comment?" asked Goodman.

Chen looked at him.

"You might want to look at your screen," she said.

"What makes you think I'm not?"

"Bob!"

"This is going to get very interesting very quickly."

"So, you might want to keep an eye on the damned screen."

"I've been here before."

"Really?"

"Are you crazy?" asked Bob. "Of course not! I need to work here now, woman, so keep your head down. This is my show."

"Go you," said Chen, not a little sarcastically.

She had no way to say how much she was enjoying herself. She had never been part of this kind of surveillance, and she knew that she never would be again, and all she had to do was observe. Bob Goodman had the reins and he knew how to hold them. He knew how to give a horse its head. He knew how to assess a situation, moment by moment.

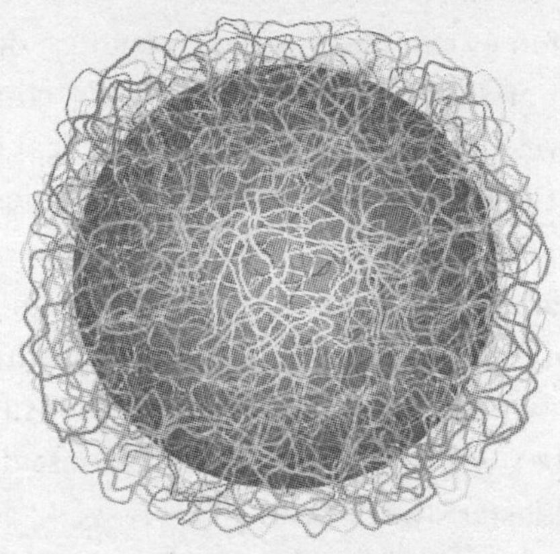

Chapter Twenty-Seven

IN HOUR SEVENTY-FIVE of the event, Control Operator Branting strode back into the conference room, clutching a bundle of printouts. He had managed a shower and a quick change of clothes, but had otherwise done everything on the run, and had not slept for twenty hours.

"The first data is in," he said to the men and women sitting around the table with him. Some were the same people who had sat with him the night before, discussing the dangers of a mind-virus that they believed was being spread via the mini-print slot.

"We have data on the Student who caused the ramp-up to Code Yellow. It is inconclusive, and we have some more legal issues," said Branting.

"What do you need?" asked Schmidt.

"Privacy law..." said Branting.

"Is a minefield," Schmidt finished.

"Operators on the ground at Master Tobe's Service Central want permission to extract emotional response data."

"They've found something that doesn't compute at the intellectual level? And yet it relates to theoretical mathematics? How can that be?" asked Professor Styles, a new member of the team brought in only this morning.

"That's what we need to find out," said Branting. "It seems counter-intuitive, but we don't know what this thing is yet, and this is only the first batch of data from the first subject exposed to Master Tobe's work. The emotional response data might not relate to the Master's work at all.

"To clarify?" asked Schmidt. "Do you want clearance for emotional response data beyond the parameters of the intellect sweep? Or, did this show up on the conventional line-check?"

Branting riffled through the data in his hands, crosschecked two pieces of information on different pages, and smiled.

"It's on the line-check. So, we can go in?" he asked.

"Providing the subject is bound by College law, and providing that the parameters of the intellect sweep are overlaid with the new emotional response data, yes, you can go in," said Schmidt.

"Let's do it," said Branting.

"There is a downside. If the subject suffers any mental health problems as a result of the methods used to extract the data, Service is entirely responsible."

"Which means?"

"It means that we could end up pensioning, for life, someone who has no function. There could be problems implementing that pension because of Civilian authorisation."

"So, if he can no longer work as a result of this procedure, we are obliged to pension him, but we have to justify that pension to the Civilian Board?"

"That's about the size of it," said Schmidt.

"We'd better hope that we don't disable him, then," said Branting. "See to it, would you Qa?"

INFIRMARY WARD ISIS was filling up with people waiting for processing. They sat around, talking, exchanging what little information they had and speculating on the rest. They ate and read, and listened to music. People were still trickling in, but the only ones with first degree contact that weren't in the infirmary were the five people still dismantling Tobe's room.

Infirmaries in Peru and Canada were also taking in possible contamination victims, beginning with the world class mathematicians, who had been the first to receive the printouts from Tobe's office.

Rosa was permanently on-screen on the Service Floor of Lima College. Workstation 3 had been tracking her for her entire College career. She had displayed erratic behaviour, via the screen, for two hours after she first received Tobe's data, and her station had gone to Code Green, but this was not considered unusual for Master Rosa, and Service had stepped down to Code Blue, overnight.

Gilles in Winnipeg had also exhibited problematic behaviour within hours of receiving Tobe's data, and Service had given him a Code Green, but his status had ramped-up, again, when his Assistant and Companion had alerted Service that they considered him to be in a dangerous state of mind.

Gilles was in the infirmary in Winnipeg, where Medtech was trying to unravel the problems.

Tobe's data was already out in the World, so a file, exactly the same as Pitu's was compiled for him, and two more for his Assistant and Companion.

Workstation 5 on the Service Floor in Winnipeg was switched out to monitor Gilles's Assistant when his turn came around. At the switch-out, Esau's screen was showing a strong blue sphere of threads, which throbbed rhythmically, and glowed in places, but had a limited corona. Named Operator Blackwater noticed an anomaly at 70, 67, about an hour into monitoring.

"Reset zoom to 70, 67," said Blackwater, rolling the sphere left and right in decreasing increments. The screen zoomed in, and the threads of light began to look like pieces of string, woven with various shades of blue, in a tangled mass.

Blackwater reached his left hand out to touch Operator Turner. There was silence as Blackwater rolled the palm-sized, rubberpro sphere again. A length of thread came into sharp focus. It was grey and fraying, a pale imitation among the stronger blue lengths of thread.

"Anomaly at sector 70," said Blackwater, hitting a button. "Tone sent." The screen in front of him blinked, and Turner tensed.

"It's in the emotional range," said Turner.

"We should check it anyway," said Blackwater. "What's the precedent?"

"Tech?"

A Tech appeared from the racks at the centre of the Service Floor, which was almost identical to the one that was monitoring Pitu, and anyone else that had seen into Tobe's room.

"We need authorisation for emotional response data on an intellectual line-check."

"Skip it," said Blackwater, not turning from his screen. An overlay was coming up on the left hand side of the screen. It read, 'Clearance for emotional response data within the parameters of the intellect sweep is granted automatically, at the discretion of the monitoring Operator'.

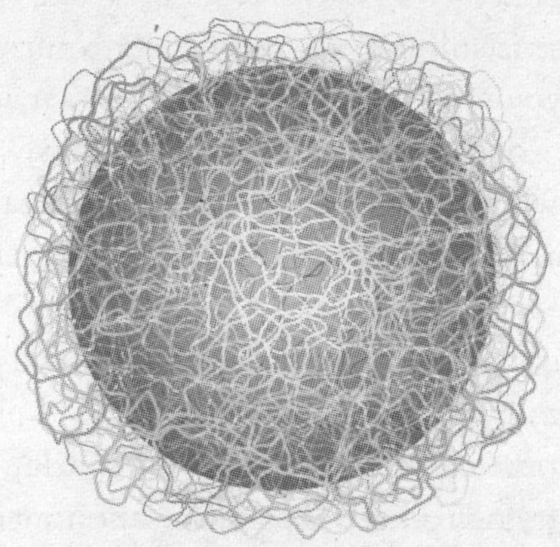

Chapter Twenty-Eight

TOBE WAS SITTING on his stool at the kitchen counter, while Metoo moved around him, clearing away his dishes. When she had finished, she sat at the counter opposite him.

"Tobe," said Metoo, "you can't go to the office today."

"Tobe always goes to the office, except on rest days."

"Service messed up, and you need to have another rest day," said Metoo, hoping that it would be enough, but knowing that it wouldn't.

"Yesterday was a rest day, because... Why was yesterday a rest day? What day is it? Why can't Tobe go to the office? Let Tobe go to the office."

"It's not up to me," said Metoo, avoiding answering too many questions in the hope that Tobe might forget that he'd asked them.

"Metoo sends Tobe to the office. It is up to Metoo."

"No. It's Service, remember?"

"Service is gone."

"No. Service is still there, but they talk to me, now, instead of talking to you."

"Tell them, Tobe is going to the office, today."

"It doesn't work like that. There is something they want you to do, though." She hoped that taking a different tack might help.

"Tobe always works in the office. What is the probability of Tobe working in the office?"

"But you worked here, in your room, yesterday," said Metoo, smiling, and trying to keep the conversation manageable, and light.

"A black swan," said Tobe, apparently deep in thought for a moment. "They used to call it a black swan. Probability."

"Probability," said Metoo.

"They want Tobe to do more probability?"

"No. They want you to answer some questions."

"Tobe's job is to answer questions, find solutions, work out the maths for things. Tobe is always trying to answer questions."

"Not those sorts of questions, other sorts."

"Other sorts? What other questions? Who wants to ask Tobe questions?"

"Well, could I ask you some questions?"

"'Could I ask you some questions?' That's a question." Tobe chuckled low in his chest, and looked over Metoo's shoulder, apparently into space. His head tipped back slightly, and he closed his eyes and began to murmur.

Metoo reached across the kitchen counter, and took Tobe's face in her hands. He dropped his head to a front-facing position and opened his eyes.

"May I ask you some questions?" asked Metoo.

"'May I ask you some questions?' That is asking Tobe a question."

"And what is Tobe's answer?"

"That is a question, too."

"I'm going to ask you some questions, now," said Metoo, smiling slightly, knowing that Tobe might be a genius, but he was a genius with limitations.

At 06:00 Goodman's screen switched out. The swirl of bright blue was like a shoal of fish with one mind, weaving a tight figure-of-eight with a throbbing halo, and flashing silver strands.

"Wow!" said Chen.

"Wow indeed," said Bob.

"You don't seem surprised."

"This was the one thing they did tell me. How else do you think they got me out of a Rest period after only six hours?"

"You know who this is?"

"Not who, but I do know what."

"Line-check?"

"I think it's better if we just observe, for now. Did you ever see anything like this in your life?"

"Did anyone?"

The figure-of-eight pulsed and throbbed in its rhythmic electric-blue and silver patterns for a few minutes, mesmerising Goodman and Chen.

At 06:03, Chen asked again, "Line-check?"

"Patience."

"Bob, what are the rules and regs for the first line-check after a switch-out?"

"It's your signature on this machine," said Bob, "I'm just the jockey, so, if you want a line-check, you should order a line-check. I'm just feeling my way, here."

They sat in silence for a few more moments as the shoal shimmered across the screen, its electrifying halo throbbing ceaselessly at them. It was the most alive entity that Bob Goodman had ever seen on screen, and he'd seen a lot of screen. He could retire after seeing this.

At 06:04 Chen asked, "So what do you think?"

Bob made an odd noise in his throat that sounded like a half-cough, half-sigh.

"'The first line-check should be completed at switch-out, but', and here's the interesting bit, 'should be completed within fifteen minutes of the switch-out'. Tell me, Chen, how long does it take me to do a line-check?"

"On this screen?"

"I take your point," said Goodman, his hand closing over the rubberpro sphere on the scuffed counter-top of Workstation 7.

At 06:05 the screen at station 7 glowed bright white, and the shoal of thready particles formed a sparkling silver sphere, reflecting light like a sequin-covered globe or a mirror ball.

"Okay," Chen managed to say without actually closing her mouth. "Okay, now it really is time for a line-check."

"Too late," said Bob Goodman, pushing his chair away from the counter and beaming. He planted his feet firmly on the floor, still sitting, and twisted his body, sending his chair spinning as he thrust his fists into the air.

"Bob? Bob..." said Chen.

Master Mohammad woke up to a new day, in Tunis, ready to get back to work on the data that he had received from Tobe. There had been no further communications or explanations.

His Assistant, Yousef, and his Companion, Sabah, ate breakfast with him, looking out of the kitchen window, across the College, with its towers and minarets piercing the early morning skyline.

"It is so beautiful today," said Sabah.

"Probability," said Mohammad.

"Has no memory," said Yousef.

"It is like a mantra with you, Yousef," said Sabah.

"If it is good enough for Eustache, it is good enough for me," said Yousef.

Mohammad looked down into his dish of oatpro and dates. He liked to listen to his Companion and his Assistant playing these verbal games, like he enjoyed listening to the birds singing, or the call to prayer. He had no way to decipher the sounds. He had a hundred, a thousand, a hundred thousand ways to decipher numbers and decrypt mathematical symbols. Maths was his music and his linguistics, and the babbling of his brook.

"Probability," said Mohammad, again.

"He will have me tossing a coin all day long," Yousef said to Sabah, "and then he will have me toss a different coin, lest the coin I tossed be unbalanced. It is the weight of his mind that is unbalanced."

"And yours is perfectly balanced, I suppose?" asked Sabah, laughing. "You feeble-minded men with your left brain this and your right brain that, and your probability. I know my Eustache too, and I'd sooner watch a cat swinging from a pendulum and call it 'Foucault's Cat'."

"Or 'Schroedinger's Pendulum'," said Yousef.

"Our jokes are too old," said Sabah, sighing.

"And too true," said Yousef.

"Off with you," said Sabah, picking up Mohammad's dish, and stacking it inside Yousef's. Go to your play, and stay away until it is time to eat. I have things to do."

* * *

WORKSTATION 4 AT Tunis College was showing a glowing blue ball of threads, throbbing rhythmically, but calmly, in front of its Operator. The Service Floors of individual Colleges had not been alerted to the global problem, and it was one Operator one screen in Tunis. The atmosphere was as sultry as the day's weather.

McBride began a line-check when he came on-station at 06:00. At 06:15 everything was normal.

IN MUMBAI, SANJEEV was roused by his Companion. He bathed quickly, and efficiently, leaving his towel on the bathroom floor as he shook his robe on over his head. His Assistant ate breakfast with him, while his Companion watched over them. Saroj, the new Assistant, was very young, and Kamla felt like her older sister or aunt, watching out for her.

"Master Sanjeev, are we to review Master Tobe's notes again, today?" asked Saroj.

"I think perhaps you might return to your own work, Master Sanjeev," said Kamla. "Let Saroj take a look at Master Tobe's musings, and put them into some sort of order before you review them again. They seem terribly taxing to me, and your own work should not be made to suffer, however notable Master Tobe might be."

"I should like that," said Master Sanjeev.

"Probability, after all, has no Master," said Saroj. Then she laughed at her pun, burned with embarrassment and dropped her face, so that her Master could not see her.

"Saroj speaks wise words," said Kamla, smiling, and happy to have got her way. "Perhaps Tobe will become the new Master of probability, but, in the meantime, you have work to discuss and share in the community, that is long past being ready. Spend this time more wisely, Master, I beg of you."

Sanjeev looked up from his breakfast, perfectly willing to do the bidding of these two chattering women. He did not understand them, and he did not mean to. He only wanted to go to his office and work on his equations, and that was all that these women seemed to want for him. The new one had a lilting sing-song voice too, although most of what she said was totally incomprehensible to him.

OPERATOR PERRETT SAT at Workstation 1 at Mumbai College. She keyed in her Morse signature, and pulled in her chair. She covered the rubberpro sphere with her left hand, and began her first line-check of the day. The ball of slightly throbbing light in front of her was a glorious shade of sky blue, not intense, but watery and beautiful. The colour was incredibly uniform, and there were no anomalies that could be seen by the naked eye. She completed the line-check anyway.

She had sat in front of this screen, four days a week, come High or Low, for four years, and she knew the subject like the back of her hand. She did not know his name, and probably never would, and she did not know his rank, although she had long-since guessed that he was a Master, probably in the sciences or maths.

Perrett had an uncanny knack with these things. She had been working station 1 since before it had been dedicated to this subject, and, although she had been relatively new to the job, then, with only two Lows under her belt, she had known that her subject had been changed. She had come back from her biennial sabbatical, but still, after six weeks, she recognised that her subject had been changed.

Perrett had queried the change, and the Service Floor for Mumbai College had been in Code Green for six hours while she was debriefed. She maintained that they wouldn't do it to her again. If they wanted to switch-out her subject, either they'd inform her, or they'd promote her. She was perfectly fine with either option.

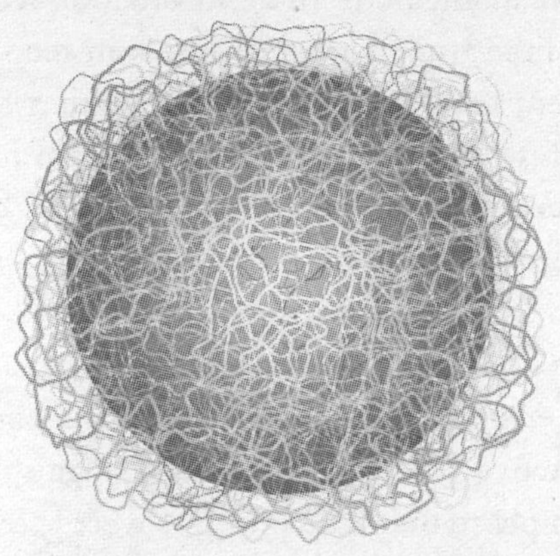

Chapter Twenty-Nine

STUDENTS ALL OVER the World pressed their buttons, at intervals, all day long: for Rouse, Roll-call, Repast, Rest, Recreation and various other elements of their routines, which were not always mandatory, but which were cycled between Students and Colleges to get the most comprehensive cover.

Service needed to monitor what was going on in each College, and how various events balanced across the globe. If an Active was down, for any reason, and they regularly were, the effect on the Student population was monitored via their buttons. They were institutionalised, and never gave their buttons a second thought. Civilians had them, Students had them, and everyone knew that the Masters' flats had them, even if the Masters, Companions and Assistants were, for the most part, spared the inconvenience of wearing them.

It was impossible for every Student who had a button to be monitored on-screen; in fact, it was rare, almost to the point of unheard of, for a Student to be monitored, on-screen. That did not mean that the Students were not monitored.

Every Student button had a hot-zone. Pitu 3 had found the hot-zone on his button when he had clamped his thumb and forefinger over it, after seeing Tobe's office.

Every Student button related to a Senior, or a Master, depending on his status, in School or in the College proper. Every Student's button could be adjusted so that a hot-zone was triggered faster or slower than average. Students in Colleges without an Active tended to have very sluggish, very limited hot-zones, simply so that false positives were rare, and the over all monitoring, globally, was as complete as possible.

Conversely, where a College had more than one Active, the hot-zone was closer to the surface, and if there was a ramp-up to a Code change, all Student buttons had their hot-zones halved. More than two hits outside the normal response to the Schedule was considered 'hot' in these circumstances.

THE FIRST TIME that Branting addressed his group of advisors, hot-hits on Student buttons were up by 8 percent. After twenty hours without sleep, Branting reviewed the hot-hits. They were up by 23 percent on the standard base level.

"At what point do we consider setting up more Service Floors?" Branting asked his team of specialists.

"What's the ramp-up?" asked Adjentetti.

"Student button responses are up by 23 percent. That's what's hitting the hot-zone. But..."

"But what?" asked Adjentetti.

"We've made them so damned sensitive that everything and anything is going to set them off. Some kid gets a cold and wants to call his Senior, and the whole system goes into meltdown."

"Any repeat offenders?" asked Adjentetti.

"By which you mean?" asked Branting.

"Can you log Students that have hit their buttons more than others. Are ramp-ups being caused by a hundred Students hitting each of their buttons once, or by one Student hitting his button a hundred times?

"Can we find that out, Qa?" Branting asked his secretary.

"I don't know. I'll check, sir."

"Good. Okay. Where are we with all this? Anything? Anyone?"

The twelve men and women sitting around the table looked to one another for inspiration; some of them stared down at the notes they had, or hadn't been taking. Several of them had been useful in various ways, but a number of them had said nothing, written nothing, contributed nothing, and sat in fear. Branting knew who they were. Everyone was monitored.

Branting reached into the underside of his lapel, and squeezed. He was hitting his button in response to his Schedule.

"If you could excuse me," he said to the assembled advisors.

They filed out, as they had filed out half-a-dozen times in the past thirty hours, or so. Those who had not participated would not be invited back into the room, but even that choice gave Branting problems, and gave Branting's superiors worse problems still.

If people chose not to participate in various sections of the briefing, did that mean they had no value? At what point did an advisor become redundant? How long would advisors wait until they chipped in with theories or voiced concerns? Six hours? Twelve? That was what had been decided. If members of the advisory team did not demonstrate some sort of engagement within the first twelve hours of their involvement they were switched out.

Six more hours, and Branting decided that he would bring back everyone who had contributed nothing during his or her twelve hour stint. How many advisors would that make? Would Global allow him to take the risk and do it? Were the most valuable people in the room those who took the time to really consider the problems? Did the fastest thinkers make the best advisors?

"Crap," said Branting. "Crap."

Qa had entered the room, and had heard both craps.

"Is there something I can help you with, sir?" he asked.

"You can find out who does the thinking, and you can find out who presses his button for no reason, and you can find out how best to sustain this whole damned fiasco without bringing down the planet!" said Branting, taking his hands out of his thick, dark hair, and staring right at Qa.

"You need to sleep, and, sir, frankly, so do I."

"You haven't slept? In how long?"

"If you work, I work."

"But that's... How long is that, Qa?"

"Too long by half... and then by some more, but I'm guessing that you're not going to excuse yourself any time soon, sir?"

"How can I?"

"You're not the only Control Operator in Global Service."

"No, I'm not, but I was the Control Operator on-call when the shit hit the fan, and this is what we do, Qa."

"What? Kill ourselves for the greater good, when more minds might make light work of the crap we're struggling with?"

"Do you really believe that?"

Qa dropped his head onto his chest. The fact was, he'd been Branting's aide for twelve years, and he couldn't think of a better man to put this thing to bed, sort it out, find the solution, and have everything back on an even keel in record time. It didn't matter that Service Global switched between almost two-dozen sites, each with half-a-dozen Control Operators. Qa believed that his boss was the man for this job, whether he'd been up to his neck in it for eight hours, or eighty.

"What can I do for you, sir?" asked Qa.

"You can find me a laundered shirt, and a cup of something stronger than the usual coffee," said Branting, "and then you can get me data on which sorry son-of-a-bitch is pressing his button, desperately, every two minutes or so."

"On it. Shall I send them back in?" Qa asked, referring to the advisors that had vacated the room.

"Do me a favour. Rouse the original twelve. Give me twelve angry men, and let's see if we can't change the World."

SEVEN HUNDRED AND forty-two Colleges had Actives in residence. Eighty-nine of them had critical problems. Eighty-nine of them were in Code Green or higher. Seventy-nine of those Codes had been caused by Assistant level members of College, or lower. The Masters were riding out the storm, for the most part, but when one fell, another followed, and if two, or three, or half a dozen fell, people would start to ask questions. What was the tipping point? At what point did this thing hit a critical mass, and who would cause it?

Branting was determined not to fall to the pressure of low-grade panic.

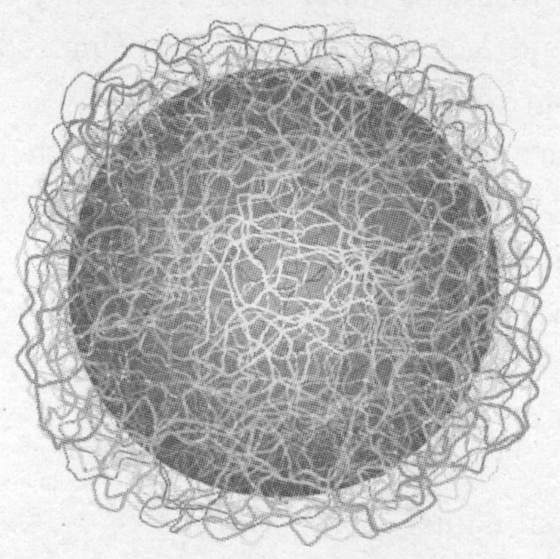

Chapter Thirty

"Do you want to sit here?" asked Metoo.

"Tobe will sit here if you like," said Tobe.

"You don't want to do this in your room?"

"Metoo doesn't come in my room. It's not Tobe's office."

"Should we wait until we can do this in your office? I'm sure it can wait until then."

"Why wait? Tobe doesn't wait."

"No," said Metoo, laughing. "You don't wait."

"Metoo wants to ask me something."

"No," said Metoo, aiming to be meticulous, "I don't want to ask you anything. Service asked if I would ask you some questions, and I said that I would, providing you didn't mind."

"So, not Metoo's questions, then?"

"Does it make a difference?"

"Will they take Metoo away? They've taken people away from Tobe before. It didn't matter so much."

"I'm sure it wouldn't matter so much if they took me away from you," said Metoo, her eyes glistening. "Who did they take away from you, Tobe?"

"Tobe doesn't know. Tobe would know if they took Metoo away."

Metoo wasn't sure that was true.

"Probability," said Metoo.

"Probability," said Tobe.

"Shall I just read the questions?"

"Ask."

"What is your name?"

Tobe laughed.

"That's a joke," he said. "Tobe knows Tobe's name."

"Of course you know your name. It's just a beginning. I think the questions are easy at the beginning. What is your name?"

"Tobe. Master Tobe, the Students call me. I call Tobe, Tobe."

"What's your title?" asked Metoo, referring to the list that had been put together, so carefully, by psychiatrists and psychologists, and behaviour specialists, for her, and for anyone else who had to put a Master through one of these undignified interviews.

"Master Tobe, my Students call me. Is Tobe Metoo's Master?" he asked Metoo, a curious expression on his face.

"Are you?" asked Metoo.

"Is that a question?"

"No. Does it make you uncomfortable?"

"Is that a question?"

Metoo laughed.

"Do you know how clever you are?" asked Metoo.

"Yes."

"How many Students do you have?"

"Some. Not a lot. Fewer than before."

"Fewer than before when?" asked Metoo.

"There seem not to be so many."

"Okay. Do you know the names of your Students?"

"Students have names. Are names important?" He looked anxiously at Metoo, for a moment. "Tobe is Tobe, and Metoo is Metoo. That's all."

"Tell me about a work day."

"Tobe gets up. Tobe goes to the office. Tobe works. Tobe works with Students, or alone. Tobe shows Students maths things. Tobe works on maths things. Sometimes Tobe sends maths things to other Masters."

"Do you know the names of the other Masters?"

"Tobe's the best. Mostly, Tobe's the best mathematician. 'The best have to teach the rest'."

"That's right. Do you like to teach the Students?"

"Tobe shows them maths things. Tobe works and Students watch. Sometimes Students show Tobe things."

"Do you remember that you gave a maths problem to a Student a few days ago?"

"That was easy."

"Why did you ask the Student to do it, Tobe?"

"SHE'S NOT ASKING the scripted questions," said Wooh. "She needs to get back on track.

Wooh and Saintout were still in the garden room. Saintout was spritzing some of the plants, wandering around the room with Metoo's pump-spray, holding it out in front of him, double-handed, as if he was pointing a gun, like a cop in the old detective movies he liked to watch.

Wooh was sitting by the door, wearing her headset. She sat with one hand over the ear that held the machine's earpiece, as if that would improve reception, and the view-screen came down over her forehead a couple of inches from her eye.

"How do you know?" asked Saintout, turning and pointing the pump-spray at her.

Wooh was concentrating so hard that she didn't see what he was doing, and when she looked up at him, she was startled. She placed her other hand flat against her chest, and exhaled through her mouth.

"Sorry," said Saintout, "but there isn't a whole lot for me to do here, now."

"What was your question?"

"Oh, right... How do you know she isn't asking him the questions she was given?"

"The questions are engineered so that they engender specific brainwave responses. The responses then show up as particular patterns on visual, and specific tones on audio."

"From that you can tell what?"

"How far out of his normal psychological range the subject has strayed."

"So," said Saintout, putting down the pump-spray, "she could be asking him the questions, and he's so far out of his 'normal psychological range' that he's just not giving you the responses you expect."

"Oh no," said Wooh, her eyes widening and her skin turning a pale, unhealthy colour.

"I'm sure it's not that. I don't know anything about this stuff. I was speculating... guessing. Don't take any notice of me."

Wooh stood up, suddenly, and reached for the door handle. Saintout put his hand out flat on the door, above her shoulder height, to prevent her opening it.

He wasn't entirely sure why Metoo would not allow them out of the garden room, but he did know that she was absolutely serious about it, and, from what Wooh had said about the situation, he guessed that she was acting impulsively and would regret entering the flat, proper, and ruining all the work she'd done.

"I'll get Service to send a tone to the flat. If you need to speak to Metoo, let's get her in here, rather than go storming out there and upsetting the apple-cart."

Wooh sagged back down onto her chair, and lifted the screen away from in front of her face.

"You're right," she said, "let's get her in here. By the way, what has any of this got to do with apple-carts? The stuff you say!"

"I'll tell you all about it when this is over, or when we've been stuck here for so long that our boredom thresholds give out, and we begin to share our life stories."

"We'd have to be pretty bored, and I doubt that's going to happen. Your life, my life, Tobe's life: it all comes down to the same thing."

"You don't believe that," said Saintout.

"Don't I?" asked Wooh.

"Well if you do now, you won't by the time this is all over."

"I'll hold you to that," said Wooh. "Now, any chance of you sending that request to Service?"

"Asked and answered."

"THE STUDENT?" ASKED Tobe.

"Yes," said Metoo. "Why did you ask the Student to do the work on the cotpro, on the linopro? The squeak? Why didn't you ask me?"

"Metoo could do it," said Tobe. "It was easy."

"Yes. So why did you have Pitu 3 do it?"

"Pitu? Pitu 3, the Student? Tobe asked Pitu to work out the linopro thing."

"Why?"

"If Tobe gives Students something to do, Students go away and do it."

"Did you want him to go away? Did you want him to go away for a reason?"

"Sometimes."

"Sometimes you want the Students to go away?"

"Sometimes."

"Why?"

"If Tobe gives Students something to do, Students go away."

"And sometimes you want the Students to go away, so that you are on your own? So that you can work?"

"Sometimes, the maths is better. Always, the maths is better."

"You like to be on your own to work?"

"Sometimes. Sometimes Students are work."

"Sometimes they are," said Metoo.

The Service tone sounded in the flat. Tobe ignored it, so Metoo ignored it too.

"When is it nice to work in your office, on your own?" asked Metoo.

"When can Tobe go to the office?" asked Tobe, as if remembering suddenly that he had an office to go to. He began to get up off his stool.

The Service tone sounded again. Metoo got up, and went around the counter to Tobe. She took his hands in hers, and pulled gently on them until he was sitting down again.

"Sit there for me, Tobe. Stay there and I'll come back in a minute. Okay?"

Tobe tilted his head back, slightly, closed his eyes, and began to murmur.

Metoo touched his cheek, gently. Tobe didn't respond to her. She knew that he would be occupied until she disturbed him, and so left the room and went to sign in with Service.

"WHY DID YOU get me back in here?" Metoo asked Wooh.

"Are you asking him the questions I gave you?" asked Wooh.

"Yes."

Wooh was still pale, and she looked hard at Metoo, holding her gaze.

"Are you asking him only the questions I gave you?"

"His name is Tobe, or Master Tobe," said Metoo, not flinching from Wooh's stare.

"Are you asking Master Tobe only the questions I gave you?"

"No."

"There, you see? Problem solved," said Saintout, smiling in vain.

"Our problems are only just beginning, if Metoo can't perform the function required."

"I tried," Saintout said to Metoo. "I got you in here, but now you're on your own. She's a hard task master."

Metoo broke her gaze with Wooh.

"You got me in here?" asked Metoo.

A Service tone sounded in the flat.

"Well?" asked Metoo.

A Service tone sounded in the flat, again, and Metoo left the garden room, afraid that the tone would wake Tobe out of his reverie, and send him looking for her.

METOO SIGNED INTO Service.

"Yes," she said.

"Please verify location of Operator Saintout?"

"He's here, in the flat."

"Please verify current inhabitants of this residence."

"That would be me, Metoo, Master Tobe, Doctor Wooh, and Police Operator Saintout."

Metoo signed out of Service and sighed. She felt as if she was being cornered, and required to perform tasks for Service that were not in Tobe's best interests. Why did they employ her, and then tell her what to do? If they didn't think she could do the job, why had she been with Tobe for six years?

She didn't want to fight the system, but they seemed to be giving her no choice, and, now, Saintout was back in the Service loop, and she could no longer rely on him for help if she needed it.

Metoo did not return to the garden room. They had let her down. She went back to the kitchen, and sat at the counter opposite Tobe.

"Hey Tobe," she said. "Would you like to go for a walk?"

"Tobe wants to go to the office."

"I thought we could just have a walk around."

"Why?"

"Because friends do what their friends ask them to do," said Metoo, looking down at her hands, clasped together in her lap.

"Tobe is Metoo's friend."

"Thank you," said Metoo.

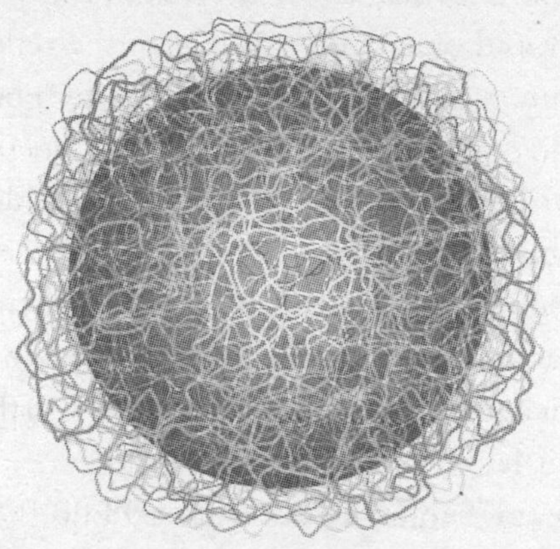

Chapter Thirty-One

CODE YELLOW REMAINED in force on the Service Floor, and all Workstations, apart from station 2, were on a two-hour switch-out. They began with the subjects most likely to be contaminated, giving each subject a two hour surveillance window. It was the biggest surveillance of its kind for over thirty years. No one on the Service floor had ever completed this procedure, apart from in Manoeuvres, and the majority of the subjects had never been seen on screens before.

AT 07:28, BABBAGE and Siemens, at Workstation 4, began their countdown for a switch-out.

"Subject switch-out at 07:30," said Babbage.

"07:30," said Siemens.

* * *

CHEN LOOKED AT Bob. The screen in front of them went from the swirling silver and blue figure of eight to the reflecting sphere, and back again, a number of times in the two hours after the switch-out.

"What is it?" asked Chen. "Who is it? Shouldn't we inform someone of this?"

"I've wanted to do this for as long as I can remember," said Bob. "I've wanted to watch this from the beginning. If I never look at another screen, it will all have been worth it."

"But what is it?"

"It's the dream. Subject switch-out at 08:00."

"08:00," said Chen.

"Three... two... one... monitoring switch-out. Okay, who's next?"

Chen looked intently at the screen, and wondered, for a moment, why she felt so disappointed. The screen showed a tangle of bluish strands. Their luminescence was low, and the corona was almost non-existent.

"How do you go from that to this?" asked Chen, gesturing at the screen.

"That's the job. Line-check?"

"Line-check at 08:02."

"Verify."

"Verify line-check. What just happened?"

"Let's get through the line-check first," said Bob, "and then we'll discuss it."

QA BROUGHT A sheaf of translucent papers into the room, in a plasticpro wallet. There were hundreds of tissue-thin sheets, each showing an image from one of the screens on one of dozens of Service Floors around the World. Anywhere that was known to have had any interface with the contaminating mathematical material was producing screen wafers, half-hourly, and after every line-check and every sent tone.

The sheets could be viewed separately, or could be superimposed on top of each other for comparisons.

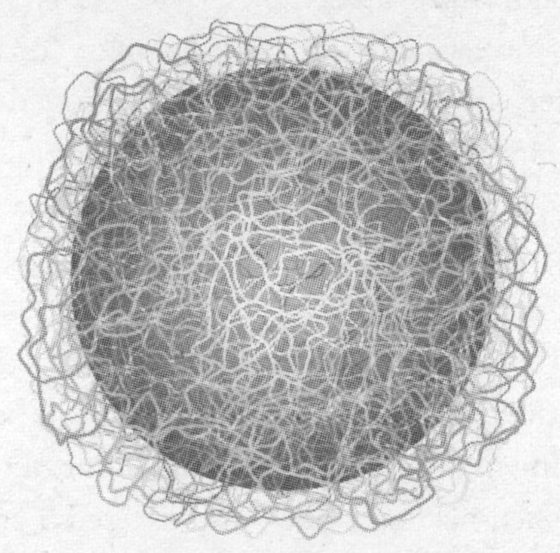

Chapter Thirty-Two

"We can't stop proliferation of this thing," said Branting. "We can't contain it, and we can't control it. This thing has a life of its own. Does anyone have any thoughts?"

"Do we have a complete rundown of the effects of this thing, yet?" asked Adjentetti.

"By which you mean?"

"Do we know the real effects of this thing on individuals or are we guessing?"

"Master Tobe has been in Code Yellow for 24 hours," said Branting, "and the crisis is now time sensitive; without a resolution, Code status ramp-up becomes automatic, unless something changes between now and then. It is, absolutely, my aim to cut this thing off."

"Have we been able to measure the effects of this thing?" asked Adjentetti, again. "And when does it get a name? We can't keep referring to it as 'this thing' indefinitely."

"We have not fully ascertained what it is yet," said Mr Ahmed. "We have ruled out certain things; for instance, it is not a computer virus of any of the old-fashioned varieties. It is not a Trojan Horse, a Wormhole, or a Psytrap."

"So, we don't know what this thing is, but we do know that it is affecting certain vulnerable people at the neurological level?" asked Adjentetti.

"No," said Branting. "We have not verified that, which brings me to the next point on my agenda. The screen, Qa."

Qa was sitting in the alcove next to the door of the conference room. He pushed his chair back and entered a code, using the switch on the facing edge of the counter. He placed his hand over the rubberpro sphere in the counter-top, and hit the switch on the bottom edge of the screen in front of him. The end wall of the conference room lit up with a screen, similar to those used on the Service Floors, but larger, and with a slightly lower resolution. There was also a menu strap down the left-hand side of the screen. There was no image on the screen.

"I'm going to show you all a series of wafers, collected from various Workstations, on a number of Service Floors, worldwide," said Branting. "Feel free to interject at any point. The time for justifying holding Master Tobe at Code Yellow is limited. If this thing ramps up, we've all got problems."

The men and women, sitting around the table, turned their chairs at an angle, so that they could all see the screen at the end of the room.

"Qa will talk you through the wafers. Qa?"

"Sir," said Qa from his seat. His back was to the room, but he was wearing a mic, attached to his headset, and his voice appeared to be coming from the screen in front of the gathered advisors.

"The first wafers," said Qa, "are a series of stills from Master

Tobe's screen, taken over the past fifteen days. They obviously include stills from his daily life before the ramp-up, and then stills from the ramp-up to Code Green and so on, until about two hours ago."

The screen filled with a blue mass of threads, more or less spherical, with a cloudy halo. The image did not pulse or throb as the moving screen images on the Service Floor did, but represented a moment in time rather than the continuum.

The wafer faded out to be replaced by a second, and then a third. The first dozen were blue, and all very similar. No one in the room, including the neurological specialists could distinguish one from another with the naked eye.

"It is not unusual," said Qa, via the screen, "for all of these wafers to be virtually identical. It does, however, prove a stability of character that one might not expect from a Master of Tobe's calibre."

The wafer faded out and was replaced by another. This one had a pale area on it, which Qa was able to zoom in on, and show as an inset, projected on top of the original.

"This wafer records the moment at which Code Green was established," said Qa. "You can all see the area of concern in detail here, and the area of the brain in which the change occurred."

"This moment represents the beginning of the problem as we recognise it," said Branting.

"Has that area of the brain been affected continuously, over the period since this wafer was shot?" asked Adjentetti.

"Do we have that information?" asked Branting.

"I'm not sure, sir," said Qa, "but we do have a series of wafers for the subject taken at regular intervals since the initial ramp-up from Code Blue to Code Green."

"Perhaps we should see them," said Branting.

Qa continued to feed the information into his screen, a wafer at a time, and it continued to appear on the large screen at the end of the room, for all those present to inspect.

The mass of threads had changed colour from blue to green, and then, again, to yellow, but the pictures appeared to be largely similar. Several members of the team, sitting around the table, leaned forwards in their seats and peered at the large screen, trying to divine anomalies in the visual information.

"Could we see the sequence again, in close-up on the affected area?" asked Adjentetti.

"Qa?" asked Branting.

Qa moved the rubberpro sphere under his hand, weaving backwards and forwards over the anomaly until it was writ large on the screen. The sequence ran more slowly, but the specialists were able to sit back and read each wafer thoroughly without having to strain.

It took two hours to cover the wafers extracted from Tobe's Service screen.

The room was silent, except for the sound of breathing, and the rustle of paper and the whispers that pens and pencils made as several of the advisors took notes or drew diagrams.

"Can we see the entire sequence again?" asked Adjentetti. "I'd really like to see all the wafers, back to back, without colour on them, and can we do it at speed so that we can see the changes?"

"Qa?" asked Branting.

"Yes, sir," said Qa, "just give me a moment to change the settings."

Qa spun the rubberpro ball under his palm, and hit a button on the counter. The menu on the left-hand side of the main screen in the room came to life, so that the advisors could see the adjustments that Qa was making, altering the contrast on the wafers, and de-saturating the colour in them. When the first image of a wafer appeared back on the screen, it was a mass of white, bright threads, with pearlescent grey hazing between them and around the corona. The surface of the screen had been blacked-out entirely, so that the subtlety of the greys and whites on the screen was more apparent than the colours had been.

"How fast do you want the wafers to feed?" asked Qa.

"Adjentetti?" asked Branting.

"Perhaps one per second, at least, so that we can scroll through the entire sequence and get an overview," said Adjentetti. "If that suits everyone?"

There were murmurs of general assent around the table, and Qa began to feed the wafers through the system.

Strung together, the wafers began to ebb and flow with light, pulsing in a staccato fashion from one to the next, and the next, right through the sequence. The entire sequence took only a few minutes to complete.

"Can you put that on a loop, Qa and fade from one wafer to the next, rather than jump?" asked Branting. "There's something odd about this, Adjentetti."

"I'm not sure yet," said Adjentetti, "but there's very definitely a pattern of some sort."

"Looping now, sir," said Qa, his voice emerging from the screen in front of the gathered experts, as his instructions were clearly visible from the menu on the left-hand side.

Some of the dozen or so men and women in the room held their collective breath for a moment or two, while the screen interpreted Qa's instructions, others took a few moments to make more notes or to consult the notes they'd already taken. Branting left the head of the conference table, and went to stand beside Adjentetti, who had risen from his seat.

"Rolling the loop," said Qa, and the large screen blacked-out for a moment, before coming back to life with the mass of white-light threads, and the pulsing grey corona of Tobe's screen. They all watched in silence as the wafers cycled through the screen, twice, three times, and, finally, when the cycle began for the fourth time, Adjentetti stepped up to the screen with a telescopic pointer, and made an imaginary circle in the air just in front of it, indicating the section of the screen that he was most interested in.

"What do you make of that?" he asked, when the wafers had cycled through to the end, again, and Qa stopped the screening.

"I think you're on to something," said Branting. "Anyone else concur?"

There was a general stirring and murmuring at the table, but it sounded mostly positive.

"It might start to become interesting," said Miss Goldstein, "if we compare this sector of scrolling wafers with those of other subjects. I'm not sure we can discuss any possibilities before we have made direct comparisons with subjects of known status."

"Qa," said Branting, "please set up a control group of wafers for Miss Goldstein. And let's see the material we've collected from anyone that we know to have been contaminated. Let's get a look at the Student's screen, to begin with, shall we?"

"Absolutely," said Adjentetti.

"Please," said Miss Goldstein.

"I can have those wafers fed through the system in a few minutes," said Qa, "but perhaps one or two of us might benefit from a break, sir?"

"Of course," said Branting. "Ten minutes, everyone."

As the advisors scraped back chairs, and collected notes, briefcases, and empty food and drink cartons, Branting took the dicky seat next to Qa, and waited for the wafers to upload.

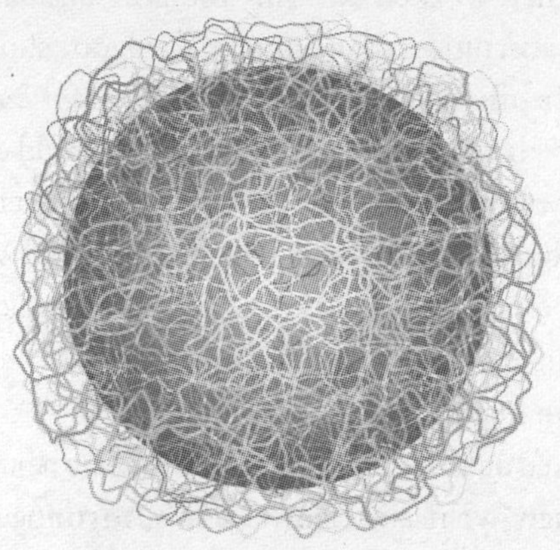

Chapter Thirty-Three

"WHAT WILL TOBE do today?" asked Tobe. They had been talking for about an hour, and Metoo was still trying to stick to the list of questions she had been given. It was useless. She was willing to try to extract the information from Tobe that they needed from him, but she wasn't sure what it was, or why they wanted it. She also found it impossible to ask a set of bald questions, which Tobe had no way to relate to. Much better, surely, to have a conversation with him that they could both learn something from.

"Can Tobe work today?" asked Tobe. He looked as if he was going to rise from his stool at the kitchen counter, so Metoo put her hand over his, stopping him in his tracks. He shuffled slightly in his seat, but didn't attempt to get up again.

"Not today," said Metoo. "You can't go to the office today. Do you want to work at home?"

"Tobe doesn't work at home."

"No," said Metoo, wearily. She had pointed out, once or

twice that he had worked at home the previous day, but this was obviously an aberration that Tobe had forgotten, or had decided, consciously, or otherwise, was a red herring. Of course, he didn't understand the concept of a red herring; he would call working at home once in twenty years, 'statistically insignificant'.

"Talk to me about statistical significance," said Metoo.

"Maths?"

"Maths."

"But, Metoo knows maths."

Metoo looked at Tobe, astonished. He had attributed knowledge to her. He knew what she knew. How? Anything out-with Tobe and his unique perception of his immediate experiences did not register in his mind. He either made assumptions or simply disregarded possibilities. He didn't even remember people's names.

"What?" asked Tobe.

THE BALL OF lit threads on the view-screen in front of Wooh's eyes began to dance and bounce all over the place, with bright lights flashing up in all areas of the cerebellum.

"What on Earth is she doing?" she asked.

"What's who doing?" asked Saintout.

"First, she wasn't asking him the questions in sequence, and now his mind's freaking out all over the place. I need to know what Metoo's doing."

"Whatever it is. I guarantee that it is in no way intended to do any harm to Tobe. I'd bet my life on the opposite: that she is doing everything in her power to improve his lot."

Wooh flipped the screen up from in front of her face, and pulled out the ear-bead. She looked at Saintout, pale and wide-eyed, with a feint sheen of sweat high on her brow.

"What do you need?" asked Saintout.

* * *

THE SCREEN AT Workstation 2 showed sudden, significant changes. The Yellow threads were weaving and pulsing, and glowing in various cortexes. Synaptic resonance showed an increase of almost twenty percent, and Operator Dudley felt cold sweat drip into the small of his back. There was no room for hesitation, and yet, he did hesitate.

A claxon sounded on the Service Floor. Every screen blinked out for three seconds, and then they began to come back on-line, one at a time, in a predetermined sequence.

Tobe's screen came back on-line after twenty-seven seconds: twenty-seven seconds in which half a litre of sweat poured out of Ranked Operator Dudley' and Named Operator Kasapi's pores. Twenty-seven seconds in which Ranked Operator Dudley found time to be grateful for his extravagant cotton garments; twenty-seven seconds in which they both rose from their seats, both completed Morse signatures, using the switch on the facing edge of the counter, and both raised their hands and called for Techs; twenty-seven seconds in which Named Operator Kasapi found time to wonder whether the sphincter to his bladder would hold fast; twenty-seven seconds in which he regretted eating too fast, sitting at his Workstation, bolting his food without looking at it, rather than switching out, in case anything interesting should happen; twenty-seven seconds in which Ranked Operator Dudley wondered whether his glee at being chosen for the job out-weighed his competence. The longest twenty-seven seconds in the history of this, or any Service Floor in over a century.

After twenty-seven seconds, when Tobe's screen came back on-line, the ball of throbbing threads was a hot, golden colour.

* * *

Wooh pressed her button and counted.

"I don't need anything," said Wooh, "3... 4... 5..."

"This is bad, isn't it?" asked Saintout.

"Take a look," said Wooh, handing Saintout her headset. "10... 11..."

By the time Saintout had disentangled the ear-bead, adjusted the strap, and placed the headset in position, feeding the bead into his ear, and finally dropping the screen down in front of his right eye, it was all over.

He blinked, flipped the screen up, and said, "You can stop counting, now, Wooh. We are at Code Orange."

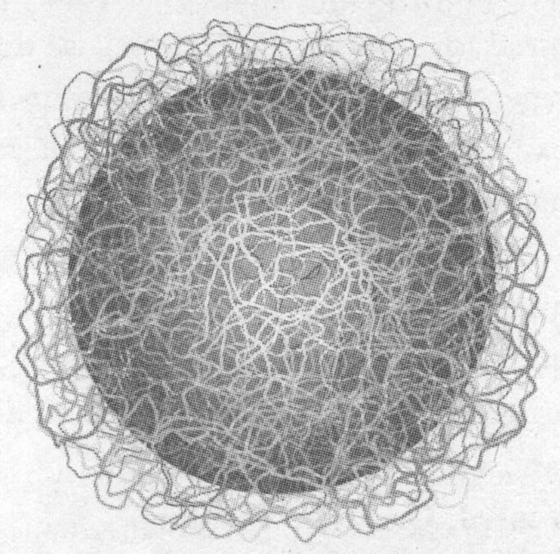

Chapter Thirty-Four

A CLAXON SOUNDED, and the dozen-or-so men and women, sitting around Branting's conference table, looked at each other. The man fourth from Branting on the left of the table turned a sickly colour, and clasped his hand over his mouth. The people on either side of him shuffled in their chairs, and he staggered to his feet. Branting was still standing, and he strode to the door and opened it for his erstwhile colleague.

"We are at Code Orange," said Branting. "Master Tobe's status has ramped up, and we need to break this problem down, and solve it." He was speaking through almost gritted teeth, his determination steelier after eighty hours than it had been after eight. "If any one else is feeling the pressure, perhaps you'd like to leave, now, so that we can bring in fresh minds. If you're not up to it, for goodness sake, go."

Branting cast a stern glance around the table, taking in each advisor as his head swung slowly from right to left. Before he was done, three more people had risen from their seats, and Branting gestured for a further three to recuse themselves.

One of the men relaxed, visibly, dropping his shoulders and rolling his head clockwise on his neck to relieve some of the tension that had built up, there.

"I'll need you back, Johnson," said Branting. "Take a Rest and Repast, and then back here, if you please."

"Yes, Control Operator," said Johnson, calmly, "of course."

Branting turned to Qa, who had stopped feeding the screen with wafers, and was awaiting instructions.

"You are excused, Qa," said Branting.

"Excuse me, sir," said Qa, "but I'd like to ask why you're dismissing me."

"You need to sleep," said Branting. "Follow Johnson, and come back to me, refreshed."

"Begging your pardon, sir," said Qa, formally, "but it could all be over by then. Can I ask, sir? Have I been underperforming, in your opinion? Have I fallen short of your needs or expectations?"

"No, Qa, you have done all that was required of you, and more."

"In that case, sir, I'd like to ask permission to remain at my post... with respect."

Branting sat for a moment, upright in his chair. Everyone around the table sat silent, watching Branting, and waiting for him to respond to Qa's request.

Service did not allow for sentiment or emotional responses to problems, in its programs of advancement. That did not mean that Operators at all levels were devoid of feelings. They might be less emotional than other castes, particularly Civilians, and they might be selected for, among other things, their pragmatism, but the past hour had proven, beyond anyone's doubt, that even Operators and Advisors at the highest Service grades could be rendered non-operational by their less rational, more emotional responses to certain stresses; Dinozzo had almost vomited, for goodness sake.

Qa was a superior aide, and Branting knew his worth. This would be a test of their combined mettle, and Branting realised, instinctively, that the two of them, working together, were more effective than the sum of their intellectual parts.

Branting looked down at the perfect, gleaming surface of the conference table in front of him, detecting a dark, but almost totally undistorted reflection of his face in the depths of its surface.

He smiled as he remembered his first Workstation on a Service Floor: the grubby beige/grey surface with its scratches and pits, and worn areas where sweaty hands had rested for decades; the tacky, grubby rubberpro ball that felt warm and matt under his hand; and the stubby switch on the facing edge of the counter, which he had used to input his Morse signature... How many times? Hundreds? Thousands?

This room might be a little more comfortable, a little more modern, a little less utilitarian than the average Service Floor, but it was merely an extension of the place where he had first been put to work.

He looked up at the large screen at the end of the room, filled with the image of the last wafer that Qa had uploaded. Then, he turned to look over his shoulder, again, into the alcove where Qa sat, looking over his shoulder back at his boss. He was sitting at, what was, effectively, a Workstation: in almost all regards, the sister of the one that Branting had started work on three decades earlier.

The job was the same.

"Permission granted," said Branting. "Thank you."

"Thank you, sir," said Qa, turning back to face his screen, and continue with his work.

"Sir?" asked Qa.

"Continue to feed the wafers," said Branting. "Unless or until we come up with something better, I see no reason to change tack, now."

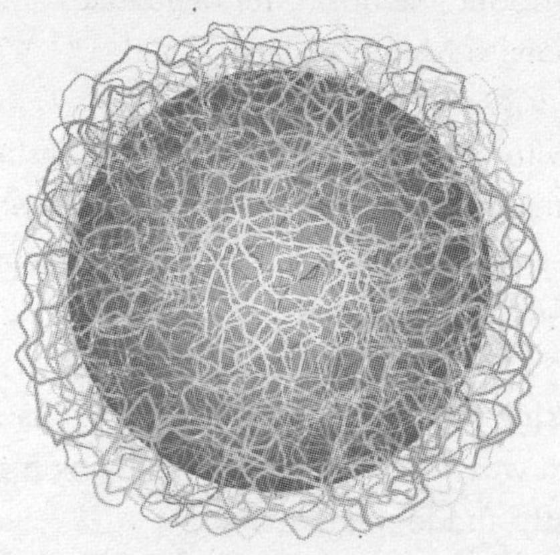

Chapter Thirty-Five

"TELL ME ABOUT me," said Metoo.

"What about Metoo?" asked Tobe.

"Anything you like."

They were still sitting at the kitchen counter, and Metoo was cradling an empty cup in her hands, the sticky remnant of her coffee coating the top inch of the cup with hardening milkpro froth.

"Metoo knows maths," said Tobe. "Not all of it, but enough."

"Enough for what?"

"Enough for Tobe."

"Okay. Does it matter that I know some maths?"

"Of course."

"Do you know why?"

"For Tobe. It matters for Tobe."

"Good. What else?"

"What else about Metoo?" Metoo nodded. "Metoo is Tobe's friend, and Tobe is Metoo's friend."

"What is a friend?"

Tobe looked puzzled for a moment.

"You don't have to answer," said Metoo. "It's not a test."

"Isn't it? It feels like a test. Can Tobe go to work now?"

"Not yet. Talk to me, some more."

"Tobe loves Metoo," said Tobe, looking down at the counter, and then looking up and beaming at Metoo. His eyes were still, but his mouth was wide, and he was showing his teeth. Metoo blushed slightly and looked down.

"What?" asked Tobe. "Why is Metoo sad?"

Metoo looked at Tobe, startled. He rarely thought about his own feelings, let alone other people's. He was an empirical soul, interested in numbers and formulae, mathematical puzzles and unanswered questions. He had never told her that he was sad, angry, elated or shy. She knew when he was curious, and she was aware that he could become obsessed. His feelings, such as they were, never seemed to relate to other people, but always to his work. He wondered about a puzzle, he was curious about a new formula, he was confident that he could deduce an answer, or he was satisfied that he had done so; anger, sadness and love were not on his radar, because they relied on others to stimulate them, and other people meant little or nothing to him.

Metoo hesitated for a moment.

"Are you ever sad, Tobe?" she asked.

"No."

"How do you know that I am sad?"

"Because Metoo looks sad."

Tobe wasn't supposed to be able to read people's feelings, or recognise those feelings from facial expressions. He wasn't very good at making eye-contact, even with Metoo, with whom he had spent a great deal of time in the past eight years. She had decided, soon after becoming his Assistant, that to get his attention and to fix his gaze, she needed to hold his face between her hands. She knew that working with a Master could be demanding, and had decided that she would need an arsenal of coping strategies if she was going to enable Tobe to perform his duties.

The first time that Metoo had taken Tobe's face in her hands in that manner, he had swatted her hands away, and cradled the back of his head, dropping his face onto his chest, closing his eyes and humming to himself. He had stayed like that for more than forty minutes. The second time she had tried to do it, she had warned him what was coming, and he had covered his ears, closed his eyes, and recited formulae to himself. She had not been able to touch him for six months, but she had persisted.

In the last year, and particularly in the last few weeks, it had become common practice for Metoo to hold Tobe's face in order to hold his attention. He accepted it, and it seemed to help him to focus on the things that Metoo needed him to focus on, so that he was able to function and accomplish what he wanted to accomplish. It was a complex balancing act: she needed to impose rules and routines on Tobe, so that Tobe could accomplish the tasks he set for himself. By working at capacity, Tobe could be a useful Master, and, who knew, even an effective Active.

In the first year after becoming Tobe's Assistant, Metoo had come to want Tobe to be drug-free, settled, and, more than anything else, she wanted him to be content. The drugs were dispensed with in short order, but the rest had been harder, and Metoo was only just beginning to feel that she was making headway.

The last few months had been very nearly idyllic for Metoo. Tobe had been incredibly stable and predictable, and almost every day had become an ordinary day, Metoo's perfect day.

Then, it had all gone wrong. Metoo was still convinced that it wasn't Tobe. If anyone knew Tobe, she felt that she did, but that wasn't enough. She didn't know what had caused Tobe to become wrapped up in probability, but she failed to see how it could possibly matter. He was content. His actions were well within his normal range. He had not retreated into himself, or put up barriers between them. He was calm and content. He was eating and sleeping, and following his usual routines.

The difference, as Metoo saw it, was that Tobe was responding to her at a deeper and more subtle level than she was used to. She wondered how that could possibly be considered to be a bad thing.

"What does 'sad' look like, Tobe?" Metoo asked, putting her cup down on the counter, and looking at him, holding his gaze.

"Tobe doesn't know. Tobe only knows that Metoo is sad. Why is Metoo sad? When will Metoo be happy again?"

Metoo placed both of her hands over one of his, still holding his gaze. He looked back at her, as if searching for answers to questions that he didn't understand.

"Very soon," she said. "I'll be happy again, very soon."

"SOMETHING'S NOT RIGHT," Wooh said to Saintout.

"You bet your life, something's not right. When was the last time we were at Code Orange? When was the last time that any College, anywhere, was at Code Orange?"

"That's not it. That's not what I meant."

"You saw the ramp-up. You hit your button."

"Yes, I did," said Wooh. "All the criteria were in place, so

I had to hit the button. When it gets to this point, there's no choice. The protocols are there for a reason..."

"What is it, Wooh? What is the problem?"

"I have absolutely no clue. This just doesn't feel right."

"Okay, rationalise it for me. Take off the headset, and just talk to me for five minutes. Tell me what feels wrong."

"We're at Code Orange, and you want me to disconnect from Master Tobe's screen?" asked Wooh, glaring at Saintout past the screen that covered most of her forward vision.

"We're at Code Orange," said Saintout, spreading his hands in a gesture of resignation. "Everyone's looking at Master Tobe's screen."

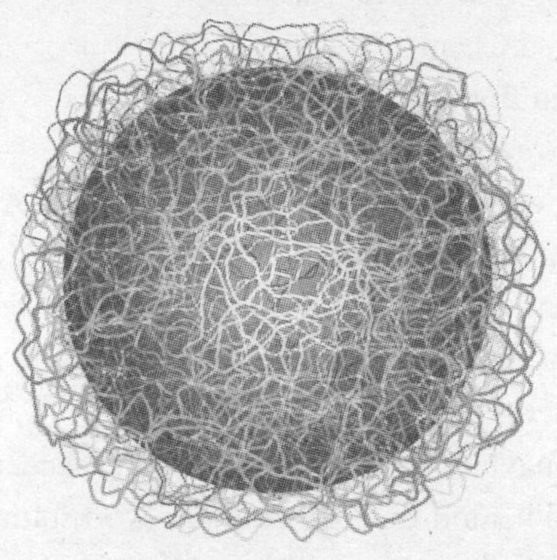

Chapter Thirty-Six

THE NINE SCREENS on the Service Floor all showed Master Tobe's data.

There were twenty-seven Named and Ranked Operators in the room, and two dozen Techs. It was standing room only. Everyone, who was anyone, in Service at College was on the Service Floor, and four Agent Operators had been drafted in, including Agent Operator Henderson.

Within minutes of the ramp-up to Code Orange, within minutes of all the screens switching out to Tobe's data, there were seventy people on the floor.

No one said a word.

Each station now had three Operators, one in the chair, one in the dicky, and one standing, watching over the shoulders of the other two. The four Agent Operators were moving around the room, from one screen to the next, but all the screens were showing the same data, and there were no comparisons to be made.

Someone had to make a decision.

"Bob?" asked Chen.

"Chen," said Bob.

"What are we looking at?"

"We're at Code Orange. We're looking at an Active's data. If it's going on in his head, we're seeing it."

"I realise that, but what's going on in this Active's head?"

"If we knew that, and we could bottle it, we'd all be out of a job."

"That's as maybe," said Agent Operator Henderson, who had come to stand behind the Operators at Workstation 7, "but you do realise that we are in a critical situation for global safety, don't you?"

"Yes," said Bob, "but I also know that, it doesn't matter how much monitoring we do of these people, we have no control over what happens."

"No," said Henderson, bowing his head, slightly, and dropping his voice, "but, unless you want to scare the shit out of everyone present, I suggest we all get to work decoding this data, beginning, Mr Goodman, with you."

"Fine, but everyone's already pretty scared," said Bob Goodman, "and it won't do you any good."

"You are excused," said Agent Operator Henderson.

"Pardon me, Agent Operator," said Chen, "but I think you're making a mistake."

"How so?" asked Henderson, looking over their heads at the screen in front of them, his hands locked together behind his back.

"Operator Goodman is to this Service Floor what an Active is to Global Security," said Chen. "He knows his stuff, sir, and, I believe that if we are to emerge, safely, on the other side of this crisis, it will be, in part, due to the very best resources being employed. Goodman is one of our best resources, sir."

Goodman and Henderson both looked at Chen, the expressions on their faces not considerably dissimilar. Henderson was surprised to be spoken to in such a way by an inferior, and Goodman was surprised to be spoken so highly of by a superior. He was the only remaining basic-grade Operator on the floor, and he fully expected to be the first to go.

"Line-check," said Henderson.

Bob Goodman hesitated.

"Line-check," said Chen.

"Line-check," said Bob.

"Verify line-check," said Chen.

"Verify." Bob began a line-check on Master Tobe's data at Workstation 7.

Henderson stepped back towards the middle of the room.

"All Workstations, line-check," he said. "I want everything on wafers, and I want every comparison made at the most minute level."

A chorus of voices repeated the line-check instructions and verifications, and the room returned to almost total quiet.

Pitu 3 sat on the cot in his room, his feet tucked under his body, for comfort, and his head in his hands. He had been discharged from the infirmary, and the quarantine ward had been closed down.

It had quickly become obvious to Service that the quarantine was pointless, and, potentially, counter-productive. The situation could only get worse if group hysteria became a problem, and rumours were already circulating around the College about what might be happening. Service buttons were being pressed, off the Schedule, as more and more Students, Seniors and Assistants became concerned about what might be happening. The extra activity on the Service buttons only confused the issues, and Service needed to nip in the bud any possibility that mass panic might ensue at the College.

Pitu 3 had left his room at the infirmary before the ward was closed down, and didn't even see Mudd on the way out. At first, it had been a wonderful adventure, and he had revelled in the opportunity to be at the centre of someone's, anyone's, attention. He had enjoyed being interviewed after he had pressed his button, standing outside Master Tobe's office. He was proud that he had pressed his button. The first couple of hours in the infirmary had been fun, too. He had felt terribly important, until his Service button had been returned to him, and the staff had stopped visiting him. Then they had simply sent him back to his room with an envelope. No one had said anything.

Pitu 3 sat on the cot, his feet tucked under his body, and his head in his hands. Two sheets of paperpro sat in his lap. One was his discharge form from the infirmary. The other piece of paperpro contained news that he was not ready for, that he might never have been ready for. In three short lines, the text on the second sheet of paperpro ended every hope, every dream that Pitu 3 had ever had, every hope that he believed Master Tobe, Metoo, and the College had all fostered in him. He had been betrayed.

Pitu 3 released his feet from under his body, and put them on the floor. He pressed the Service button hanging around his neck to acknowledge Recreation, and stood up. The sheets of paperpro floated from his lap, landing on the linopro between his feet.

Pitu 3 lifted his robe off over his head, gathered it up in his hands and wiped his face with it. He had been crying, but had stopped now.

His face dry, Pitu 3 calmly shook out his robe, and took hold of the neckline, with both hands, close together. He twisted the hem of the neckline until a small tear appeared in it, and then he spread his arms wide, tearing the robe asunder from top to bottom. He moved his hands around the neck of the robe, and began the process again, until he had three long strips of cloth. He tied the ends together and began to plait the light-weight strips of silkpro cloth to form a strong, thick cord. When the plait was complete, he tied the loose ends together.

Pitu 3 pushed the tied ends of the plait through the strands of the plait about a third of the way along the cord, to form a loop. He stood on the cot and reached up to tie the end of the cord to the bracket in the ceiling that his light-source hung from.

Standing on the edge of the cot, Pitu 3 was too short. He stepped off the cot, and made his way to the shared kitchen, his feet slapping heavily on the worn, cracked linopro as he darted along the corridor, apparently unaware of his nakedness. There was no one in the kitchen, so he took the top stool off the stack in the corner, and padded back to his room.

Pitu 3 placed the stool on the floor, up against the edge of the cot, where one of its feet anchored the two sheets of paperpro to the linopro. It didn't matter.

Pitu 3 stepped onto his cot, and then up onto the stool. Then he took hold of the loop in the cord, and made it as wide as he could by threading the cord between the strands of silkpro. He placed the loop over his head, and pulled it snug around his neck. The cord got tangled in his Service button, so he loosened it slightly, to release the knot, and then slipped the Service button from around his neck, and dropped it onto the floor beside the cot. He pulled the cord snug around his throat a second time.

Without a moment's thought or hesitation, Pitu 3 stepped off the stool, knocking it over, as he did so, with his trailing foot. The leg of the stool that had been standing on the sheets of paperpro ripped through them, and sent them skidding across the linopro, torn and creased. The Service button was knocked under the cot.

The tips of Pitu 3's toes scrabbled slightly in the air, as if trying to find the edge of the cot, to stand on. His body convulsed slightly, and then turned, anti-clockwise on its cord. The bracket in the ceiling creaked, but held firm.

The drop was not long enough to break Pitu 3's neck, but it didn't matter. His Service button did not need to be pressed again until Repast, and there was no reason for anyone to seek him out; no one had ever sought him out before.

There was plenty of time for Pitu 3 to die.

MUDD HELPED TO wind down the quarantine at the infirmary, and hit his button for Rest about two hours after the first of the quarantine subjects was discharged. He had quite enjoyed the experience, but would, he thought, be eternally grateful for the fact that he had not been incarcerated with Pitu 3. The time Mudd had spent piggy-backed to Pitu, in the corridor outside Master Tobe's room, in the interview with Bello, and then on the walk to the infirmary was all the time he ever wanted to spend with the kid.

Mudd was off-duty when the Service Floor ramped-up to Code Orange, and, suddenly, everyone was on standby. As a Medic Operator, Mudd was used to being on standby, it was a regular feature of his job. In his time as a Medic Operator, Mudd had never been called out on standby.

When the call came through, Mudd was plugged into a vid-port, watching re-runs of some of his favourite tv comedies. They still made him laugh, even though nothing new had been made for almost a decade.

Mudd pressed his button, and went to the nearest Service point.

"Medic Operator Mudd," said Mudd.

"You are required at Student Accommodation Tobe, room 14," said Service.

"Anomaly status?"

"Unknown."

Mudd wasn't thrilled; another of Tobe's Students was in trouble, or Pitu 3 was in trouble, again, and he didn't relish either prospect. He signed out of Service, picked up his kit, and zipped himself into his regulation jacket.

Mudd arrived at the room in Tobe's Student accommodation, and knocked on the door. There was no answer. He knocked again.

After three or four minutes, Mudd checked the shared bathroom and kitchen. Both were empty. The Student's colleagues obviously hadn't noticed that he was missing, and had gone about their usual business.

Mudd knew, instinctively, which Student had been overlooked, because he knew that he would have done the same.

Mudd knocked on the door again, and called Pitu's name. There was no answer. He tried the handle.

The door to Pitu's room was not locked. It opened onto the bed, and was partly blocked by the stool that Pitu had knocked over when he had stepped off it, into space.

With no way to step into the room, Mudd got on his hands and knees, and manoeuvred the stool, in the cramped space, so that he could pull it into the corridor. He stood up, and shoved the door open with one hand. It wouldn't open all the way, and was pushing against something heavy, but mobile, behind it. Mudd stepped into the room, sideways, and pulled the door towards him. Pitu's limp body thumped against the back of the door, dead weight.

"Bugger," said Mudd, as he saw what the obstruction was. He

dropped his bag on the floor, and hit his Service button. There was no point trying to resuscitate the boy, it was far too late for that, and if no medical attention was needed, Mudd was required not to interact with the body at all. As the first Service Operator at the scene, however, Mudd was expected to begin to process the surroundings.

He closed the door, and took a step back, looking the body up and down. He took in the cord around Pitu 3's neck, and the pieces of paperpro on the floor, one of which, he was partially standing on. He bent down to pick up the pieces of paperpro, and, as he did so, he noticed the cord to Pitu 3's Service button, lying on the floor, only inches below Pitu's dangling feet. Mudd pulled the cord towards him, at full-stretch, with one finger, disinclined to get close to the body. He dropped the Service button into a sterile bag from his Kit, and bent again to pick up the sheets of paperpro. He tried to decipher what was written on them, through the creases, tears and dusty footprints. The first was simply Pitu's discharge form from the infirmary. The second was from College administration. It had a serial number at the top, and Mudd read:

Assessment and Re-assignment complete.
Subject unsuitable for furtherance.
Return to School and register as Senior Stanley.

Mudd took another step back, and leaned against the far wall of the tiny room. He didn't want to look at Pitu 3. He didn't want to believe that he had let the boy down.

Mudd waited for Service to send someone, the form from Admin still in his hand.

"Bugger," he said. "They didn't even let him keep the name."

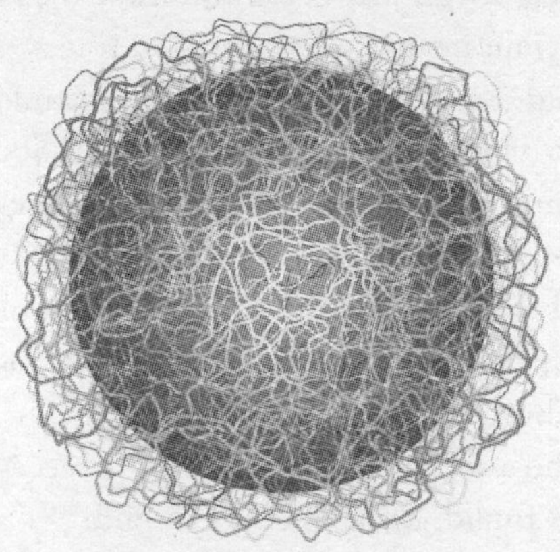

Chapter Thirty-Seven

A TONE SOUNDED in Tobe's flat. Tobe looked at Metoo across the kitchen counter. She looked back at him.

"I should answer that," said Metoo.

"Service?" asked Tobe.

"Service."

"Tobe doesn't do Service."

"No he doesn't," said Metoo, rising from her stool, and turning to leave the kitchen. "Lucky Tobe."

"Lucky? Why?"

"Just lucky, that's all," Metoo said, over her shoulder as she went to sign in.

"Metoo," said Metoo.

"Anomalies?" she asked, after Service had failed to acknowledge her sign-in for a minute or two.

"Wait," said Service.

"Why don't you send another tone when you've got something

for me? Or better, yet, why don't you leave me alone to do the job that you want me to do?"

"Wait," said Service. There was another short pause, in which Metoo realised that she was, unconsciously clenching and unclenching her fists.

"We have to inform you that one of Master Tobe's Students is dead," said Service.

Metoo stopped unclenching her hands. She placed her fists in front of her chest, the knuckles touching.

"What?" she asked.

"Pitu 3 was found, hanged, in his room."

"And what do you suppose I should do about that?" asked Metoo, aghast at the baldness with which the news was delivered.

She turned and left the way she had come, without waiting for an answer from Service, and without signing out. She was back in the kitchen, seconds after her outburst, but felt her stress levels continue to rise. She didn't know what she was feeling, but she did know that, beyond the sadness and guilt that she felt for Pitu, and the wonder she felt at how damned crass Service announcements could be, she also felt a deep and abiding frustration that could only be attributed to her relationship with Tobe.

"Metoo is unhappy," said Tobe, as she strode past him, snatching her cup from the counter as she went. She leaned down to put it in the auto-clean, and then turned back to Tobe. She sighed.

"I'm not unhappy, Tobe," she said, "not really."

"Good. Can Tobe go back to work, now?"

"No," said Metoo, slumping down onto her stool opposite Tobe, her head bowed. "You can't go to work today."

Tobe got up from his stool and walked around the counter

to her. He placed one of his hands on each side of her face, and lifted it, so that he could see her. Metoo kept her eyes downcast for a long moment, before lifting them to look at him. A tear escaped the lower lid of her left eye, and trickled down over Tobe's hand.

Tobe let go of Metoo's face, suddenly, and started rubbing the back of his right hand, where the tear had been, with the palm of his left. He went to the sink and ran the water, but was soon splashing it all over himself and the kitchen.

Metoo collected herself, and went to Tobe at the kitchen sink. She leaned past him as he backed away from her, and turned off the tap.

"I'll run you a bath," she said, as brightly as she could.

Tobe said nothing. Still rubbing his hands, he left the kitchen, and walked down the corridor to his own little room.

Metoo went to the bathroom, and began to run Tobe's bath, relieved to have something practical to do. The tone sounded again. Metoo put her hand under the stream of water, running into the tub, to check that it was at the right temperature. Then she dried her hands and sorted out a towel and a robe, ready for when Tobe got out of his bath. The door to the bathroom was open, so that the bath could steam, happily, without causing condensation everywhere, and Metoo sat down to enjoy a moment's peace, listening to the running water, and thinking about Tobe.

The tone sounded again.

Metoo turned off the tap, and made her way out of the bathroom. She turned when she heard footsteps behind her, and saw Tobe coming out of his room. She stopped to watch him. He was still wearing his robe.

Metoo waited for Tobe to start peeling his robe off over his head, as he usually did in his room, and, if not, always on his way to the bathroom. Before she had come to live with Tobe, Metoo had never seen a naked man, and it had taken her several weeks to get used to his total lack of self-consciousness. She had not given it a second thought for years.

Tobe went into the bathroom, still wearing his robe. She followed him back to the bathroom, just as he was closing the door.

Tobe never closed the bathroom door. He never closed any door. Tobe liked to be able to see the space around him, especially in the flat. The only door that was kept closed in the flat was the garden room door.

A Service tone sounded in the flat.

Metoo couldn't think. She was tense, and everything around her seemed, suddenly, much less predictable than she was used to.

Pitu 3 was dead, and Metoo did not know what to think about that. A Medtech doctor and a Police Operator were hiding out in her garden room, and she didn't know what to think about that. She was, effectively, in lockdown, because of something that Tobe was supposed to have done, and she didn't know what it was. Tobe was acting out of character, or, out of his character at least.

Tobe appeared to be transforming into something approaching a normal person.

If all of that wasn't enough for Metoo to deal with, the Service tone sounded again.

Metoo had to sign-in, or was it -out? She hardly knew any more.

SAINTOUT AND WOOH had spent more than five minutes rationalising what was going on: much, much more. The ramp-up was complete, and Wooh had been part of the process that had altered Code-status to Orange. Saintout was right, all the screens on the Service Floor, not to mention screens all over the World, were tuned in to Tobe, collecting his data in ever-increasing detail. More mind-hours than anyone could imagine were being devoted to assessing, manipulating and cross-checking data, and all of it was streaming from Tobe: one man, one Master, one Active.

The entire World of Service now revolved around Master Tobe.

Wooh did not need a view-screen in front of her face, or a bead in her ear; other people were doing that job. Wooh was on the ground, and she was a specialist, and Saintout was on the ground, and he was a specialist.

After many minutes, hours, even, spent discussing Tobe, they finally decided what they needed in order to make any real progress.

"You know what we need?" asked Saintout, smiling.

"Yeah," said Wooh, "we need an expert. We need someone that can decode Tobe's brainwave from the inside out, but, if he's out there, you can be pretty sure that he's already working on this particular problem."

"It's not a 'he'," said Saintout.

Wooh and Saintout visibly jumped as the garden room door crashed open with no warning, and Metoo bowled in on them.

When they had gathered their wits about them, and Metoo had closed the door behind her, Saintout was the first to speak. He looked at Wooh, and smiled.

"It's not a 'he', it's a 'she'," said Saintout, "and she's not 'out there'..."

"She's in here," said Wooh.

"What?" asked Metoo.

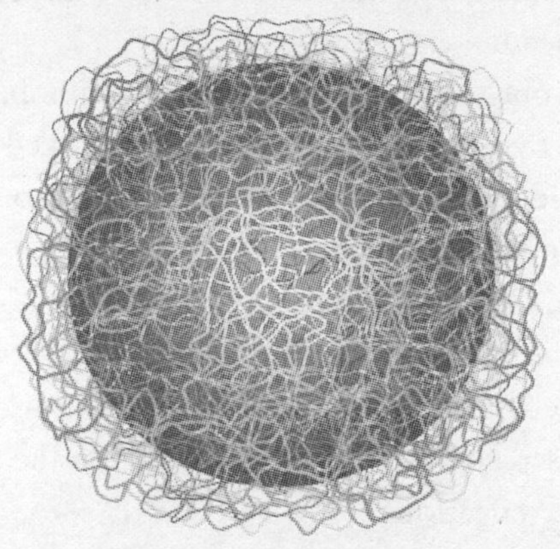

Chapter Thirty-Eight

HENDERSON TOOK THE message that Pitu 3 had been found hanged, apparently by his own hand, and that the Student was an associate of Master Tobe's and one of the last people to see him before his home isolation. He did not know what it meant for the Code status.

"Chen?" said Henderson.

"Yes, sir," said Chen.

"No. It's nothing," said Henderson, pausing with his right elbow cupped in his left hand, and his right hand to his mouth.

"Not a good look, sir," said Bob Goodman.

"What, Operator? Are you speaking to me?" asked Henderson.

"Yes, sir. Sorry, sir."

"What's not a good look?"

"Classic defensive, concerned posture, and, if your legs are crossed, too, we're really in trouble."

Henderson uncrossed his feet and looked hard at the back of Goodman's head.

"I can see your reflection on-screen," said Bob.

"Why aren't you looking at the screen?" asked Chen.

"I am," said Bob, "that's how I was able to see Operator Henderson's posture."

"Bob!" said Chen, shocked.

"What? Doesn't everyone do that?"

"Are you telling me that you can monitor everything that's going on on-screen, and still keep an eye on the Service Floor, via the screen reflections?"

"Can't everyone?"

"No, Mr Goodman, they can't," said Henderson. "So, you know a little something about body language, do you?"

"It's all part of the same thing. Looking at peoples' heads on-screen is no different from having a person in front of you. The two can be read in much the same way."

"Really?" asked Henderson.

"Sure. What? You didn't know that?"

"I didn't."

"Me either," said Chen.

"Anyone else?" asked Henderson.

There was quiet on the Service Floor, for a few seconds, and then Bob spoke again.

"I'm pretty sure the Operators are concentrating on what they're doing. Put a request up on their screens."

"I'll be right back," said Henderson.

WITHIN MINUTES OF Henderson leaving the Service Floor, every Workstation on every Service Floor, in every College on the planet had a rolling questionnaire appearing on the left-hand side of its screen. There was no time to put together a brand new psychometric test for what Henderson was looking for, but it was possible to take one of the basic aptitude tests and insert questions from one of the personality tests used on infant and latent Actives. Individual scores wouldn't be conclusive, but comparisons might prove interesting.

Branting began to get the results of the Operator tests through in less than thirty minutes.

Every Operator on the local College Service Floor was reviewing Master Tobe's data, and one Workstation on every College Service Floor globally had also been given over to checking his output. The whole World was working on the problem. The whole World had to; by the time Code status had been ramped up to Orange, thousands of Students, Seniors and Assistants had ceased to function within their remits, hundreds of Companions were out of action, and more than two dozen Actives had been suspended, or had stopped processing.

The ever-changing mind threads that wove the synaptic Shield that kept the World safe and secret from the Universe were fraying; the warp and weft of the mental net was wearing away and perforating, and holes were beginning to appear in it.

Everyone knew about the domino effect. One domino falls, and others must follow suit, until all the dominoes have fallen. Everyone knew about ripples on a pond. Throw the tiniest of pebbles into the middle of a pool of water and the ripples will grow to fill the pool, water waving and splashing at its perimeter.

There had been no external view of the Shield for over a century. For the first hundred years of the College system, one, lone, stealth-satellite had monitored the Shield from beyond the Earth's atmosphere, which was contained within the Shield. Some tumult in the solar system, which was never fully explained, had knocked the satellite out of orbit, and the only external eyes on the Shield were lost forever. The only way to monitor the integrity of the Shield, now, and for the past century, was to monitor the Actives. The Shield was invisible to Earth, but the Actives were alive and kicking, and could be housed, and controlled by Service Global.

Master Tobe, and his probability problem constituted the flick of the first domino, the pebble. The maths was out there, and as the ripples spread and grew they gained speed and momentum. There was no way to contain the problem. There was no way to plug the holes in the Shield, or weave the synaptic threads back together.

Qa had processed and input hundreds, maybe thousands of wafers, and the data never stopped coming.

The Operator tests came through as data, which needed to be translated into a graph.

"Let's process this lot then, shall we, and see what the graph looks like?" asked Branting. "Obviously, we don't have enough to do already."

"Sir?" asked Qa.

"Sorry. I'm getting a little punchy, I know. I'm just going to sit for a minute."

Branting's advisors were on one of their short breaks, and he still had ten minutes to collect his thoughts. He sat down at the conference table and dropped his head, lacing his fingers together on the back of his neck. He could see his reflection in the shiny surface. Dropped over, his face was slack, and he barely looked like himself. He thought for a minute or two, and then said, "Qa, sit here for a minute."

Qa got up from his seat in the alcove, and sat down next to Branting at the table.

"Sir?" he asked.

"Look down."

Qa dropped his head onto his chest, misunderstanding his boss's instruction.

"No, look down at the table. What can you see?"

"Oh," said Qa, leaning over. "I see the table-top, and the reflections in it."

"Yes, you do. Now look at me." The two men lifted their heads and looked at each other.

"I don't get it, sir," said Qa.

"Try again," said Branting.

Both men looked down into the mirror surface of the table. Branting watched the expression on Qa's reflected face change. He put his hand on his shoulder, and said, "That's right, Qa. What do you think of that?"

"I think it means you have to put together a new team," said Qa.

"So, find me the people I'm looking for," said Branting, almost smiling.

Branting put through an instruction to dismiss all his advisors, and sat on the dicky-seat at Qa's Workstation.

"You can input the data here, right?" asked Branting.

"It'll take a few minutes," said Qa.

"Minutes, we have," said Branting, "let's just not take hours over this, okay?"

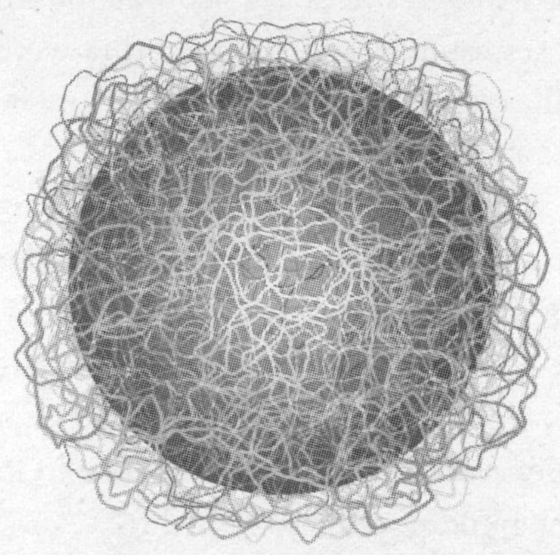

Chapter Thirty-Nine

THE QUARANTINE HAD not proven effective, and it had probably contributed, to some degree, to the unease that seemed to pervade the atmosphere in every College in the World.

After close to a hundred hours, Patel and her teams were finally allowed to leave Tobe's office building. They had completed their task in short order, but had not been allowed to leave their posts for another ten hours, and none of the material that they had painstakingly collected from Tobe's room and collated, bagged up, documented and checked, had been removed from the building during the entire time they spent in the offices. Patel's photographs were the only evidence that had made it back to Service.

The teams were demoralised; more than thirty hours of work had gone to waste, and another ten, sitting doing nothing had not improved their moods.

The quarantine had applied to everyone, but the lifting of it did not. It was lifted in stages. Service was the first department to be entirely re-instated, and all Operators were free to move around at will, except that they were all on incredibly tight Schedules because of the Code status.

The School was more-or-less a closed environment, so it was easy enough to end the quarantine there, and the Students and Seniors hardly noticed the difference, even if they were relieved that they were no longer under orders to remain in the building. Many of them wouldn't have chosen to leave it, anyway; many of them only left very rarely, but it was nice to know that they could leave the building if they wanted to.

The College proper proved the most problematic. There was some question as to whether it was a good idea to re-instate pre-quarantine rules and regs, straight away. Students, Assistants and Companions had caused the most problems throughout the ordeal. They were the most fragile personalities, and they responded badly to stress, particularly when it was associated with change. The Code changes and the quarantine had affected them more than any other group, and what affected them invariably affected the Masters, which meant that Actives were put at risk.

Another change, even a reversal, out of quarantine, might be too difficult. It was another twelve hours before a decision was made; twelve hours in which the bags and boxes filled by Patel and her team were removed from the corridor outside Master Tobe's room, and taken away for processing by Service. There would be no teaching timetable, which had been suspended when the quarantine was imposed, but all members of College were free to move around, and Masters could return to their offices, if they chose to. The library was also re-opened, but lecture halls remained closed.

The food hall was up and running again two hours after the

quarantine was lifted, but its opening hours were restricted. Many Students, who'd been living off very basic rations in their rooms and dorms, were relieved to be able to spend their coupons again. They were also allowed to use any coupons that had gone out of date during the quarantine, and, within a few hours of the food hall opening, the atmosphere was beginning to change for the better. Small groups of Students were beginning to relax together. Decent food and good company began to calm the Student body, and Observer Operators, judiciously placed among them, were happy to report that Student-life seemed to be returning to better-than normal.

TOBE'S QUARANTINE WAS not lifted. Tobe, Metoo, Wooh and Saintout would remain in the flat.

"We might as well be under house arrest," said Metoo.

"It's not so bad," said Saintout, smiling.

"Not for you," said Metoo. "This just turned into a walk in the park, for you, but I've still got Master Tobe to deal with, and it isn't getting any easier."

"We'll help in any way we can," said Wooh.

"Help by staying out of the way, then. Help by allowing me out into the garden for an hour."

"Okay," said Saintout, "we can do that." Wooh cast a frown in his direction; she wasn't entirely sure that it was up to them to decide the conditions of Metoo's quarantine.

"No," said Metoo, "I can't." Saintout shrugged at Wooh, behind Metoo's back, but he knew exactly what he was doing.

"I don't think you'll be here for long, anyway," said Wooh. "I wanted to warn you in advance..."

"What?" asked Metoo, an anxious expression crossing her face.

"Shouldn't we wait for Service?" Saintout asked Wooh.

"Oh, come on. You, of all people, ought to see that telling Metoo is –"

"No, you're right," said Saintout, interrupting Wooh, and holding his hands out, to take Metoo's.

"Let me explain what's going to happen," said Saintout, sitting Metoo down on one of the chairs in the garden room, still holding her hands. "Our assessment of the situation, mine and Doctor Wooh's, is that you are the key to solving this mess."

"How do you mean?"

"The thing is," said Wooh, approaching Metoo, "we don't really know why, but Saintout and I have come to the conclusion that you are closer to the sub – to Master Tobe, than anyone, and you might hold the key to answering the questions that this situation has posed."

"What situation?" asked Metoo. "What's she talking about?" she asked Saintout.

"We're at Code Orange," said Saintout. "Master Tobe's status has been degrading for days. No one seems to know why, and no one seems able to reverse the problem."

"There's nothing wrong with him," said Metoo, dropping Saintout's hands, and rising, as if to flee.

"I believe you," said Saintout, "but we're still at Code Orange, and you're not so naive as to think that a problem like that will just go away."

"I'm not naive at all," said Metoo. She sank into the chair that Saintout was standing next to. "What do you need from me?"

Doctor Wooh stepped forwards, saying, "Service will require your presence at one of the Service Central Offices. We don't know where, but we assume it'll be as local as possible, given everything that's happening."

"I can't just sign in and talk to them that way?"

"They want to see you," said Saintout, kneeling by Metoo's side. "The interview could be quite... intrusive."

"Intrusive, how? How could anything be more intrusive than chipping me, and you've already done that," she said, glaring at Doctor Wooh. "They can get into my head any time they damned well please. They don't need to see me. My place is here, with Master Tobe."

Doctor Wooh looked at Metoo with pity.

"Why are you looking at me like that? What the hell do they think I've done?"

"They don't think you've done anything," said Saintout, still low to the floor, on one knee. "The fact is... You do realise... They might decide to interview Tobe."

"That's what I've been trying to do! You gave me the questions. I said I'd do it. I'll do it," she said. "They can try to ask him questions, but what are they going to do? Take him somewhere he doesn't know? Surround him with people he doesn't know? Ask him questions he doesn't understand?"

"She has a point," said Saintout, rising to his feet, and looking at Wooh.

"Did you do this?" asked Metoo. "Did you decide that I should be thrown to the lions? Bullied and questioned, and God only knows what else? How could you?" she said, looking up into Saintout's face. "How could you do that?"

Metoo left without waiting for an answer or an explanation. She left the garden room, and took a couple of steps, and then turned her head in the direction of Tobe's room. She wasn't even aware that she was doing it, but she did it a dozen times a day when Tobe was in the flat, in his room. She liked to keep an eye on him. It was her job.

The door to Tobe's room was closed.

Metoo's hand came up to her open mouth, but she didn't utter a sound. She lifted the hem of her robe with her left hand, and, her right hand already stretched out in front of her, bolted for the door.

She did not knock or wait; she simply opened the door, without stopping, and walked into the room. Tobe was sitting on his bed, looking at his wipe-wall. He turned to face the door when Metoo entered.

"What?" asked Tobe.

"Tobe?"

"Tobe," said Tobe, placing one hand on his chest.

"Sorry," said Metoo, abashed, and she stepped back out through the door, and closed it behind her. She didn't know what to do. She never went into Tobe's room when he was in the flat. It was his space, and she didn't invade it. On the other hand, the door was never closed, ever. She looked around for the wedge with the little owl on it that had been used to prop the door open for the past six years, at least. She could not see it. She made her way to the kitchen to wash her hands and calm down.

The door-wedge with the owl on it was sitting on the counter, on top of a piece of paper, where Tobe would normally sit. Metoo lifted the wedge. The piece of paper simply read:

Tobe's room, please knock.

Her face pale, and her eyes wide, Metoo staggered back to the garden room, barely able to breathe. She pushed through the door, and stumbled into a chair, almost collapsing.

"Christ!" said Saintout. "What is it, Metoo? What the hell's going on?"

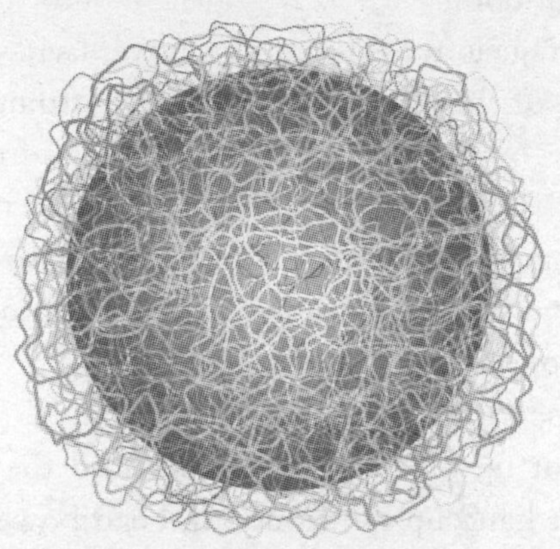

Chapter Forty

By the early hours of day 5, Qa and Branting were looking at a bell curve.

"Now all we have to do is decide where we want the cut off," said Qa.

"We have nine hundred and eighty-seven Colleges worldwide, and we have data for all the Operators who are at their stations, what about all the others? The ones that are eating, sleeping and playing?" asked Branting.

"Service Global has put out instructions to have completed questionnaires from all Service Operators within two hours," said Qa. "The questionnaire is short, so it doesn't take long to answer the questions."

"OK, but I don't want to wait that long."

The two men sat staring at the data for a few minutes.

"We want the rarities, the oddities, right?" asked Qa.

"Right, but do we want the top of the graph or the bottom,

or do we want both?"

"If Joe Average is at the top of the curve, I say we start at the opposite end of the curve to the Actives. Although, to be on the safe side, you might want to take samples from both ends of the curve."

"And how many of them do you suppose there are?" asked Branting. "And what if they don't work on Service Floors? Can we test everyone?"

"Not in time for this."

Branting got up off his dicky, and paced the width of the room, his left hand up to his mouth, head bowed in thought. He stopped, stood still for a second, and dropped his hand from his mouth. Then he smiled.

"I really am getting punch drunk," he said. "It's staring us right in the face. Get me the Service number of the Operator that started all this... Goodman, was it?" asked Branting.

"Using his Service number, we extract his data, and make him the control, go a point or two either side, and with any luck, we'll have our sample group. Brilliant!" said Qa.

"I hope he is. I'm going to get him, on-line, right now."

"No, I meant..." Qa began, but Branting was already on his way out of the room, and Qa returned to upload Goodman's Service number, and find out where on the curve his results sat.

Bob Goodman left the Service Floor, accompanied by Ranked Operator McColl. He had been told nothing. Henderson had asked him to sign out, and hand over to Chen. Chen tried to ask Henderson why Goodman was being removed from his post, but Henderson simply waved her concerns away. She had confronted him once, and did not feel able to do so again.

McColl and Goodman left the Service Floor, exited onto the

exterior gallery, and went into the interview room that McColl had previously visited with Strazinsky.

"I'll be observing," McColl said to Goodman, as they walked into the room.

"Great, that's fine," said Bob, "but I'm still not sure what I'm doing here."

"I'm not sure if anyone really knows why you're here, but you certainly seem to have impressed someone," said McColl.

"Or pissed someone off," said Bob Goodman, smiling bravely.

McColl pressed his hand firmly against Goodman's back, by way of reassuring the Operator, and smiled at him.

"You'll be fine," he said.

The vid-con screen on the wall opposite a table and a pair of chairs, lit up with drifting snow, and then settled, showing a chair and a computer array in an anonymous-looking room.

McColl and Goodman sat down facing the screen; the screen vibrated slightly and a man walked into the shot, his back to the camera. He turned to sit in the chair, but Goodman didn't recognise him. The man wore a dark suit with a light shirt and a dark tie. The picture seemed indistinct, and, while he didn't recognise him, Goodman thought that the man on the screen could be mistaken for almost anyone. He had an anonymous, regular face. He was of medium height, medium weight and average colouring, apparently without any identifying marks or features.

The man looked out of the screen at Goodman and McColl.

"Control Operator Branting, interviewing," he said. Before he had finished speaking, Goodman was on his feet, knocking his chair over and almost getting tangled in it.

"What the..." he began, kicking at the chair to free his legs so that he could flee.

"Sit down, please, Operator Goodman," said Branting.

"Perhaps you could give him a hand," he continued, gesturing at McColl and shuffling the pieces of paper that were visible in his hands. "I can't see you if you stand up, Goodman."

McColl hurried to help Goodman, but he only seemed to make things worse, and it was several sweaty moments before McColl and Goodman were both seated again. "Interviewee?" asked Branting.

There was a pause before Goodman turned to McColl and said, "Is that me?"

"It is," said McColl. "Just take a deep breath and answer the man. Goodman leaned forward slightly, in his chair, and, speaking more slowly and clearly than usual, he said, "Operator Bob Goodman, Control Operator, uh, Branting."

"Observing?" asked Branting.

"Ranked Operator McColl, sir," McColl said, briskly. "Should I get someone in here of a higher rank, sir?"

"Oh, I think I've got sufficient rank for all of us, don't you, McColl?" said Branting, smiling and trying to put the two men a little more at their ease. He looked into their faces, and then realised that his ploy couldn't possibly work, because of the reverse-recognition filter in the system.

"Hold on," he said, rising from his chair, and moving towards the recording device, his dark suit and pale shirt filling the screen in front of Goodman and McColl until they could see only a pale grey blur.

The man that sat back down didn't look anything like the man who had introduced himself as Branting. He was short and stocky, and swarthy, with a shock of very dark hair, and eyes that turned down slightly at the corners.

"Sir?" asked McColl.

"Let's start again, shall we?" said Branting. "Control Operator Branting, interviewing."

The formalities were over quickly, and Branting was able to put McColl and Goodman at their ease, with his sympathetic approach and his winning smile. A large part of any Control Operator's job was communication. All political posts were filled according to ability, but one key factor in measuring how effective a politician might be was by gauging his popularity. Branting was likeable.

"You filled in a questionnaire for us," said Branting.

Bob looked at McColl and then back at the screen before answering, "Yes, sir, a psychometric test, as far as I could tell. Not the usual, though."

"No, not quite the usual," said Branting. "You said something to Agent Operator Henderson when you were on the Service Floor; something about body language."

"I could see his reflection on my screen. I didn't mean any disrespect."

"I wanted to know if there's a connection, for you, between people and their screen readings."

There was a pause. Goodman looked down, and then at McColl. He looked briefly up at the screen, but not for long enough for the Agent Operator to hold his gaze.

"By which I mean," said Branting, "for instance, if you were to meet someone for the first time, could you say what their screen might look like?"

"I don't know," said Goodman. "It would depend."

"What would it depend on, do you suppose?"

"I guess it would get easier the stronger the personality. When I first arrived at the College, thirty-odd years ago, I used to play this little game..." His voice trailed off. "...I don't want to waste your time," he said, looking at Branting.

Branting smiled.

"No," he said, "this is very interesting. Go on. Please."

"I used to play 'spot the Master'. I'd walk around College, and when I saw someone that I thought might be a Master I'd say 'good morning' or 'good afternoon, Master'. Mostly they didn't reply, and sometimes they'd get a bit jumpy, which was a good sign that I'd hit the nail on the head."

"And how often were you wrong?"

"Oh, I don't know that I was ever wrong," said Goodman, "except it did get harder, because pretty soon, I'd spotted all the Masters and I switched to Companions. Same game: 'good morning, Companion', or 'good afternoon, Companion'."

Branting looked at Goodman, intently, and said, "How long did this little game last?"

"Oh, things changed pretty soon after I got here. Everyone knew pretty much everyone, and when she found out that I wasn't spending all my time in the School, my Senior got a bit difficult and started keeping an eye on me.

"Then I joined Service, and it's not so interesting with Operator types. We're all pretty much alike, and we all know each other. You can only play the game with people you don't know."

"So, you started playing this game when you were in the School?" asked Branting.

"Pretty much as soon as I got here, after being Drafted. I was just a kid," said Goodman.

Branting flicked through the file, on the desk in front of him. He stopped to check a fact, and then looked out at Goodman. He smiled.

"You were eleven," he said.

McColl looked at Goodman. Goodman didn't notice.

"Does that surprise you, Operator McColl?" asked Branting.

Goodman looked at McColl, surprised by the question.

"Excuse me, sir, but I thought I was just here to observe," said McColl.

"Then offer me your observations on the matter," said Branting.

"I don't know. Either it's pretty impressive, or it's a good party trick. I don't know which. How does a kid work people out that quickly, though?"

"Good question," said Branting. "Would you like to answer that for us, Bob?"

"I don't know," said Bob. "I just thought everyone did it. Can't you tell what a person's like just by looking at them?"

"Not always, no," said Branting, referring back to his notes. "You've been an Operator for over thirty years?"

"Sounds about right."

"You've never put in for a promotion. Why is that?"

"I don't know. I like the screens. I like the people on the screens. It's not like mind-reading, but some of the minds I've seen in my work have been pretty cool."

"How so?"

"You know. You can tell when you're looking at a Master's brain. Totally different to when you're looking at a Senior's brain, say."

"Yes," said Branting, "the rate of pulsation might be different, the intensity of the corona... that sort of thing."

"I suppose so, but it's more than that. A Master's mind works differently. His emotions are scattered in different places in his brain, and are diffuse, so you get to see more of the intellect at work. With most people you can see how happy or sad they are, or angry, or bored. Sometimes I fancy that someone's in love. You can tell when someone's thinking about something mathematical or visual, or whether they're having a good memory, or listening to music.

"If I was watching a Master's screen while he was listening to music, I might only pick up intellectual stuff about the mathematical puzzle of the music, rather than how he feels about it. Stuff like that.

"Usually, of course, we don't know what they're doing. We're not supposed to know. Anyway, Masters' patterns are different to all the others."

McColl looked at Goodman again.

"You can tell all that?" he asked.

"I think so."

"Can you gauge personality types?" asked Branting. "You claim that you could tell, by looking at people, who was a Master, and you can tell that on-screen, but what about everyone else?"

"What about everyone else?" asked Goodman.

"If I showed you some screen footage, or wafers, could you tell me what's going on in the subject's head?"

"I don't know. I don't think we're supposed to do that. Aren't there privacy laws or something? We're not supposed to know whose screen we're watching, after all, are we?"

"No, you're not, but you do understand that we're in a very difficult situation."

"The Code Status, you mean?"

"Yes, the Code Status," said Branting, looking slightly distracted for the first time since the interview started.

"You're really worried about it, aren't you?" asked Goodman.

"I realise," said Branting, "that you aren't expected to understand all the implications of our current Code status, and it isn't your concern, of course, as a basic-grade Operator, but, yes, I am worried. We are all very worried, and we don't have much time to get to the bottom of all this, and find some solutions."

"I thought it was a test," said Goodman, looking at McColl. McColl shrugged his shoulders. "Because of the Master's screen."

Branting leaned forward in his chair, filling the screen in front of McColl and Goodman.

"What about the Master's screen?" asked Branting.

Goodman looked a little confused, and then his face started to turn white.

"I was joking with Agent Operator Henderson..." he said, his sentence tailing off. He looked from Branting to McColl. "I thought he was acting... I thought he'd learnt some basic body language, and was using it to keep us all fooled... I thought..."

"Calm down, said Branting. "Bob, calm down and just look at me."

Goodman could hear a muffled voice as if from a long way, away, or through a terrible loudspeaker turned to minimum volume. He put his head in his hands, and then ran his hands down his face. The colour in his cheeks began to come back a little.

"Calm down, Bob, and concentrate, for me," said Branting. "We are at Code Orange. The Code status has been ramping up for several days, and, no matter what we do, we don't seem able to control the situation. We haven't even worked out, yet, what the situation is."

"Code Orange. Not because of the Master, though," said Goodman.

"One of our Actives has been undergoing some mental/emotional changes," said Branting, "and the balance of his mind appears to be in danger. We also believe that he has transmitted his problem via the mini-print slots to other Masters and Actives, globally."

"Not our Master," said Bob. "Not the screens on the Service Floor." He hesitated again, and then turned his head to look at McColl. "Why are all the screens on the Service Floor looking at our Master, here, if an Active is in such trouble?" he asked no one in particular. "Why aren't we working on the Active's screen?"

Bob got out of his chair again. He looked from McColl to Branting and back again, and then gestured, wildly with his arms.

"I have to warn them," he said. "I have to get back on the Service Floor and tell them they're looking in the wrong place."

"McColl," said Branting, "you need to help me with Operator Goodman. I need him to calm down."

Bob Goodman seemed almost entirely oblivious to Branting and McColl, and what was going on in the interview room. He was fighting with his chair, standing up and sitting down, by turns, and wiping down the length of his face with his left hand. His composure was utterly gone.

"Yes, sir," said McColl, half-standing, and taking Goodman by the elbow. "Bob," he said, pulling himself upright. "Bob?"

McColl turned Bob towards him, and got hold of both of his elbows in his hands. He held him firmly, and spoke right into his face.

"Bob, we've got a job to do," said McColl. "You've got a job to do. Control Operator Branting is going to ask you some questions, and I need you to answer them, okay?"

"But it's wrong," said Bob Goodman. "They've got it all wrong, and there's no time!"

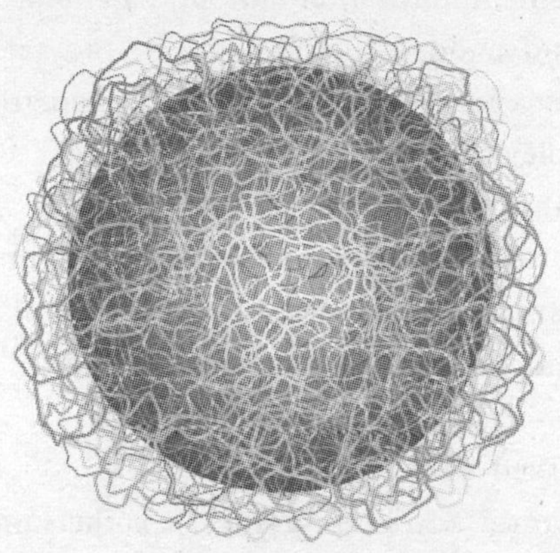

Chapter Forty-One

Tobe and Metoo had not left the flat for forty-eight hours, and Tobe had only worked one day in the cycle so far.

Metoo got up a little before her regular time and delivered eggpro, toast and cereal to the garden room, for Wooh and Saintout.

"Are you ready for this?" asked Saintout, taking the tray from her.

"No," said Metoo. "I don't know." She turned and left the room, and Wooh shrugged at Saintout.

"We'll see," she said.

"I hope so," said Saintout.

At 06:00, the shower was running, and Tobe's eggpro was sitting on the counter waiting for him. Metoo had watched him open the door to his room, and walk down the corridor to the bathroom, still wearing his robe. The bathroom door had closed behind him, but Metoo didn't hear the lock turning and shutting him in. She breathed a sigh of relief.

Three or four minutes after 06:00, Tobe emerged from the bathroom, and padded to the kitchen. He sat on his stool and tucked into his breakfast, apparently hungry. He finished within a couple of minutes.

"It is the same," he said.

Metoo stopped filling the auto-clean and stepped up next to Tobe. She leaned over and took the dish from in front of him.

"You've said that every morning this week," said Metoo. "What do you mean?"

"What?" asked Tobe.

"'It is the same.' You keep saying, 'It is the same'."

"It is the same," said Tobe.

"What is the same?"

"Breakfast."

Metoo crossed to the other side of the counter, so that she was facing Tobe, still holding his dish in her hand.

"I can make you something else, for breakfast, if you like."

"Why?"

"Because it's the same. Perhaps it's time for a change."

Tobe looked at her.

"But it's the same," he said.

Metoo wasn't sure what Tobe was driving at, and didn't want to upset him ahead of the long day that they both faced. She left it alone.

By 08:30 everyone had eaten, except Metoo, who couldn't face food, but she had managed to have a conversation with Tobe about what the day would bring, and he seemed very settled, sitting at the kitchen counter with his empty tea-cup in front of him.

A tone sounded in the flat, and Metoo went to sign in, her heart beating a little faster than usual. This was it; this was the call.

Metoo signed out and went to the front door of the flat, where Saintout was waiting to be let in. Metoo called Tobe out of the kitchen, and the three of them stood in the hallway.

"You remember Saintout," said Metoo.

"French," said Tobe.

"A long time ago," said Saintout, smiling, but keeping his hands in his pockets. Metoo had primed him as best she could in the time available, and he knew that trying to shake hands with Tobe was out of the question.

METOO HAD DECIDED that, if she was going to do this at all, she was going to do it on her own terms, or as close to her own terms as humanly possible. Her attempts to interview Tobe, the previous day, using Wooh's questions, had failed, and she felt like she was losing control of the situation. She clung, in vain, to the small amount of influence remaining to her.

Saintout climbed out of the garden room window, and walked around the outside of the building to the front door of the flat. Doctor Wooh remained in the garden room.

Metoo spent some time, after breakfast, explaining to Tobe that she needed to go out for a little while, that Service wanted to interview her, and that it was strictly routine, and nothing to worry about.

Tobe had insisted that he wasn't worried about anything. Never-the-less, Metoo had explained, she wanted her friend to stay in the flat with Tobe, just to make sure that he was safe. It would be fine; her friend could stay in the garden room, out of the way. Tobe wouldn't even know that he was there.

It was more than an hour before Metoo was comfortable about the whole arrangement. Tobe seemed fine with it pretty quickly. Metoo told herself that it was because Tobe didn't understand what she was saying to him, but nothing she said seemed to frighten or disturb him.

"SAINTOUT WILL STAY with you while I go to see Service," said Metoo. "I'm so sorry about this, Tobe, I'll be back as soon as I can manage."

"We'll be okay, won't we, Master?" asked Saintout. "The Master and the Frenchie."

"Frenchie," said Tobe, smiling broadly. "Master Tobe and the Frenchie."

"God, it sounds like one of those bad straight to vid police-thriller-romance things," said Metoo.

"Seriously," said Saintout, "what could possibly go wrong?"

"What could possibly go wrong?" asked Master Tobe.

"Maybe, while she's gone," said Saintout, leaning in to Tobe, and speaking to him conspiratorially, "you and I can play a game."

Tobe stepped back from Saintout, unable to bear anyone, let alone a comparative stranger, in his personal space. He stepped away, but he didn't panic.

"What game?"

Saintout took his cue, and kept at arms-length from Tobe.

"A get to know you game," he said. "We take it in turns to ask each other questions, and answer them, and then we have a contest to see who knows the most about the other person."

Tobe looked at Saintout, quizzically. Metoo took hold of Tobe by the face, one small hand on either cheek.

"I probably won't be gone that long," she said to him. "If Saintout bothers you, or you don't like him being here, he'll go into the garden room, okay?"

"And if you really can't stand me, I'll leave," said Saintout.

"Frenchie leave," said Tobe, his face expressionless. Saintout punched Tobe lightly on the shoulder, still at arms-length, and laughed at the suggestion.

"Not yet, Buddy, surely," he said. Tobe jolted sideways, slightly, from the play punch, taken unawares, but the expression on his face didn't change.

"Buddy?" asked Tobe. "Who's Buddy?"

Metoo held Tobe's gaze for a moment.

"I won't be long," she promised, casting a determined gaze in Saintout's direction. "Look after each other."

"We will," said Saintout, "won't we, Buddy?"

"Who's Buddy?" asked Tobe.

Metoo shot Saintout another look, and then left the flat.

Doctor Wooh remained in the garden room. She put on her headset, positioned the bead in her ear and dropped the little screen down in front of her face. In the hour between breakfast and the appointment time, while they waited for Metoo to prepare Tobe, more equipment had arrived via the garden room window. Saintout had inserted a mini-bead into his ear, and fixed a comm-camera, fashioned in the shape of a Service badge, on his lapel. Both should be totally undetectable, unless Saintout got very unlucky.

Doctor Wooh had the text of all the questions that Service wanted Master Tobe to answer; it was her job to relay them to Saintout, via the mini-bead. She would whisper in his ear, and monitor everything from Saintout's point of view, or from the point of view of Saintout's lapel, at least. She was grateful that he was taller than Metoo and Tobe; maybe, she'd be able to pick up some of the Master's facial expressions, which might help her to decode his answers. In the meantime, she knew that Service would be watching. All screens on the Service Floor would be on Tobe.

Saintout stood where he was after Metoo left. He didn't want to cause Tobe any problems by moving around too quickly, or going somewhere he wasn't wanted. Tobe stood next to him, in the hallway. After three or four minutes, Saintout decided that he'd have to make some sort of move.

"I'd like a drink, if that's all right?" he asked. "Can we go into the kitchen?"

"Kitchen," said Tobe, turning and making his way down the corridor. He entered the kitchen first, walked around the counter, and sat down on his stool. Saintout hung in the doorway until Tobe was sitting down. There was one other stool in the kitchen, opposite Tobe's, on the other side of the counter: Metoo's stool.

"Can I sit here?" asked Saintout.

"Metoo's," said Tobe. Saintout took that to mean 'no', so he stood at the counter next to the stool.

"Can I make you a cup of coffee?" asked Saintout. Tobe laughed, as if Saintout had said something foolish.

"Metoo drinks coffee," said Tobe.

"Lots of people drink coffee."

"Tobe drinks tea at breakfast time, or water."

"Fair enough. We'll have water, then, shall we?"

Saintout stood for a moment, waiting for an answer, but none came. So, he walked around the counter, giving Tobe a wide berth, and made his way to the sink. Four or five glasses stood next to the tap for drinking water. Saintout hesitated again. All of the glasses were different shapes and sizes. He knew that if he picked up the wrong glass anything might happen.

"Which is your glass?" he finally asked Tobe.

"The big one, of course," said Tobe. Saintout began to wish that Tobe was more capable of hiding his disdain, but at least the Master seemed to feel in control of the situation, which might make him more tolerant of the Operator's presence. Tobe obviously didn't view Saintout as any kind of threat.

Saintout picked up the largest glass, and began to fill it from the tap.

"No. No. No!" said Tobe, suddenly, almost making Saintout jump. "Too full. Too full," he said, thumping the side of his head lightly with the knuckles of his fist.

Saintout looked over his shoulder at Tobe, but couldn't read the expression on his face.

"It's okay," he said. "Look, I'll pour it away. It's fine." He poured the water into the sink.

"No!" shouted Tobe, again, thumping the side of his head more deliberately.

Saintout took a breath, and said, "Why don't you tell me how to do it? Look, I won't do anything until you're calm and we can work this out, properly. You know how to do it, don't you? So, you can make sure that I do it right."

After three or four minutes, Tobe stopped thumping the side of his head, and looked back at Saintout, who was standing as still as he could, his hand clasped around Tobe's glass.

"Do it like Metoo does it," said Tobe.

"And how is that?" asked Saintout.

Doctor Wooh watched on her screen as Tobe talked Saintout through the pouring of water. When it was wrong, Saintout was not allowed to pour the water down the sink. He should've known better. Water was conserved at all costs, drinking water, especially. If the water in the glass was wrong, he was to pour it into a large jug in the fridge, which Metoo always used to fill her glass.

The large glass that Tobe used was moulded with a series of scalloped ridges, running up the sides, like an old-fashioned soda glass. The water had to be poured in one go, and should come up to the curved tops of the ridges. Too much and the water was poured into the jug, too little and the water was poured into the jug. If the water was poured incorrectly, the glass had to be rinsed and dried thoroughly with a blue tea-cloth.

How the hell does she manage this? Saintout wondered, packing the glass with the cloth and then rotating it to thoroughly dry the inside. *Is he the same with everything?* He decided that when this was over, he'd have a lot of questions to ask Metoo.

Saintout poured the water correctly on the third attempt.

POLICE OPERATOR STRAUSS greeted Metoo on the other side of the door, and led her out of the building and across the site to Service. She didn't speak to her escort, not out of rudeness, or because she didn't care for her, but because she was worried about Tobe, and nothing seemed to take that worry away. At least, she wasn't worried about Tobe; she was worried about so many other people worrying about Tobe.

Metoo and her escort rode the elevator to the exterior gallery, and entered a small interview room. It was the room where Pitu 3 had been questioned, although there were no signs of the room's previous use.

"Take a seat," said Police Operator Strauss. "I'll be observing the interview, but I'm just going to step out for a moment."

Metoo sat alone for a few minutes, unaware that she was being watched. The vid-con screen in front of her was black, apparently inactive. She sat, quietly, looking into the black screen, almost as if she was in a trance. She was counting her breaths, slowing them down, so that she could think clearly, so that she wouldn't be caught off guard, so that she wouldn't appear flustered or incoherent. She just wanted everything to return to normal, and if being interviewed by Service would make that happen, she would endure the indignity.

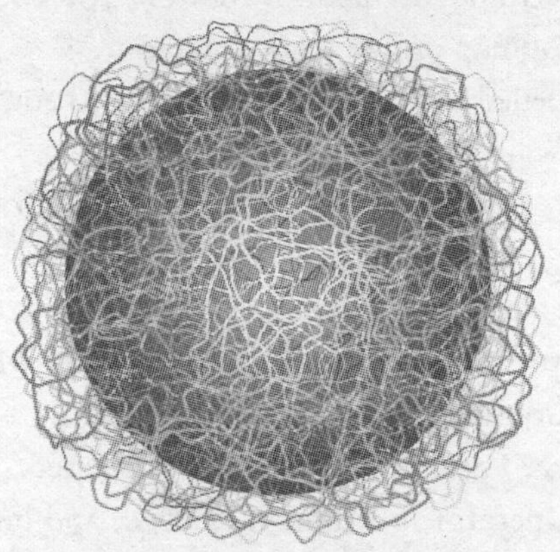

Chapter Forty-Two

BRANTING WAS LOOKING intently at the vid-con screen, deeply concerned for Operator Goodman, and for the implications of his breakdown in the light of the crisis.

The door into the little room opened, and McColl saw Branting raise his head. The Control Operator appeared to be looking over the top of him and to the right. He gestured at something that McColl couldn't see, except that he was almost tempted to turn around, and look behind him.

The door opened into Branting's interview room, and Qa thrust his head around it, holding a piece of paper up in his hand. Branting looked over the top of the screen at him, read the scrawled message on the piece of paper that Qa was holding up, and waved a hand. Qa retreated.

"If you could just stay there for a minute or two, gentlemen," said Branting, getting out of his seat, and nodding to McColl. Goodman had still not recovered his composure. "I won't be long. Perhaps, Ranked Operator McColl, you could try to calm Operator Goodman down, while I step out."

Branting opened the door of the interview room to find Qa in the corridor, waiting for him.

"Okay, Qa, you've got my attention," said Branting. "What is it?"

"We've got another one."

"So your little message said, Qa, but another what?"

"Another Goodman."

"You're sure?" asked Branting, visibly excited.

"She's an Operator in Mumbai College, and her score on the test was exactly the same as Goodman's. Her profile didn't seem remotely similar, but then I checked her Codes," said Qa, smiling.

"And?"

"Operator Perrett had been working a station on the Service Floor when she put through a query. She recognised that the subject at her Workstation had been changed."

"That happens," said Branting. "What makes her unusual?"

"She was young, she'd been in the job two Lows, she was fresh back on the Service Floor after a six week sabbatical, and she'd spotted a difference between two control subjects, who, for all sensible purposes, had the same screen."

"She picked up minute differences after a gap of six weeks?" asked Branting.

"She couldn't explain it, but she was adamant that the subject had been switched-out, and nothing could persuade her otherwise."

"And, she was right?"

"And she was right."

"Get her into an interview room, now," said Branting, "and splice her vid-con onto mine, so that I've got her and Goodman on at the same time."

"Done and done. Can I get you anything?"

"I'm fine. Good work, Qa, this'll all be over before you know it."

"Not before time, sir."

"Just one thing. When do we begin interviewing the Assistant-Companion?"

Qa looked at his watch, and said, "Any time now, sir, if she's on time for her appointment."

"Does she strike you as the type that would be late?"

"No, sir, she doesn't."

"You'd better make that a three-way split on the vid-con, then. I want them to be able to see her, so let's keep multiple channels open between the three locations, please."

"Four."

"What?"

"Four locations, sir. Your room, one in Mumbai, and two at College Ground Zero."

"Is that what we're calling it now?"

"Yes, sir."

"Four, then," said Branting, turning back to the door he'd come out of only minutes before.

A TONE WAS sent to Perrett's room. It was 13:40 in Mumbai, and she was in a Repast/Recreation cycle. She'd hit her button for Repast only two hours ago, and wasn't due back on duty for another six hours. She signed in.

"Operator Perrett," she said.

"Repast cycle terminated, await escort to Service Floor," said Service.

"What for?"

"Please await your escort."

Perrett signed out. She cleaned up a little, and changed her robe. If she was being called back into Service, it wasn't to go back on the Service Floor; the first to be called back in an emergency would be the group completing a Rest cycle. The Global situation might be complicated, but there was no reason for her to be called back to her Workstation. Something else was happening, and Operator Perrett wanted to make sure that she was prepared.

A Police Operator arrived to escort Perrett back to Service.

"Can you tell me what's going on, Police Operator...?"

"Black," said the tall, dark female Operator. "I can't tell you. Apparently this is all 'need to know', and the powers that be haven't deemed it necessary to bring me in on their plans."

"Oh."

"I wouldn't worry. I'm just the escort; I've got to hand you off to Ranked Operator Chandar. Do you know him?"

"I know of him," said Perrett, her small face pinching into a strained expression. "Thanks."

Black escorted Perrett into the Service building, up to the exterior gallery, via the elevator, and into a small interview room, half a storey below the Service Floor. Perrett had not been in one of the rooms before. It was small and windowless with only one entrance/exit. There was a table in the room, and two chairs, one of which was already occupied by a large, older man with broad white streaks in his dark hair. Perrett didn't want to assume that the other chair was for her. She turned to Black, but she had already retreated, and the door closed a split second after Perret turned, her mouth half-open to speak to her escort.

"Take a seat," said the large man, without looking at Perrett.

Perrett pulled the chair out, and smoothed her robe over her behind as she sat down. Stress almost made her appear prim to anyone that didn't know her, and she hated it.

"What's happening?" asked Perrett.

"Haven't a clue," said the large man, who seemed remarkably unbothered by the whole episode.

"You're Ranked Operator Chandar?" asked Perrett, tentatively.

"That's right."

With that, the vid-con on the wall opposite flickered brightly into life before settling into a drifting snow-scape of white noise. It made Perrett jump.

When the fuzz cleared, the screen blinked into life, showing a small, dark-haired man, sitting in a chair with a pile of documents on a table in front of him. The man appeared to be looking over her left shoulder, and was mouthing words that she couldn't hear.

The screen blinked again, and this time, she saw a room just like the one she was sitting in, but facing her were two men, one of whom looked ill, and appeared to be being consoled by the other. Again, she couldn't hear what was being said, but they didn't appear to be looking at her.

BRANTING SWITCHED HIS point of view between the three rooms. He hadn't introduced himself to Operator Perrett, yet, but he could see her sitting in an interview room with Ranked Operator Chandar. Chandar seemed very relaxed, and Branting made a note to check out his file, in case the man could prove useful in the future, providing, of course, that they had a future.

He then switched to the second interview room at College Ground Zero. The room was empty. The time signature at the top of his vid-con suggested that his third subject was not yet late.

He kept the empty room on screen and waited. As the time

signature clicked over to the hour, the door to the empty room opened, and Branting caught his first sight of Metoo. She entered the room alone, as he had requested, and he had three minutes just to look at her, before her escort was due to return. He downloaded those three minutes of her in the room, ready to make the footage available to Goodman and Perrett, if required.

Police Operator Strauss closed the door to the interview room, and stood outside for the allotted three minutes. Then, she tapped lightly on the door, and let herself in.

Metoo appeared to be totally calm. Strauss entered the room, closing the door behind her, and sat down in the vacant chair.

The vid-con blinked and fizzed, and then drifting snow appeared to fill it for three or four seconds. When it had cleared, Metoo could see a small, dark-haired man sitting behind a desk. He smiled out at her.

"Hello, Metoo," said Branting. "I am Control Operator Branting, and, with your permission, I'll be interviewing you, today."

"You're tired," said Metoo.

"Excuse me?"

"You're tired," said Metoo, looking hard at Branting's image on the screen. "You've been working too hard for too long, and you're tired."

Branting sighed. "You're right, of course, but maybe, if you can see your way clear to helping us out, we can put all this behind us, and I can get some Rest."

"Maybe," said Metoo, calm, but still a little wary. "Tell me first, why am I here?"

Branting looked at Metoo, and put down the pieces of paper that he was holding in his hands.

"All right," he said. "That seems only fair."

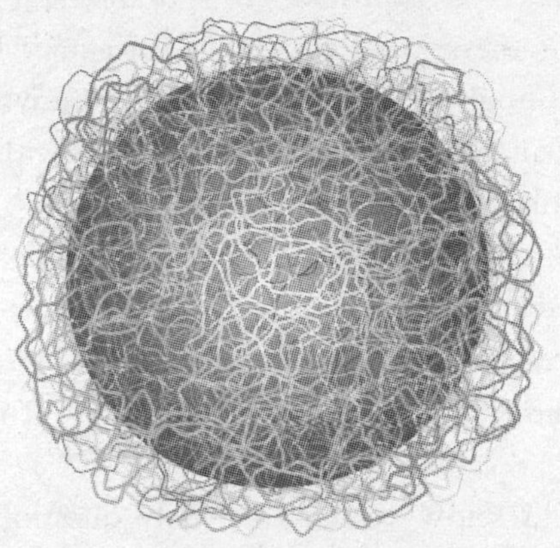

Chapter Forty-Three

MASTER TOBE AND Saintout sat on either sides of the kitchen counter. It had taken over an hour, but Tobe had finally indicated that Saintout could sit on Metoo's stool.

Doctor Wooh sat in the garden room, more than a little frustrated. She kept whispering the first few questions on the test into Saintout's ear, but he wasn't responding. To begin with, she thought that perhaps he couldn't hear her, so she asked him to cough if he was picking her up on his ear-bead. He coughed on cue.

It was almost eleven o'clock before Saintout decided that it was time to ask Master Tobe the first questions and see what happened. He had spent two hours with the Master, more-or-less, and he was already beginning to understand what Metoo went through on a daily basis. He was really beginning to think that the woman must be a saint.

"So, shall we play our little game, then?" asked Saintout.

"What game?" asked Tobe. "Tobe doesn't like games."

"Remember the getting to know you game? Come on, it's easy, and you might have some fun. Ask me anything."

Tobe looked at Saintout for several seconds without speaking. The silence started to get to Saintout.

"Okay," he said, "I'll start. What's your name?"

Tobe looked at Saintout, but the Police Operator still couldn't read his expression.

"Metoo told you Tobe's name," he said. "Tobe knows his name."

"You should know your name. Silly question really, but I thought we should start with easy stuff. What is your name?"

"Tobe. Master Tobe, the Students say. I call Tobe, Tobe."

"Now you get to ask me a question," said Saintout, tapping out a rhythm on the kitchen counter in front of him, unconsciously.

Tobe looked at Saintout, and asked, "Why do you tap?"

Saintout stopped tapping, and thought for a moment. "I don't know. It's the William Tell overture... I like it. My turn. What's your title?"

He already knew the first half-a-dozen questions; Doctor Wooh had been whispering them in his ear for almost two hours. These dull questions had been carefully chosen by a group of mental-health specialists to calibrate something-or-other. Saintout failed to see what good it could do, though, asking this man his name. It was all so undignified.

"Master Tobe, my Students call me," said Tobe. "I'm their Master, but I'm not your Master."

"Do you know how clever you are?"

"Yes. That's two questions. Now I get two questions. Who is 'William Tell' and what is 'Overture'?"

"Music," said Saintout. He wanted to ask whether Tobe

knew anything about music, or even liked it, but Wooh was whispering the next question urgently into his ear.

"How many Students do you have?" asked Saintout.

"Some. Not a lot. Fewer than before. There seem not to be so many. Does Saintout have Students?"

"No. Do you know the names of your Students?"

There was a long pause. Saintout assumed that Tobe was thinking about his answer to the question. He couldn't read the expression on the Master's face, and waited for a long time for a reply. He was about to give up, and ask the question again, when Tobe spoke.

"What is the probability that Saintout and Metoo would ask Tobe exactly the same questions?" asked Tobe.

Saintout was unsure what to do. Tobe hadn't answered his question, but the Police Operator knew enough about what was going on to know that maths was somewhere at the root of it all. Was Tobe giving him some clue about how to approach the global problem? What part did probability play in the crisis? Was maths the problem or the solution?

Doctor Wooh was whispering in his ear again.

"You have to try to ignore what he says and move on to the next question," she said. "I think you should ask him the question again." Saintout did nothing for several seconds.

"Ask him, again," said Wooh.

Saintout reached into his ear, and removed the bead. Tobe watched him. The bead was only a few millimetres across, and Saintout was able to pull it out by the tiny thread that nestled in the crevice above his earlobe, and palm the device without Tobe seeing it. With a bit of luck, Tobe would think that he was simply scratching his ear. He squeezed the ear-bead between his thumb and forefinger, and deposited the useless residue, nonchalantly, in his pocket.

Doctor Wooh could not see what Saintout was doing; she could only watch Tobe, watching Saintout, and his facial expressions weren't giving anything away.

"What is the probability that Saintout and Metoo would ask Tobe exactly the same questions?" Saintout asked Tobe. "Tell me about probability."

"Follow me," said Master Tobe, getting up from his stool, and passing Saintout on the way out of the kitchen. Saintout got up and followed Tobe down the corridor, and in through the door to the Master's tiny room. Tobe was almost bustling, and seemed, so far as Saintout could tell, to be in his element.

"What does Saintout know about probability?" asked Tobe.

"Nothing, really. I know that it's a way of working out how likely it is that something will happen."

"Good," said Tobe, in a tone that suggested an avuncular teacher. He started to draw a probability tree.

"If I toss a coin, it will land head-up or tail-up," said Tobe. Saintout wanted to laugh at Tobe's attempts at the vernacular, but bit his lip, and looked very seriously at the tree diagram. "Obverse or reverse. Each branch represents a toss of the coin, so the first stage is two branches: one for obverse and one for reverse. Each of the two branches has two branches: one each for obverse, one each for reverse. Tobe continued to draw as he explained.

Once he had the basic diagram with four branches, Tobe started to write along the branches.

"What is the chance of getting obverse with the first coin?" asked Tobe.

"It has to be one, or the other," said Saintout, "so, it's fifty-fifty."

"Or a half," said Tobe, writing 1/2 on the line, and the same for reverse. "So I've got an obverse with the first throw, what are the chances of getting an obverse with the second throw?"

"I don't know," said Saintout. "Less?"

"Yes, less, but every time the coin is tossed it's fifty-fifty that it's obverse." He wrote 1/2 on the second branch. The chance of getting obverse twice in a row is a half times a half."

"Which is what? My maths is shocking."

"Then, Frenchie must be very clever," said Tobe. "Tobe's maths is very clever, but it is logical, and not shocking at all."

Saintout smiled slightly. He tried to hide his responses, because he didn't want to offend Tobe. He'd completely forgotten that Tobe couldn't read expressions, and didn't know how to feel offence. He liked Tobe, and he wanted Tobe to like him.

"A half times a half is a quarter," said Tobe. "So the chance of getting two in a row of the same, obverse, or reverse is one in four."

"So the more times you toss a coin the less likely you are to get more heads in a row," said Saintout. "That's just common sense, isn't it?"

"It's not true."

"You just showed me that it was true, though."

"I tried tossing a coin. I tossed it a lot."

"And, what happened?"

"Fifty-fifty, except not every single time."

Saintout thought for a moment, more-or-less understanding, but hoping that Master Tobe might continue.

Tobe's head dropped and he started to giggle into his chest. It wasn't a man's laugh, but the noise a clever child might make, or the way a child might laugh at a joke.

"What is it?" asked Saintout, ducking under Tobe's shoulder height to try to catch his eye.

"Not ever on the odd numbers," said Tobe, giggling some more.

Saintout thought about that, and finally said, "Because you can't have half an obverse."

"Or half a reverse."

"Funny," said Saintout, smiling at Tobe. "Good joke, Buddy."

"Who's Buddy?" asked Tobe, suddenly serious again. "It's not true."

"You said that before. Tell me what isn't true."

"Can Tobe go to the office?" asked Tobe. "Tobe's work is at the office. There isn't room here."

"You want to look at your maths?"

"Tobe wants to look at the maths."

"You can't go to the office, today, but what if I got you a print-out from the mini-print slot? Would that do?"

"Tobe would like that."

"Okay, Buddy," said Saintout, "I'll see what I can do."

DOCTOR WOOH SOON realised that the sound was down on her system, and that, for whatever reason, Saintout couldn't hear her. She could hear him, though, and see what he and Tobe were doing. He wasn't asking the questions.

Doctor Wooh was soon signing into Service, urgently. She was horrified by what she was seeing. She had no idea what Saintout thought he was doing, but she knew that she had to stop it.

THE SHIELD WAS at risk of perforating, the Earth was at Code Orange, there was a maths virus loose in the mini-print system that no one had been able to get to the bottom of, and, now, some renegade Police Operator was offering to give the cause of it all a whole lot of new toys to throw out of his pram. This could not possibly end well.

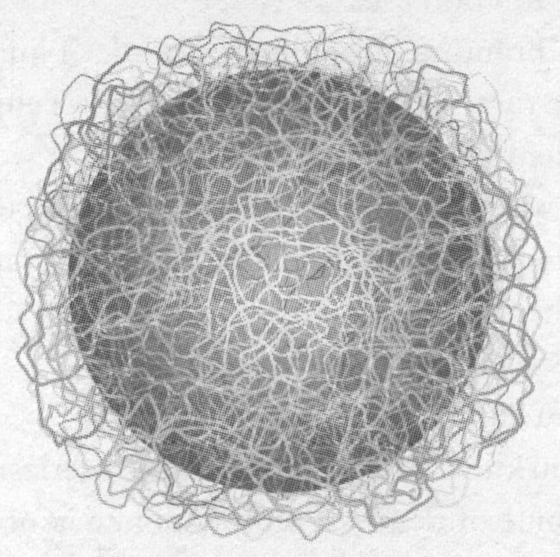

Chapter Forty-Four

BRANTING LEFT PERRETT with Chandar, and Goodman with McColl, and concentrated on Metoo.

"Why am I here," asked Metoo, again.

"Mostly, because you know Master Tobe better than anyone, and we're hoping that you can answer some questions for us," said Branting.

"We could have done that via Service; I could've stayed in the flat. We could've had a conversation without you putting a chip in my head."

"To be fair, you already thought you had a working chip."

"That's not the point," said Metoo, wearily.

"No, it isn't."

"So, why don't you trust me?"

"It's not a question of trust. If you lied to us, we wouldn't necessarily know that's what you were doing, even with the chip."

"The point is. I don't lie."

"No," said Branting, dropping his head, "I know you don't. You're a very rare young woman. Very few people have their chips permanently de-activated."

"So I understand, but you had a reason for de-activating it, and you had a reason for replacing it, and, as yet, you haven't explained either to me."

"Do you remember the selection processes?"

"I was just a child."

"Well, as you know, everyone undergoes a series of tests during childhood. Some of them are simply done via observation; we have lots of early-learning teachers who monitor children while they're still in their families.

"Then there are a series of intelligence tests, which begin when a child reaches about two years old, followed by a series of written tests, which begin when a child is eight or ten, depending."

"Depending on what?"

"The system isn't entirely regularised, globally. So, for example, a child who doesn't start day-school until he is seven will take written tests later than a child who begins at five."

"Okay, go on."

"Most children fit into a kind of average score system, and about two-thirds of those are not selected. Those who show a particular talent or intelligence level are automatically selected..."

"And the rest?"

"The rest fall into two further categories. At one end of the spectrum, the children continue to be tested, and about one in a thousand of those fall into the Master/Active bracket. Most of those children have already been selected, and the final tests are simply verification of what we already believed."

"And the other end?"

"That's where it gets complicated, because we really don't yet know what the people at the other end of the spectrum are truly capable of."

There was another long pause.

"Is that me?" asked Metoo.

"Sort of."

"Are you being deliberately obtuse? What is it that you're not telling me?"

"You fall into the rarest category of all. Do you understand the concept of altruism?"

"Of course. It's about doing good for its own sake, without reward."

"Yes."

"Although, I've never understood that. Doing good is its own reward."

"Exactly. You have answered your own question, and that is why your chip was de-activated. You are reliable. You have formed a bond with Master Tobe, which is, for all sensible purposes, permanent, indestructible, even."

"That's nothing."

"That's everything."

"Only to me."

Branting coughed and looked at his watch. He was aware that time was moving on, and he still had a great deal to do, not least with Metoo.

"I'm terribly sorry, Metoo," said Branting, "but we have a great deal to do, today, so I'd just like to ask you for your co-operation, and we can begin."

"I am more than happy to co-operate. Just promise me that Master Tobe is in safe hands, and that nothing bad is going to happen to him."

"The point of this exercise is to preserve Master Tobe at all costs," said Branting. "Rest assured, we have no intentions of harming him in any way."

"Good. What would you like me to do?"

Agent Operator Henderson paced the Service Floor. Service Central had let him know that Master Tobe was being interrogated, using a specified set of questions that constituted a particular psychometric test. A time signal was set to appear on-screen when the questions began. The nine screens tuned in to Tobe's mind appeared not to change at all, other than a few glitches between 09:00 and 09:30. They were within the normal parameters for Tobe, given that someone new had entered his environment. The glitches were, in fact, smaller than anyone on the Service Floor had anticipated.

It was close to 11:00 before the time signature lit up in the top right hand corners of the screens, and the line-checks began, in rotation, around the room. Workstation 1 began a line-check at 11:00, which Workstation 2 picked up as soon as One had finished, at 11:07. It would take about an hour for all the Workstations to complete consecutive line-checks, and then the process would begin again.

It was during the second line-check that things began to happen on the Service Floor.

The line-check wasn't necessary to show the changes in Master Tobe's mental/emotional activity. All twenty-seven Operators sucked breath in through clenched teeth as they saw the fizzing synaptic changes in distinct areas of the screen.

"Simultaneous line-check," said Agent Operator Henderson.

Armed with headsets of various styles and dates, Tech's danced around the Service Floor, providing the Operators with whatever they needed. Nine rubberpro spheres, set into scratched and greying counter-tops, rolled under nine hands, some of them sweating, or trembling slightly, one or two sticking.

The Operator at station 5 threw his hands in the air. The Operator standing behind him, pulled him off his chair, unceremoniously, and toggled the switch on the facing edge of the counter; he had taken over in less than ten seconds, but it could still prove to be ten seconds too long.

Babbage was one of the first to complete the line-check, but within four minutes, all nine Workstations concurred. The activity was in the emotional range, and scattered.

The readings were highly unusual for an Active.

"Get me Branting," Agent Operator Henderson said to no one in particular.

No one on the Service Floor looked in his direction. Then a Tech came up beside him, and handed him a headset.

"Here, sir," said the Tech.

"Thank you," said Henderson. "Okay, everyone, as you were."

QA WAS WORKING in his alcove, trying to find more Operators with test scores similar to those achieved by Goodman and Perrett. It was proving more difficult than he anticipated. He'd had about a dozen false positives: Operators with exactly the same scores as Goodman, who didn't appear to follow any of his traits. Qa hadn't ruled them out entirely; it was possible that they simply hadn't been in an environment where they could prove themselves. Goodman obviously took his skills for granted, and Perrett had only shown up because her scores were identical to Goodman's and she had a history of Codes that tied in with their hypotheses.

Qa found his third candidate with the second batch of tests, as they came through, an hour after the first batch. Operator Juan Marquez was working in Service in a College on the outskirts of Rio de Janeiro, and had filled in the questionnaire during his regular shift. He was not working Master Tobe's station on his College Service Floor, and did not understand why he was being escorted to one of the interview rooms adjacent to the Service Floor. A Ranked Operator, called Burgess, had simply come onto the Service Floor and escorted him off, leaving his Workstation temporarily vacant. It worried Marquez; Workstations were always manned, and everybody knew that the World was in crisis, so why would a working Operator be relieved of his duty and not replaced?

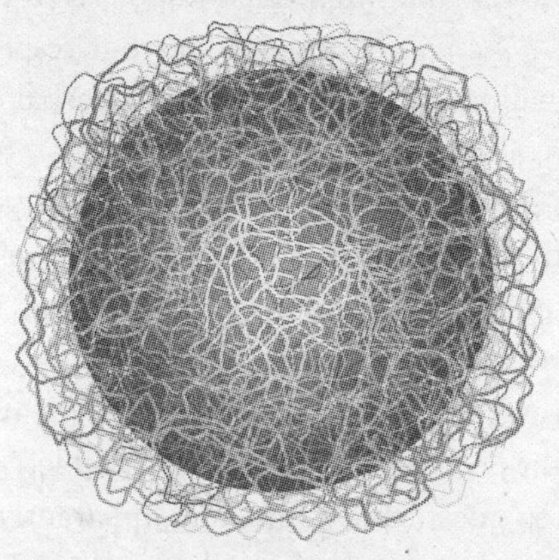

Chapter Forty-Five

BRANTING SWITCHED HIS vid-con so that Perrett and Goodman could both see and hear him, but could not see or hear each other.

McColl had spent some time calming Goodman down, and reassuring the Operator that Service knew what it was doing. He reminded Goodman of Control Operator Branting's status, and that Branting was by no means the last link in the chain of command. A lot of people were assessing the situation, people with a lot more training and knowledge than Goodman or McColl could claim to have.

"I know you've been working the screens for years," said McColl, "and you're a specialist in your field; that's why they're consulting you. Trust me; they know what they're doing."

Branting let him finish.

"Okay," he said, and McColl and Goodman, and Perrett and Chandar faced their respective vid-cons, expectant. "I'd like to test your emotional and intellectual responses to some images," said Branting. "We will be monitoring your responses via your chip, but we will verify those results with verbal questions and answers. Are you ready?"

"Yes," said Goodman.

"Yes," said Perrett, her voice a second or two behind Goodman's, because of the time lag on the vid-con from Mumbai.

"Pictures are going to appear on your screen, and I'd like you to categorise the people in them, if at all possible," said Branting. "If you want to guess, that's fine, too; apparently we can tell a lot about a person by the guesses they make." Branting's tone was light, and he smiled a lot, but neither Goodman nor Perrett was fooled; they could both feel the tension emanating from the Control Operator.

The first picture that appeared on-screen was of Bob Goodman.

"No comment," said Goodman.

"He's probably Service," said Perrett. "He's a bit old, but I wouldn't be surprised if he sat at a screen all day."

The second picture was of Perrett.

"Young, serious, ambitious," said Goodman. "She won't be reading screens for long."

"I'm not going to talk about me," said Perrett, a few moments later.

Branting showed slides of twenty or thirty individuals, from Service Operators to Politicians, and from Students to Civilians. Some of the faces were known to Goodman and Perrett, some were not. Neither subject commented on all of the faces, but, of those they did comment on, they were close to a hundred percent correct in their responses; more importantly, perhaps, on occasions when Goodman' and Perrett's evaluations did not match Service Findings, the two Operators had a better than eighty percent chance of agreeing with each other. Goodman scored a little higher than Perrett, over all, but Branting put that down to Goodman's age.

While they were undergoing the test, Perrett and Goodman were being monitored, as Branting had warned them, and Qa was processing wafers from their screens.

One of the last pictures that the Operators were shown was of Pitu 3.

"Miserable loner, poor sod," said Goodman.

"This boy needs help," said Perrett. "People don't like him, but he doesn't know why, and he's lonely. I guess he's a Student, not very bright, though."

The final picture was of Tobe.

"Master or Active," said Goodman.

"Definitely a Master," said Perrett, "sciences, or maths, maybe."

"Wait..." said Goodman. "... No, it's nothing."

"Would you like to explain?" asked Branting.

"No, sir," said Goodman. "It's just that he seemed familiar, somehow."

"Okay," said Branting, "thank you very much. We're going to break for ten minutes, and then I'm going to show you some film footage that I'd like you to comment on. The third part of the test will consist of a series of wafers that I'd like your thoughts on; the same applies: Say what you think, and guess if you like."

Metoo sat in the interview room for almost an hour, while Branting began testing Goodman and Perrett. He wanted at least three similar subjects, if he could possibly get three, before he started working with Metoo, in earnest. Half-way through the testing, Marquez was brought on-line, and his vid-con connection was completed in time for the second part of the test. He could catch up on the first section of the test, later.

Metoo could not hear Branting speaking to Perrett and Goodman, but she could see the pictures of faces that they could see.

"Are the pictures important?" she asked Police Operator Strauss.

"I have no idea," said Strauss. "I think everything is important at the moment.

"Yes, you're probably right," said Metoo. She sat, facing the screen, watching the faces coming and going.

She was monitored from the moment she walked into the room, and she was being filmed, although she was not aware of that. Her screen was being uploaded as continuous feed, and wafers were being produced at regular intervals.

Metoo looked intently at the pictures, and did not address Strauss again.

"He died," said Metoo when Pitu 3's picture came up on-screen. "I was so angry. I thought I was angry with him, but I wasn't. I was angry because I knew it; I knew how much pain he was in, and I did nothing. I should have done something."

Branting appeared on Metoo's vid-con screen a few moments after the last of the pictures was shown.

"Metoo," said Branting, "I'm going to ask you some questions, now. Just answer them in any way you can. This won't take long."

"I'm ready."

"The last picture you saw, how did that make you feel?"

"The picture of Tobe? I thought how unlike him it looked. It was nice to see his face, though, after being confronted with Pitu 3's picture."

"Tell me something about that."

"I should have done something, but he wasn't very likeable. I was too worried about Tobe to think about Pitu 3. I'll make an effort to get to know the Students. I know how hard it can be, but for him, especially, it must've been very lonely."

"Yes, I suppose it must. Do you feel responsible for his death?"

"I don't feel responsible," said Metoo, "I am responsible... I suppose we're all responsible, but it only takes one person to intervene. I could've made a difference to his life if I'd tried."

Branting asked Metoo a few more general questions about her gardening, and about how she felt about Police Operator Saintout and Doctor Wooh. Then he began to ask about Master Tobe.

"Have you noticed any changes in Master Tobe, recently?"

"How recently?" asked Metoo, buying time to frame her answer. She would not lie, could not, but she was determined to give cautious, measured responses to the more probing questions.

"In the last seven days, say."

"Yes. I have noticed some changes in him."

"Would you like to tell me what they were?"

"You have to understand that Master Tobe is a complicated person, and the things I am going to tell you might not be what you're expecting; this might not be what you want to hear."

"I only want to hear the truth."

"All right," said Metoo, still unsure of what she was doing, and how it would affect her relationship with Tobe in the future. She didn't answer his question.

Branting began again.

"Do you know Tobe's status?"

"He is a Master at the College."

"For how long?"

"Twenty years, I believe," said Metoo. "He must have been one of the youngest to have been made Master."

"He was. Does that mean something to you?"

"I suppose it makes me proud, although I had nothing to do with it, of course."

"How long do you think you'll be Tobe's Companion?"

"Assistant-Companion," said Metoo, stressing the word 'Assistant'. "I imagine that, after this is over, I will be relieved of my duties." She dropped her head, and Branting thought for a moment that she might be crying. He was surprised to realise that he felt terribly sorry for Metoo, and slightly horrified that it appeared he could not be impartial, at least where she was concerned.

"That is by no means a foregone conclusion," he said. "What do you understand to be the difference between a Master and an Active?"

"I don't understand the difference at all," said Metoo. "Are you asking me if I believe that Master Tobe is an Active?" she asked.

"No," said Branting, taken aback.

"Then, I don't understand where these questions are leading."

Branting sighed. Metoo was being honest with him, and it compelled him to be honest with her. They had so little time, perhaps it was better to get to the point, and hope that she could enlighten them.

"I'm trying to get as much information from you as I can," said Branting. "We need to know what's happening with Master Tobe; we need to know the cause of several thousands of people leaving the reservation."

"I'm sorry," said Metoo, "I don't understand."

"I need to know, from you, how to protect the Earth."

* * *

PERRETT, MARQUEZ AND Goodman watched Metoo on their screens. They watched continuous feed of her conversation with Branting, although, there was no sound, and they were not aware that she was in conversation. Neither did they know that the feed was live.

Goodman turned to McColl.

"That's got to be her," he said. "I never thought I'd see the day." He could not help but be thrilled by Metoo's presence in front of him. He had never thought to see an Empath's screen, let alone the face that belonged to the mind.

"Who is that?" Perrett asked. There was no answer; Branting was, apparently off-line.

"Excuse me?" asked Chandar.

"Nothing," said Perrett. "It's just... Do you know who that is? I don't remember seeing her face before, but..."

Chandar looked up for the first time since Perrett had entered the room. He looked at Perrett, and then at the vid-con screen. He took his glasses off and peered into the screen.

"No, no idea," he said. "She's beautiful, though, isn't she?"

"Very," said Perrett, "but that's not it. She's extraordinary. I've never seen anyone like her. Does Service know who she is? Does Branting?" Perrett had pushed her chair away from the table in front of her, and was getting to her feet. Chandar took hold of her arm, and pulled, gently, encouraging her to sit down.

"I'm guessing," he said, quietly, "they know exactly who she is. Do you?"

"I know that I've never seen anyone like her," said Perrett. "There are rumours, obviously..."

"Rumours?"

Marquez sat in front of his vid-con screen, still a little bewildered by what was going on. There had been no real preamble, and he was thrust into watching the vid-con screen without knowing what he was supposed to be doing.

"Good-looking isn't she?" said Burgess, casually.

"Yes," said Marquez, staring at the screen.

Ranked Operator Burgess did not know why he was escorting Marquez, but he was sure that, whoever he was, the young Operator was going to figure pretty seriously in the outcome of the crisis.

"What are we looking at?" asked Burgess.

"The Mother of all things," said Marquez.

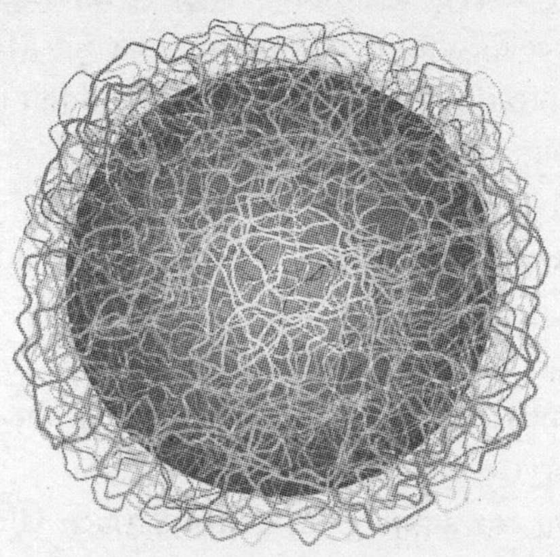

Chapter Forty-Six

"YOU KNOW YOU'VE got people worried," said Saintout, casually.

"Worried?" asked Tobe.

"The maths. People think that the World will end because of it."

"The maths? Tobe's maths?"

"Yes."

Master Tobe's chin dropped down onto his chest, and he began to giggle in a way that was most unnerving to Doctor Wooh, who was trying to watch her screen, listen to the audio, and get through to Service Global all at the same time.

Part of her desperately wanted to tear off the headset, and hurtle out of the garden room to find Police Operator Saintout, so that she could rip his head off.

Tobe eventually lifted his head. He didn't look at Saintout, but at the wipe-wall in front of him.

"The World will not end because of Tobe's maths," said Tobe.

"Why not?" asked Saintout. "They're talking about you at the top. Service Global is talking about you. Metoo has been summoned to testify about you. Why shouldn't the World end because of your maths?"

Wooh finally signed on to Service Global.

"Are you people watching this?" she demanded. "Why aren't you stopping it? Someone has got to stop him!"

There was no answer for several seconds, and Wooh was about to launch into another tirade when she finally had a reply from Service Global.

"Thank you for signing in," said Service Global. "Service will resume shortly."

Wooh breathed hard. She could feel her chest tighten as her body began to panic. She knew that she must keep herself in check if she was going to succeed, and she knew that she must succeed, at all costs. Wooh exhaled long and hard through her mouth, and then inhaled long and slow through her nose. She felt better in seconds.

"Anomaly status on Master Tobe?" she asked.

"That information is not currently available," said Service Global.

Saintout stood in front of the mini-print slot in the wipe-wall in Master Tobe's room.

"Isn't this thing hooked up to the wipe-wall in your office?" he asked.

"Tobe doesn't know."

"This is an older model, though, right?"

"Tobe doesn't like change. The mini-print is the same."

"The same as what?"

"The same as when Tobe came."

"Okay. Is this the slot that was in the wall when you moved in here?"

"Tobe doesn't like change."

Saintout took that to mean that the slot had not been replaced for a long time.

"And the slot in your office?" he asked, "Has that been there since you moved in?"

"Tobe doesn't like change."

"Well, it looks like this is your lucky day, then, Buddy," said Saintout, squinting at the keypad on the mini-print slot. "There's no compress button on this thing."

"It's not true."

"That's the third time you've told me that, and I still don't understand what you're saying. What isn't true?" asked Saintout, as the slot started to spit out pages of material that the Police Operator could never hope to understand.

Tobe watched, intently, as the slot spewed out page after page of his workings out.

It was all there. Tobe could see it in his mind's eye, and now it was all there, right in front of him. The mini-print slot was so ancient that it couldn't distinguish one set of instructions from another, and had automatically uploaded everything that was on the wipe-wall, and everything that had been lifted by the newly installed slot in the floor of Tobe's office.

"What is all this stuff?" asked Saintout, holding a ragged, disorderly sheaf of papers out to Tobe.

"Maths," said Tobe, in a tone of voice that suggested that Saintout was stupid. "The maths is all here! The maths from the linopro. All Tobe's maths is here." He took the sheaf of papers and began to look at them, putting them in order, counting them, and then re-ordering them.

"Now tell me something I don't know," said Saintout.

Tobe looked at him.

"It's not true," he said.

"You know what," said Saintout, grabbing the sheaf of papers back in one swift motion, "you're going to sit on that cot and you're going to explain exactly what you mean when you say, 'it's not true'. I'm sick of hearing 'it's not true', so explain yourself or be damned."

"It's not true, but Tobe doesn't know why."

"Hence the maths."

TOTALLY POWERLESS TO do anything, Doctor Wooh watched Tobe, and listened to both of them, via the comm-camera in Saintout's lapel. The bead was in her ear, and the view-screen was only a couple of inches from her face, yet she leaned over, in her seat, as if she was trying to get closer to what she was watching. Sitting in the chair in the garden room, her body was almost bent double; her forearms were resting on her thighs, close to her knees, and her neck was extended in front of her as if she was craning forwards to see something more clearly. He hands were clenched into tiny, tight fists that were jammed under her chin.

"That's it!" she cried, jumping up from her seat, and beginning to pace while she got back to Service. "That's bloody it!"

"LET'S GO BACK to first principles," said Saintout. "What was your initial hypothesis? Tell me the question that you were hoping to answer."

A tone sounded in Tobe's flat. Saintout looked up. He thought to ignore it, but knew that he shouldn't. The tone sounded for a second time, almost before the first had ended. Saintout pointed at Tobe.

"Stay there. Don't move. I'll be back in a minute."

"Service?" asked Tobe.

"Service."

Saintout signed in to Service.

"Master Tobe must be confined to the kitchen," said Service.

"Why?"

"Master Tobe must be confined to the kitchen," said Service. "Escort him, and remain with him."

"Great," said Saintout. He signed off.

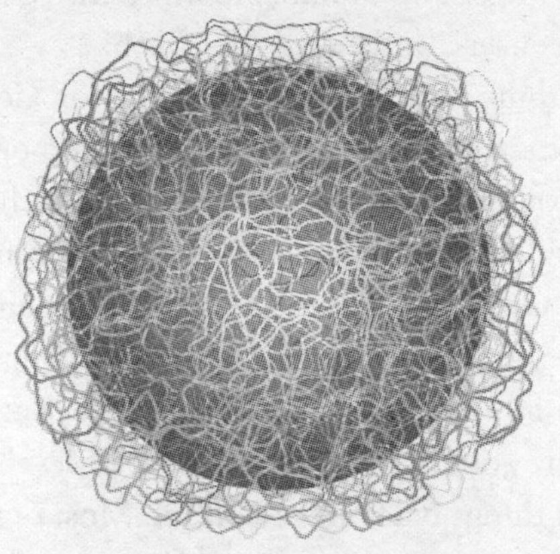

Chapter Forty-Seven

CLAXONS SOUNDED ON the Service Floor. The artificial light, set to a very particular bandwidth, pulsed violently for several seconds. One of the Operators at Workstation 8 vomited copiously all over the counter-top in front of him. The screen he was working at was pebble-dashed with old, undigested food. He looked at what he had done with huge, damp eyes, peering out of a grey face, and slid off his chair. Henderson stepped forward to replace him.

He looked once over his shoulder, and said, very loudly, "Anyone else?"

There was no reply.

The lights on the Service Floor stopped pulsing, and the pitch and frequency of the claxons changed dramatically, as if the working parts had been dropped into a very large basin of water.

Henderson keyed in his Morse signature, using the switch on the facing edge of the counter in front of him. He felt vomit on the tips of his finger and thumb. He wiped the residue off on the thigh of his trousers, and called for a Tech.

"Get something to clean this up with, for God's sake," he said. The woman in the dicky seat had been mopping gingerly at the edges of the pool of sticky yellow sick, but was afraid that if she tackled it wholesale, she would either incur the wrath of the Agent Operator, whom she suddenly found sitting next to her, or she would succumb to her weaker impulses and join her colleague in a stupor on the floor. Neither appealed to her very much.The good auspices of a couple of level-headed Techs soon brought things back under control. Most of the vomit was removed through the suction cleaner hoses under the counter, and one of the Techs rummaged around in the racks until he found a damp cloth that smelt of vinegar, which he used to wipe the last of the mess off the countertop.

The work surface still felt oddly tacky under Henderson's hands, but he managed to ignore the flecks of green and orange matter that had wormed their way into the mount that held the rubberpro sphere in place on the surface of the counter. Under almost any other circumstances, the whole incident would have been vile to Henderson. In the middle of a crisis, he was unflappable.

The ramp-up was happening again. The claxons and light pulses told everyone on the Service Floor that the system was approaching critical mass. Code Red was imminent.

If Code Red was reached, the Shield would no longer be impenetrable. The Earth would be visible to the Universe, and would, almost certainly, be destroyed. The planet would, at the very least, have to 'Go Dark'.

There were protocols in place for practising 'Darkness'. For four days a year, everything was switched off. In a new 'Dark Age', anything that required power would be disengaged from the source of that power. The World would be rendered dark and quiet. Manufacturing would cease. Travel by any method other than human or animal energy would end. The lights would go out. The only source of heat would be fire. Communications between nations, towns, and even people, would cease. Food would have to be grown locally, pipelines would stop pumping, turbines would stop turning. Survival at an individual level would become paramount, and there would never be an opportunity to return to a world of light.

Even in a new Dark Age, the Earth would be visible. It would not sparkle like a rich gem in the heavens, as it would, now, without the Shield, but it would not be hidden behind the magical cloud of synaptic energy that had been harnessed to render the Earth safe from prying eyes.

METOO FLINCHED, AND twisted in her chair.

"What's that?" she asked. "Is Tobe safe?" She could sense the faint wail of the claxons, beyond the near-soundproof walls of the interview room, and registered the ebb and flow of light at the edges of her vision.

Police Operator Strauss reached out and touched the back of Metoo's hand.

"I don't know," she said. "If it's important, Service will inform us."

Branting's face appeared on Metoo's vid-con screen. He had opened channels to all four of the interview rooms he was communicating with globally, and gave them all the same information.

"Okay," said Branting, "you might be experiencing some minor audio and/or visual disturbances. There is no need for immediate alarm.

"However, it is my duty to inform you that, without a resolution to the current global problem, the Earth will 'Go Dark' in approximately six hours. Time is of the essence. Good luck."

THE SCREENS IN the interview rooms went black. The interviewees stayed in their chairs, but Marquez was sweating and fidgeting in his seat, and Perrett was chewing her left thumbnail. Goodman was looking at McColl.

"This is it, then, is it?" he asked.

"Let's hope not," said McColl. "What can you give them? Can you give Service any hope at all?"

"Hope of what?" asked Goodman, his tone resigned. "They're not listening to me."

"Explain."

"They think this entire crisis has been caused by Master Tobe, right?"

"I suppose so. That certainly seems to be the assumption."

"Well, they're wrong. I'd stake my life on it."

"Go on, then."

"Go on, what?"

"Stake your life on it."

"Maybe I would, if I knew how the hell I could get them to listen."

McColl rose from his chair. He looked at Goodman, and then stepped, with one foot, onto the chair he had vacated, and, with the other, got himself onto the table they'd been sitting at. He raised his arms in the air and started shouting, and jumping up and down on the table.

"Aaaaaarghhhhhhh!" he screamed.

Goodman looked up at him. McColl seemed not to be

breathing, and the scream sounded like it would never end. Then, as abruptly as he'd begun, McColl stopped screaming, and leaned over, bracing his hands against his knees. He smiled down at Goodman.

"What the hell was that about?" asked Goodman.

"I wondered if I could get them to listen," said McColl, stepping off the table. "Seems not."

METOO GOT UP and began to pace up and down the little room, her eyes never leaving the vid-con screen.

"You need to remain calm," said Strauss. "We all need your help, and you won't be able to give of your best if you're in a state."

"How could I not be in a state?" asked Metoo, dropping back down onto her chair, ringing her hands together on the table-top in front of her. "Tobe has changed. I've noticed the changes, of course, but I've tried to ignore them. I only want him to be the person he was born to be, but that doesn't seem possible any more. He was Active, wasn't he?"

"I'm not privy to that information," said Strauss, "not many of us are."

"He was Active. I know that he was, and I've done something wrong. I've ironed out his specialness. I've made him ordinary. God forgive me, what have I done?"

BRANTING CAME BACK on-line on Perrett', Goodman' and Marquez's vid-con screens.

"Time is of the essence, Operators," he said. "You are one of three Service personnel that have been tracked down for their skills in reading screens, and people. We cannot verify that these skills are genuine, but early tests suggest that they might be useful, and, frankly, we have to try everything and anything we can to get through this crisis."

"I've got something to say," said Goodman. Perrett and Marquez couldn't hear him, but he managed to stop Branting in his tracks.

"You've got two minutes," said Branting.

"Master Tobe is not the perpetrator of this... whatever it is." said Goodman. "I have worked on his screen, and there is nothing wrong with him. His mental state is not deteriorating, if anything, it is stable and possibly even expanding.

"Whoever or whatever is causing the ramp-up, it isn't Master Tobe. You've made a terrible mistake."

"How sure are you of that?" asked Branting.

"As sure as I can be," said Goodman. "I just don't know if I can prove it."

Branting's vid-con screen went black. He stared at it, bewildered. The screen fizzed to life with drifting snow, and then blinked before recovering to show a small, elegant man in a very sharp suit sitting in front of him. Branting did not need an introduction. The man on the screen in front of him was responsible for the Earth's safety. He was the Minister for Global Security, and, possibly, the most important non-Active on the planet.

"Branting," said Special Operator Tibbets, "we need to consolidate, and we need to do it fast. Your department is the only one that seems to be making any kind of headway, so we are increasing your resources. We are also monitoring all of your activity, minutely. Be aware that you can be removed from your post without notice."

The screen fizzed again, and the Minister's face disappeared.

The wall adjacent to Branting's seat slid slowly back to reveal a bank of vid-con screens, arranged four high and six wide. Branting leaned to his left and hit a button on the wall. The screens fizzed to life to reveal swirling snow; slowly, one by one, Branting assigned them.

"Qa in one," he instructed, "Goodman in three. Then Service screen-feeds in seven and thirteen, Wooh's feed in eight, and Perret in nine. Finally, let's have Assistant-Companion Metoo's live-feed on fourteen, and put Marquez on screen fifteen."

Branting had organised a square of three screens, with Wooh's feed of Saintout and Master Tobe in the middle. Metoo's feed was directly below Tobe's, and the three screen Operators had the column of screens to the right of Tobe' and Metoo's. The two screens on the left were Service screens.

"Cross feed all screens," said Branting. "I want to make sure that anyone I choose has access to anything I choose.

"Qa, I need you to feed images to various vid-cons, as and when I tell you, okay?"

"OK," said Qa. "This is going to take a few minutes to set up. Do I have clearance?"

"This is all on me, but, if I get this wrong, none of that will matter any more."

"Yes, sir. What's first?"

"Put me through on Assistant-Companion Metoo's screen," he said, "and line up Master Tobe's feed."

Metoo watched the screen as Branting spoke to her.

"I know this is very hard for you," he said, "and I'm sorry that I have to keep you here, but, I am going to show you live feed of Master Tobe, during the time when I cannot be talking to you directly. I hope that it will help."

"Thank you," said Metoo, but she was not sure that Branting heard her; the screen had already switched to footage of Tobe.

Branting switched back to Qa.

"I want Metoo's wafers on screen thirteen, and Tobe's live screen-feed on seven," he said. "Then split feed them to Perrett, Marquez and Goodman, prioritising Goodman. I'll need to speak to them, so put me on their audio."

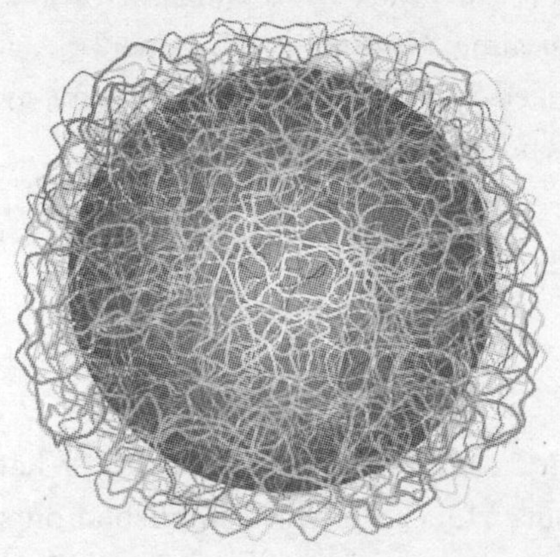

Chapter Forty-Eight

"TOBE KNOWS MATHS," said Tobe. "Metoo knows some maths, too, but Metoo knows everything else."

"Okay," said Saintout, "I can buy that, from your point of view, at least."

Master Tobe was sitting on his stool, on his side of the counter in the kitchen, looking up at Saintout. Saintout stood with his back leaning against the kitchen door, his feet crossed on the floor in front of him. He held the print-out, from the slot in Tobe's room, in his hands.

Doctor Wooh couldn't see Saintout, but he sounded far too relaxed for her comfort. On the other hand, she was relieved that Tobe seemed settled, and not at all bothered by the conversation that Saintout had foisted upon him. She just wondered whether the Tech team could get into and out of Tobe's room without Tobe realising it, either now, or later; later mattered less, since no one knew how much time was left to them.

"It's the same, every day," said Tobe. "I wanted to know how it could be the same. Nothing is the same."

"What?" asked Saintout. "What is the same every day?"

"Eggpro," said Tobe.

"And that's bad? I had some of Metoo's eggpro, and I thought it was brilliant."

"Not bad," said Tobe, "impossible."

"I DON'T GET it," said Branting to himself. "What the hell is he going on about?" Once Qa was established on screen one, he had tuned in to screen eight, to see Master Tobe, live. Screen seven then blinked into life, streaming Tobe's Service screen. Screens three, nine and fifteen all came to life at the same time, showing the Operators in their interview rooms, and, finally, Branting cued screens seven and thirteen.

SPLIT SCREENS APPEARED on the vid-cons in the Operators' interview rooms. The left hand screen started to fill with wafers that made Perrett and Marquez sit up and take notice. Chandar put down what he was doing, and looked up, too, when he heard Perrett's gasp. None of them had ever seen anything like it.

"That's got to be her," said Marquez, staring at the screen.

"Who?" asked Burgess. "No, don't tell me; that's 'the Mother of all things', isn't it?"

"Oh, yes," said Marquez, staring intently at the screen.

"That's her," said Goodman. "I never thought I'd see her screen twice."

"Wow!" said McColl. "You didn't tell me about this!"

"It's the girl," said Goodman.

"The girl?" asked McColl.

"The beautiful girl we were looking at when they showed us all that footage."

"This is her? How do you know?"

"I just know. Frankly, it comes as a surprise that other people don't know."

The right hand screens in the interview rooms fizzed into life, but instead of wafers blending from one to the next, this looked like a live Service screen.

"And we've all seen that," said Goodman.

"The Master," said McColl.

"I think we can probably cut the crap, now, can't we? And call him the Active."

"When did you know?" asked McColl.

"I don't know, but it doesn't matter, it's not him that's causing this bloody crisis."

Goodman looked again at the screens, his eyes flitting from one to the other.

"I need a line-check," said Goodman. He looked up slightly and said more loudly, "I need simultaneous line-checks on these two subjects, now!"

Branting's voice was calm, as he spoke to Qa. He left Goodman's audio channel open.

"Request concurrent line-checks on Master Tobe, and Assistant-Companion Metoo, Agent Operator Henderson," he said.

"Prep station 7," said Goodman, getting out of his seat. He left the room without further ceremony, and ran back onto the Service Floor as quickly as he could. He was a big man, but fit, and Chen barely had time to reset the switch on the facing edge of the counter-top, and vacate the seat, before Goodman was striding towards Workstation 7, the first place where he had seen Metoo's mind at work.

"He's right," said Perrett, from her interview room in Mumbai. "Look in the 60 to 80 range. There'll be an anomaly, on both sides. You'll see something in both subjects."

Marquez joined in. He was peering, intently, at the split screen vid-con in front of him.

"It's not the same, though," he said. "The intellectual and emotional cortexes are... I don't know... cross-pollinating, somehow. You won't find the same data in both subjects. Think laterally."

"Thank you, Operators," said Branting. He could not keep up with what they were suggesting, and could not see what they could see on the feeds in front of him, but the tests, so far as they had gone, had convinced Branting that these three Operators were a rich seam when it came to interpreting Service screen data. He secretly promised himself that he would never allow any of them to read his own Service screen.

Goodman completed the change-over in thirty-five seconds, a record, even by his standards.

"Who's doing the line-check?" he called over his shoulder.

"Who do you want?" asked Henderson.

"Mayer," said Bob, rolling the rubberpro sphere around under his hand. "Is Mayer on the Floor?"

"Here," said Mayer, bouncing out of the dicky seat at Station 9. "I've got the Active."

The glistening figure of eight was swirling on Bob's screen as he began the countdown for the simultaneous line-check.

"Line-check," they said, together.

"Verify," said the Operators in the dicky seats at Workstations 9 and 7, on cue.

"Verify line-check," said Goodman and Mayer, together.

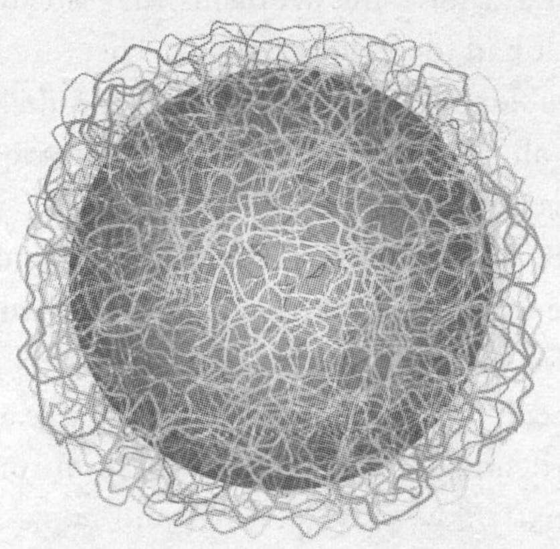

Chapter Forty-Nine

SCREEN 6 IN front of Branting fizzed into life. Snow drifted across the screen, and then it blacked out. There was no visual signal, but a jagged line crossed the screen, pulsing up and down, and back and forth to the sound of Qa's voice.

"Patching through Doctor Wooh, redirected from Service Global," said Qa. "Screen 6."

"Okay," said Branting. "Doctor Wooh, can you hear me? This is Control Operator Branting."

"Sir," said Wooh, breathily, the jagged line squeezing up with the frequency of her excited voice. "All of the maths is pouring out of the mini-print slot in Tobe's room, here in the flat. Send in a Tech team, and get the information out into the World."

"Done," said Branting signing off. The maths had been sent around the World via the mini-print slot in Tobe's office, without anybody knowing how the print-out related to the actual material in the office; perhaps sending the work out in its entirety would solve the problems that it had caused in its partial state. It had to be worth a try.

Wooh was able to relax, knowing that the Techs were in the flat, and that all possible information concerning Tobe's maths was being disseminated.

Metoo watched the same pictures that Doctor Wooh was watching. She too felt more relaxed than she had since leaving the flat, but for different reasons. She could relax, because she could see Tobe; it only remained for her to be reassured that he was his old self, and not some shadow of his former Active self.

"I TELL YOU what," said Saintout, "why don't I make us some eggpro?"

"It's not the same," said Tobe.

"Okay, Buddy, so talk me through it."

"Tobe gets up at the same time, every day. Tobe has a shower. Then Tobe comes here," he said, patting the kitchen counter in front of his stool. "The eggpro waits for Tobe, and Tobe eats it."

"So, every day, you come in here and eat the eggpro that Metoo makes for you. I don't get it. Why is that impossible?"

"Probability."

"You've lost me, Buddy."

Tobe looked up at Saintout, and said, "Who's Buddy?"

Metoo smiled at the screen. If it looked like her usual Tobe, and it talked like her usual Tobe, maybe it was her usual Tobe.

"What has breakfast got to do with probability?" asked Saintout.

"A coin," said Tobe in teacher mode, "has an obverse and a reverse. How many elements are there in breakfast?"

"I don't know," said Saintout. "No, hang on, I do know. I'm pretty sure Metoo told me how she makes Eggpro... What was it, again?"

"Tobe doesn't know," said Tobe, answering Saintout's rhetorical question. "There are more than two elements in breakfast. I know that. More than just obverse/reverse."

"I suppose so," said Saintout, but he wasn't really listening; he was trying to remember Metoo's eggpro recipe.

"Tobe doesn't understand cooking," said Tobe. "The more elements there are, the less likely something is to be the same."

Saintout was still trying to remember what Metoo had said, and didn't answer Tobe.

"Like a dice," said Tobe. "A dice has six elements, so the probability of throwing a one is one in six, or one-sixth. The probability of throwing two ones in a row is one-sixth times one-sixth, which is one-thirty-six. Should Tobe draw you a probability tree?"

"Two scoops of eggpro powder to one of powdered milk," said Saintout, hesitating for a moment before going on. "A pump each of salt and pepper, out of the dispenser, and let the steam do the rest: 45 seconds."

METOO LOOKED AT Strauss.

"I know what he's doing!" she said, beaming.

"We'd better tell someone, then," said Strauss, unable to keep a broad smile off her face.

GOODMAN AND MAYER worked through the line-check, while the rest of the Operators and Techs on the floor stood or sat in silence, barely able to move, hanging on with bated breath.

Every time either man called out a sector number the other checked the corresponding position on his screen.

The sparkling blue shoal that wove its way in a magical infinity symbol, like a figure of eight or a mobius strip, across Goodman's screen, was difficult to implement a line-check on; nothing on Goodman's screen remained static for long enough to read it thoroughly, even at the speed Goodman could work at, and the intensity of the pulsing lights obscured Goodman's view, even when he was able to home-in on something. It was also extremely difficult to track sectors in the line-check, since they seemed to be constantly on the move.

Operators Goodman and Mayer reset, zoomed in, and hovered, according to each other's instructions, but coordinating the two very different screens was proving impossible.

"Abort line-check," said Goodman. "This isn't working." He threw the switch on the facing edge of the counter, and got up out of the seat. "Stay on her, though," he said, as Chen took over.

Goodman walked up behind Mayer, and looked at Tobe's screen over his shoulder.

As soon as Goodman left the interview room, Branting filled screen twelve with live feed from the Service Floor, so that he could keep an eye on progress. When Goodman aborted, Branting apprised Perrett and Marquez of the situation.

"The line-check has been aborted," said Branting. "I need any ideas you might have, and I need them fast."

Perrett and Marquez acknowledged Branting, and went back to work, scrutinising the screen-feeds in front of them.

* * *

Ranked Operator Chen keyed in her signature using the toggle switch on the facing edge of the counter. She sat watching the screen for a few minutes, mesmerised by the ebb and flow of the light and colour, and the sparkling of the particulars as they followed each other around and around, forming a perfect figure of eight. She rested her hand on the rubberpro sphere set into the counter-top in front of her.

Chen had seen Metoo's screen before. She had been with Goodman when he had reviewed the screen; it seemed like months ago. She remembered suggesting that Goodman do a line-check, and she remembered him resisting her suggestions. Then the screen had...

"Oh my God!" said Chen, almost under her breath. She sat for a moment, staring at the screen.

"Goodman," she said, still barely making a sound, and then, "Goodman", a little louder this time.

Several seconds passed while the twenty-seven Operators on the Service Floor stared at their screens.

Branting switched audio out to Henderson's headset.

"Check out Ranked Operator Chen, at Station 7," said Branting.

"Goodman, sit here," said Henderson, throwing his switch, and leaving his seat.

"You're the boss," said Goodman, "but I should be –"

"Don't worry about it," said Henderson, cutting him off.

Agent Operator Henderson walked up behind Chen at Workstation 7.

"What is it, Chen?" he asked. "Control Operator Branting wants to hear what you have to say."

Chen stared more intently at the screen, partly because she couldn't take her eyes off it, and partly because she was willing herself not to turn around and look Henderson in the eye when she told him what she needed to say. She wanted to make sure that he listened to her, and took her seriously.

"It's this screen," said Chen. "The last time Goodman and I viewed this screen, there was a massive change, to a form that might be easier to complete a line-check on."

"Explain," said Henderson.

"She can't," Goodman called from across the room. Chen's voice had finally carried to him, and he rose from the seat that Henderson had just vacated. He crossed the room in barely a couple of strides, and was behind Chen before she'd had a chance to throw her switch. She did it now.

"I don't need to sit," said Goodman. "We just need to work out what triggered the switch from this pattern," he said, indicating the screen, "to the spherical pattern that followed it, the last time we had Metoo on screen."

"No names," Henderson said, trying to maintain discipline on a Service Floor that seemed to be heading dangerously towards a free-for-all.

"Goodman, my station will be reset to the Assistant-Companion's screen. Go... Sit until we have further instructions," he said, relaying Branting's instructions. Then he stepped back to the centre of the room. Branting had acknowledged that he was right to try to maintain Service Floor protocols, and he placed Henderson at the centre of the Floor with precisely that end in mind.

"Qa," said Branting, switching back to his aide, "I want new feeds for Master Tobe and Metoo. Scroll back through activity on Station 7, take the time signature for the section from 06:00 on day 4, and marry it to Master Tobe's time signature. Synchronise the feeds and get them up on my screens seven and thirteen as quickly as possible."

"They'll appear on Goodman's vid-con," said Qa, "and Perret's, and Marquez's."

"Good," said Branting, "the more the merrier.

"Wait," he said, and switched back to Henderson's audio channel.

"Goodman, Control Operator Branting wants you back in the interview room," said Henderson. Goodman threw the switch on the facing edge of the counter in front of him, rose from the chair, and crossed the floor in a blur. He left the Service Floor as quickly as he had arrived, and was sitting back in his seat in the interview room when the screen fizzed and snow drifted across it.

The vid-con screens in three of the interview rooms showed side-by-side feeds from 06:00 on day 4 of the event.

Perrett, Goodman and Marquez watched them intently.

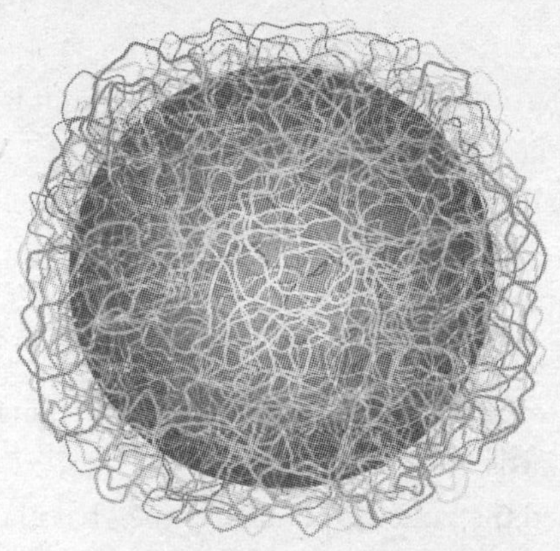

Chapter Fifty

"HELLO," SAID METOO, "can you hear me? Tobe has changed, but I think I know how, and I think I know why."

Assistant-Companion Metoo sat back in her chair, watching the vid-con, and talking to it, but not to her Master. She waited for a reply, but none came.

"Hello," she said again. "Hello?"

"I'll press my Service Button," said Strauss, beside her, "perhaps we can raise someone that way."

"No," said Metoo. "Just take me home." She rose from her chair, and raised her hand to the vid-con, as if waving goodbye to it.

Strauss rose, too, a little more hesitantly.

"It's okay," said Metoo, smiling. "Everything's going to be fine, really."

Metoo and Strauss exited onto the gallery, and left the building without anybody on the Service Floor realising that they'd gone.

* * *

"So," said Saintout. "It is your hypothesis that it is impossible to make eggpro the same every time?"

"It is impossible," said Tobe, "but it is the same."

"And you understand maths, but would you agree that I understand life?"

"Life? Tobe doesn't know about life."

"My point exactly," said Saintout, rummaging through the kitchen cupboards.

Tobe watched the Police Operator, somewhat alarmed by what was going on. Saintout anticipated the problem, though, and said, "Now, don't you worry about me looking through here. I'm just collecting the stuff I need for our little experiment. You understand experiments, don't you, Buddy? You do experiments with numbers all the time."

"Experiments with numbers," Tobe repeated. He tilted his head back, slightly, closed his eyes, and began to murmur under his breath. Saintout saw what he was doing, and started snapping his fingers right in front of Tobe's face, so close that Tobe could feel the disturbance the sound-waves made in the air around him. He opened his eyes.

"Stay with me, Buddy," said Saintout. "Watch this."

Saintout took the box of eggpro powder, and, using the scoop inside, measured out two level scoops full of the stuff into a dish. He took the powdered milk, and, using the same scoop, measured out a level scoop full of that, before adding it to the dish.

Tobe watched as Saintout took the dish over to the dispenser on the wall and pressed the salt pump once, followed by the pepper pump, once.

"That's it," said Saintout, vacuum sealing the eggpro into the steamer, setting the time to 45 seconds and closing the door.

"That's it?" asked Tobe.

"That's it, and now we wait for..." He watched the time counting down on the steamer clock. "... ten, nine, eight, seven, six..." He reached his hand into the drawer in the counter, and pulled out a spoon. He held it out to Tobe. "... three, two, one!"

The steamer stopped cooking, and Saintout opened the door. He took out the dish of eggpro, and put it in front of Tobe.

Tobe looked from Saintout to the dish of eggpro. He put his spoon in the egg and lifted it to his mouth.

"Ah!" he said, spitting Saintout's eggpro out, and jumping off his stool at the same time, dropping his spoon, and spilling the dish of eggpro down the front of his robe.

"Ah!" he shouted again, as the hot eggpro soaked through his robe, burning his chest.

"Oh no!" shouted Saintout, crossing to Tobe's side of the counter, and pulling at his robe to get it off over his head as quickly as he could, so that the Master didn't get badly scalded.

"Oh, Buddy, I'm sorry," he said.

"Hot."

"Yes. Why didn't you leave it a minute to cool down before you started eating it? You should've known it'd be too hot to eat."

Metoo had heard the commotion as she opened the door to the flat, and waved Strauss away. She rushed straight to the kitchen, where she found Tobe hopping up and down, while Saintout wrestled with his robe.

"Let me," she said, approaching them. Saintout stepped back, and watched while Metoo soothed Tobe. "Get me a cold, damp towel."

Saintout went to the sink and soaked a towel in water. He squeezed out most of the liquid, and handed it to Metoo, who pressed it against Tobe's chest. Tobe held his robe crumpled up in his hand, over his genitals, so that Metoo couldn't see him, and jiggled furiously on the spot while Metoo tried to calm him.

After five or six minutes of Metoo saying soothing things, and rolling the towel over his chest, every so often, so that the coolest part was always against his skin, Tobe grabbed the towel out of her hand, and waddled out of the kitchen, the towel and robe pressed against his body.

GOODMAN, PERRETT AND Marquez watched their vid-con screens.

Exactly five minutes into the footage, Metoo's screen coalesced into a sparkling mirror-ball of reflective silver particles. Marquez and Perret were taken aback, Marquez literally throwing his head back when the screen changed, as if suffering from whiplash.

Goodman was the first to see it.

"Open the channels between interview rooms," said Branting, watching the three screen Operators at work.

"That's it, right there!" Goodman exclaimed. He switched to look at Tobe's screen, and pointed at a glowing thread in the lower right hand portion. "There, again, around sector 120," he said.

"Got it," said Perrett. Goodman hadn't realised that he was talking to anyone, except Service Global, or maybe Control Operator Branting, but he didn't have time to be surprised or to ask who he was talking to.

"There's something around sector 80," too, said Marquez. "Wow, the sparks are flying all over the place."

"How did this happen?" asked Perrett, "and why have I never seen this before?"

"No time," said Goodman. "Are you there, Control Operator?"

Branting fed his audio to the three interview rooms, excluding Metoo's.

"What have you got for me, Goodman?" he asked.

"They need to be together."

"He's right," said Marquez. "It's symbiosis!"

"It can't be," said Perrett. "I know she's... She's..."

"The Mother of all things," said Marquez.

"Get them together," said Goodman, again, "and then get them on a couple of Workstations on the Service Floor so that I can do that damned line-check and verify this."

Tobe returned to the kitchen. He had changed, but was still clutching the towel to his chest, making the front of his clean robe wet.

"If you give that to me," said Metoo, "I'll make it cool for you again; it'll be more comfortable."

Tobe looked at Metoo, and then handed her the towel. He lifted the silkpro of his robe away from his chest, where it was clinging to his skin with the damp.

Metoo soaked the towel in cold water, and squeezed out the excess, twisting the towel between her hands. She walked over to Tobe, pulled out his stool, and handed him the towel. He sat down. Metoo walked around the counter, and sat on her stool, opposite Tobe.

"I'll... just..." Saintout said.

"Thank you, Saintout," said Metoo. "You can stay, or go, as you like." Metoo sounded very calm, and Tobe seemed relaxed, despite his scalded chest, but Saintout decided to stay anyway, just in case. He leaned on the kitchen wall adjacent to Metoo, so that he was out of her way, and faced Tobe, so that he didn't embarrass the Assistant-Companion.

"What about the equivalence relation?" asked Metoo.

"I did that," said Tobe.

"Difficult, though," said Metoo. "Some people would have taken the eggpro to a lab, and got down to the molecular level. That would've proved that it wasn't the same, of course."

"Yes. It was the same to Tobe."

"Was that what mattered? That it was the same to you?"

"Yes," said Tobe.

Branting switched audio and visual to screen fourteen on his square. He began to speak before he looked up.

"Sorry to have ke –" he said, stopping suddenly, mid-word. "Oh no... Where the hell are you?" Screen fourteen showed an empty interview room. Metoo and Strauss had gone, and both of their chairs were neatly tucked under the table as if they had never been there.

"Screen thirteen," said Branting, "what's on screen thirteen?"

Screen thirteen fizzed into life to show a great sparkling sphere, like a Christmas decoration, or a mirror-ball.

Bob Goodman sat at Workstation 7, waiting for the switch-out. He wanted to get on with the line-check, but he couldn't help enjoying the sight of the silver sphere in front of him.

"Ready," he said, still waiting. "Ready at station 7."

"There will be a short delay," said Branting.

Operator Goodman could not help himself. He began a line-check on the screen, in front of him, assuming that it was the old footage that he had been watching in the interview room. As he did the line-check, he began to notice things that contradicted what he had just been viewing on the vid-con.

"The footage on station 7," said Goodman, "when was it shot?"

There was no answer. Goodman waited for several seconds, which began, very quickly to feel like minutes.

"Control Operator Branting," he said, and waited, again for an answer.

"Mayer?" he asked.

"Here, boss," said Mayer.

"Do a line-check with me, right now," said Bob Goodman. "Three, two, one."

"Line-check," they said, in unison.

"Qa, get Strauss," said Branting. "I've lost the Assistant-Companion. We must find Metoo."

"72, 84," said Goodman.

"Check," said Mayer, a moment later.

"102, 82," said Goodman.

"Check," said Mayer.

"This isn't a coincidence," said Goodman. "This is live. Check."

"Sir," said Qa,

"Have you got Strauss?" asked Branting.

"No, sir, I –"

Branting cut him off, saying, "I need to find Assistant-Companion Metoo,"

"No, sir, she's at home," said Qa. "We're streaming her screen live to the Service Floor."

"That's what I can see on thirteen?" asked Branting.

"That's what you can see on thirteen, sir," said Qa. "Are you all right, sir?"

Branting had cut Qa off, and had opened a channel to Goodman.

"Station 7, Goodman, we are ready for your line-check."

"Line-check complete," said Goodman.

"Line-check complete," said Mayer.

Mayer and Goodman rose from their seats, neither of them bothering to throw their switches. They strode towards each other across the Service Floor, and when they were within a yard of each other, Mayer stuck out his hand for Bob to shake. Bob took a small step forwards and threw his arms around the smaller man.

"Stuff your bloody handshake," he said. "Do you know what we did? We bloody saved the World! That's all!"

"We bloody saved the World," Mayer agreed.

"YOU'VE CHANGED, TOBE," said Metoo.

"Tobe doesn't understand it. It's not like maths,"

Metoo and Tobe sat opposite each other for several minutes, until Saintout could bear it no longer.

"What's not like maths?" he asked.

Tobe looked up at the Police Operator and said, "Life."

Metoo leaned across the counter, and took Tobe's face in her small hands.

"Don't try to understand life, Tobe. Nobody understands life."

"But..." Tobe began, not knowing what he wanted to say.

"You can have feelings without having to understand them," said Metoo. "It's nice to have feelings. You'll like it.

"Saintout," she said, "can you go into Tobe's room and get me the Eustache, the maths book without its cover. I want to show him something."

A few moments later, Saintout came back with the book, and handed it to Metoo. She turned to the end papers and handed the open book to Tobe.

"'Probability extends beyond the mathematical. In the real world, probability has no memory'," he said. "I don't understand."

"Not yet," said Metoo, "but you will, very soon."

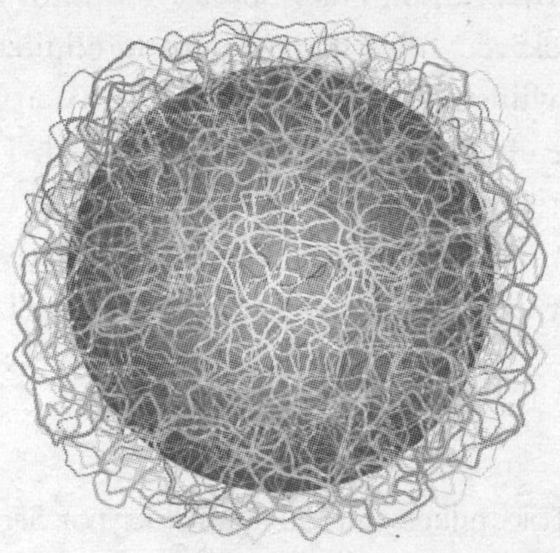

Epilogue

THE SERVICE FLOOR erupted in chaos as Operators and Techs jumped up and down, screaming, crying and embracing each other, with Bob Goodman and John Mayer at the centre of the storm.

His bank of screens in front of him, Control Operator Branting removed his headset and mic, and ruffled his own hair. Qa walked into the room, and Branting stood up and offered his hand. They shook hands firmly, solemnly for several seconds, and then beamed at each other.

"Is it over?" asked Qa.

"Take a look at that," said Branting, pointing at screen seven. "It's not just over, it's going to change the World."

Eight of the screens on the Service Floor blinked, and turned black, before shifting to scenes of drifting snow. They blinked again, in unison, and when they cleared a bright-white, tightly knit ball of threads emerged, gleaming and pulsing with an incandescent halo.

Around the World, on every Service Floor, in every College, one screen flickered, filled with snow, and blinked to reveal the same bright-white ball.

Tobe's screen had changed. He had changed. The World had changed.

The Earth no longer needed a thousand Actives. The Earth had Assistant-Companion Metoo and Active Tobe, and that was enough.

METOO AND TOBE talked until a small army of Service personnel arrived to take them away. Saintout had left after retrieving the book for Metoo. Their conversation seemed far too intimate to tolerate an eavesdropper for long.

He had retreated to the garden room. As he stepped over the threshold, Doctor Wooh threw herself into his arms. She embraced him fiercely, and then pounded her small fists into his chest.

"You scared me you... You..."

"I scared me, too," said Saintout.

Saintout and Wooh were debriefed while they waited for Service to arrive at the flat.

"Will I see him again?" Metoo asked Saintout, as he escorted her from the kitchen.

"Are you kidding me?" said Saintout. "You're a bloody hero, woman. You will have to undergo some pretty intensive debriefing, and I gather that scholars are queuing up to interview you. Your screen data will be studied from here to eternity... Now that we have an eternity."

"We do?" asked Metoo.

"That's what they tell me," said Saintout.

* * *

When Active Tobe was interviewed, which he often was in the weeks, months, and even years that followed, he was invariably asked how he had come to feel. He didn't know how, and he said so. He also said that he only knew that someone had taught him to feel.

When Active Tobe was asked who had taught him to feel he didn't hesitate. He simply beamed and said, "Empath Metoo taught me."

Empath Metoo was studied and questioned, and did everything that she could to help develop a program for the training and nurturing of others like her, and the integration of Empaths into Active households. There was no longer any need for the secrecy that surrounded Actives.

Tobe and Metoo were the first, but there would be others. An Empath paired with the right Active could create a Shield that would remain impenetrable for as long as they lived.

Service had barely changed for two hundred years, and when a crisis had occurred its conditions were unprecedented. Service would change now, and probably for the better, but, if another crisis ever did occur, it too would come with its own unprecedented conditions.